Young Blood

E. W. Hornung

Alpha Editions

This edition published in 2024

ISBN : 9789362995391

Design and Setting By
Alpha Editions
www.alphaedis.com
Email - info@alphaedis.com

As per information held with us this book is in Public Domain. This book is a reproduction of an important historical work. Alpha Editions uses the best technology to reproduce historical work in the same manner it was first published to preserve its original nature. Any marks or number seen are left intentionally to preserve its true form.

Contents

CHAPTER I.   THE OLD HOME. ....- 1 -
CHAPTER II.   THE BREAKING OF THE NEWS. ....- 7 -
CHAPTER III.   THE SIN OF THE FATHER. ....- 13 -
CHAPTER IV.   THE NEW HOME. ....- 21 -
CHAPTER V.   A WET BLANKET. ....- 27 -
CHAPTER VI.   THE GAME OF BLUFF. ....- 38 -
CHAPTER VII.   ON RICHMOND HILL. ....- 47 -
CHAPTER VIII.   A MILLIONAIRE IN THE MAKING. ....- 56 -
CHAPTER IX.   THE CITY OF LONDON. ....- 62 -
CHAPTER X.   A FIRST OFFENCE. ....- 72 -
CHAPTER XI.   BEGGAR AND CHOOSER. ....- 79 -
CHAPTER XII.   THE CHAMPION OF THE GODS. ....- 87 -
CHAPTER XIII.   THE DAY OF BATTLE. ....- 96 -
CHAPTER XIV.   A CHANGE OF LUCK. ....- 105 -
CHAPTER XV.   IT NEVER RAINS BUT IT POURS. ....- 110 -
CHAPTER XVI.   A DAME'S SCHOOL. ....- 115 -
CHAPTER XVII.   AT FAULT. ....- 122 -
CHAPTER XVIII.   MR. SCRAFTON. ....- 127 -
CHAPTER XIX.   ASSAULT AND BATTERY. ....- 133 -
CHAPTER XX.   BIDING HIS TIME. ....- 140 -
CHAPTER XXI.   HAND TO HAND. ....- 145 -
CHAPTER XXII.   MAN TO MAN. ....- 153 -
CHAPTER XXIII.   THE END OF THE BEGINNING. ....- 161 -
CHAPTER XXIV.   YOUNG INK. ....- 172 -
CHAPTER XXV.   SCRAFTON'S STORY. ....- 178 -
CHAPTER XXVI.   A MASTERSTROKE. ....- 189 -

CHAPTER XXVII.   RESTITUTION. ....- 196 -
CHAPTER XXVIII.   A TALE APART. ....- 203 -

CHAPTER I.

THE OLD HOME.

Harry Ringrose came of age on the happiest morning of his life. He was on dry land at last, and flying north at fifty miles an hour instead of at some insignificant and yet precarious number of knots. He would be at home to eat his birthday breakfast after all; and half the night he sat awake in a long ecstasy of grateful retrospect and delicious anticipation, as one by one the familiar stations were hailed and left behind, each an older friend than the last, and each a deadlier enemy to sleep. Worn out by excitement, however, he lay down for a minute between Crewe and Warrington, and knew no more until the guard came to him at the little junction across the Westmoreland border. Harry started up, the early sun in his sleepy eyes, and for an instant the first-class smoking-compartment was his state-room aboard the ship *Sobraon*, and the guard one of his good friends the officers. Then with a rush of exquisite joy the glorious truth came home to him, and he was up and out that instant—the happiest and the luckiest young rascal in the land.

It was the 19th of May, and a morning worthy the month and the occasion. The sun had risen in a flawless sky, and the dear old English birds were singing on all sides of the narrow platform, as Harry Ringrose stretched his spindle-legs upon it and saw his baggage out of the long lithe express and into the little clumsy local which was to carry him home. The youth was thin and tall, yet not ungainly, with a thatch of very black hair, but none upon his sun-burnt face. He was shabbily dressed, his boots were down at heel and toe, there were buttons missing from his old tweed coat, and he wore a celluloid collar with his flannel shirt. On the other hand, he was travelling first-class, and the literary supplies tucked under his arm had cost the extravagant fellow several shillings at Euston book-stall. Yet he had very little money in his pocket. He took it all out to count. It amounted to five shillings and sixpence exactly, of which he gave half-a-crown to the guard for waking him, and a shilling to a porter here at the junction, before continuing his journey in the little train. This left him a florin, and that florin was all the money he possessed in the world.

He was, however, the only child of a father who would give him as much as he wanted, and, what was rarer, of one with sufficient sense of humour to appreciate the prodigal's return without a penny in his pocket or a decent garment on his back. Whether his people would be equally pleased at being taken completely by surprise was not quite so certain. They might say he ought to have let them know what ship he was coming by, or at least have sent a telegram on landing. Yet all along he had undertaken to be home for his twenty-first birthday, and it would only have made them anxious to know that he had trusted himself to a sailing-vessel. Fifty days instead of twenty from the Cape! It had nearly cost him his word; but, now that it was over, the narrow margin made the joke all the greater; and Harry Ringrose loved a joke better than most things in the world.

The last two years of his life had been a joke from beginning to end: for in the name of health he had been really seeking adventure and undergoing the most unnecessary hardships for the fun of talking about them for the rest of his days. He pictured the first dinner-party after his return, and the faces of some dozen old friends when they heard of the leopards under the house, the lion in the moonlight, and (when the ladies had withdrawn) of the notorious murderer with whom Harry had often dined. They should perceive that the schoolboy they remembered was no longer anything of the sort, but a man of the world who had seen more of it than themselves. It is true that for a man of the world Harry Ringrose was still somewhat youthfully taken up with himself and his experiences; but his heart was rich with love of those to whom he was returning, and his mind much too simple to be aware of its own egotism. He only knew that he was getting nearer and nearer home, and that the joy of it was almost unendurable.

His face was to the carriage window, his native air streamed down his throat and blew a white lane through his long black hair. Miles of green dales rushed past under a network of stone walls, to change soon to mines and quarries, which in their turn developed into furnaces and works, until all at once the sky was no longer blue and the land no longer green. And when Harry Ringrose looked out of the opposite window, it was across grimy dunes that stretched to a breakwater built of slag, with a discoloured sea beyond.

The boy rolled up his rug and changed his cap for a villainous sombrero preserved for the occasion. He then made a selection from his lavish supply of periodical literature, and when he next looked out the train was running in the very shadow of some furnaces in full blast. The morning sun looked cool and pale behind their monstrous fires, and Harry took off the sombrero to his father's ironworks, though with a rather grim eye, which saw the illuminated squalor of the scene without appreciating its prosperity. Sulphurous flames issued from all four furnaces; at one of the four they were casting as the train passed, and the molten incandescent stream ran white as the wire of an electric light.

After the works came rank upon rank of workmen's streets running right and left of the line; then the ancient and historic quarter of the town, with its granite houses and its hilly streets, all much as it had been a hundred years before the discovery of iron-stone enriched and polluted a fair countryside. Then the level-crossing, without a creature at the gates at such an hour; finally a blank drab platform with the long loose figure of the head-porter standing out upon it as the homeliest sight of all. Harry clapped him on the cap as the train drew up; but either the man had forgotten him, or he was offended, for he came forward without a smile.

"Well, David, how are you? Your hand, man, your hand! I'm back from the wilds. Don't you know me?"

"I do now, sir."

"That's right! It does me good to see an old face like yours. Gently with this green box, David, it's full of ostrich-eggs, that's why I had it in the carriage. There's four more in the van; inspan the lot till we send in for them, will you? I mean to walk up myself. Come, gently, I say!"

The porter had dropped the green box clumsily, and now sought to cover his confusion by saying that the sight of Master Harry, that altered, had taken him all aback. Young Ringrose was justly annoyed; he had taken such care of that green box for so many weeks. But he did not withhold the florin, which was being pocketed for a penny when the man saw what it was and handed it back.

"What, not enough for you?" cried Harry.

"No, sir, too much."

The boy stared and laughed.

"Don't be an ass, David; I don't come home from Africa every day! If you'd been with me you'd think yourself lucky to get home at all! You just inspan those boxes, and we'll send for them after breakfast."

The man mumbled that it was not worth two shillings. Harry said that was his business. The porter hung his head.

"I—I may have broken them eggs."

"Oh, well, if you have, two bob won't mend 'em; cling on to it, man, and don't drop them again."

The loose-limbed porter turned away with the coin, but without a word, while Harry went off in high good-humour, though a little puzzled by the man's manner. It was not a time to think twice of trifles, however, and, at all events, he had achieved the sportsmanlike feat of emptying his pockets of their last coin. He strode out of the station with a merry, ringing tread. Half the town heard him as he went whistling through the streets and on to the outlying roads.

The one he took was uphill and countrified. High hedgerows bloomed on either hand, and yet you could hear the sea, and sometimes see it, and on this side of the town it was blue and beautiful. Our wayfarer met but one other, a youth of his own age, with whom he had played and fought since infancy, though the families had never been intimate. Harry halted and held out his hand, which was ignored, the other passing with his nose in the air, and a tin can swinging at his side, on his way to some of the works. Harry coloured up and said a hard word softly. Then he remembered how slow his old friend the porter had been to recognise him; and he began to think he must have grown up out of knowledge. Besides accounting for what would otherwise have been an inexplicable affront, the thought pleased and flattered him. He strode on serenely as before, sniffing the Irish Sea at every step.

He passed little lodges and great gates with never a glance at the fine houses within: for to Harry Ringrose this May morning there were but one house and one garden in all England. To get to them he broke at last into a run, and only stopped when the crest of the hill brought him, breathless, within sight of both. There was the long front wall, with the gates at one end, the stables at the other, and the fresh leaves bulging over every intervening brick. And down the hill, behind the trees, against the sea, were the windows, the gables, the chimneys, that he had been dreaming of for two long years.

His eyes filled with a sudden rush of tears. "Thank God!" he muttered brokenly, and stood panting in the road, with bowed bare head and twitching lips. He could not have believed that the mere sight of home would so move him. He advanced in an altered spirit, a sense of his own unworthiness humbling him, a hymn of thanksgiving in his heart.

And now the very stones were eloquent, and every yard marked by some landmark forgotten for two years, and yet familiar as ever at the first glance. Here was the mark a drunken cabman had left on the gatepost in Harry's school-days; there the disused summerhouse with the window still broken by which Harry had escaped when locked in by the very youth who had just cut him on the road. The drive struck him as a little more overgrown. The trees were greener than he had ever known them, the bank of rhododendrons a mass of pink without precedent in his recollection; but then it was many years since Harry had seen the place so late in May, for he had gone out to Africa straight from school.

As for the dear house, the creepers had spread upon the ruddy stone and the tiles had mellowed, but otherwise there seemed to be no change. It would look its old self when the blinds were up: meantime Harry fixed his eyes upon those behind which his parents would still be fast asleep, and he wondered, idly at first, why they had given up sleeping with a window open. It had been their practice all the year round; and the house had been an early-rising house; yet not a fire was lighted—not a chimney smoking—not a window open—

not a blind drawn—though close upon seven o'clock by the silver watch that had been with Harry through all his adventures.

His hand shook as he put the watch back in his pocket. The possibility of his parents being away—of his surprise recoiling upon himself—had never occurred to him until now. How could they be away? They never dreamt of going away before the autumn. Besides, he had told them he was coming home in time to keep his birthday. They were not away—they were not—they were not!

Yet there he stood—in the sweep of the drive—but a few yards from the steps—and yet afraid to ring and learn the truth! As though the truth must be terrible; as though it would be a tragedy if they did happen to be from home!

It would serve him right if they were.

So at last, with such a smile as a man may force on the walk to the gallows, Harry Ringrose dragged himself slowly to the steps, and still more slowly up them; for they were dirty; and something else about the entrance was different, though he could not at first tell what. It was not the bell, which he now pulled, and heard clanging in the kitchen loud enough to rouse the house; he was still wondering what it was when the last slow tinkling cut his speculations short.

Strange how so small a sound should carry all the way from the kitchen!

He rang again before peering through one of the narrow ruby panes that lighted the porch on each side of the door. He could see no farther than the wall opposite, for the inner door was to the right, and in the rich crimson light the porch looked itself at first sight. Then simultaneously Harry missed the mat, the hat stand, a stag's antlers; and in another instant he knew what it was that had struck him as different about the entrance. He ought not to have been able to peer through that coloured light at all. The sill should have supported the statuette of Night which matched a similar representation of Morning on the other side of the door. Both were gone; and the distant bell, still pealing lustily from his second tug, was breaking the silence of an empty house.

Harry was like a man waking from a trance: the birds sang loud in his ears, the sun beat hot on his back, while he himself stood staring at his own black shadow on the locked door, and wondering what it was, for it never moved. Then, in a sudden frenzy, he struck his hand through the ruby glass, and plucked out the pieces the putty still held in place, until he was able to squeeze through bodily. Blood dripped from his fingers and smeared the handle of the unlocked inner door as he seized and turned it and sprang within. The hall was empty. The stairs were bare.

He ran into room after room; all were stripped from floor to ceiling. The sun came in rods through the drawn blinds: on the walls were the marks of the pictures: on the floors, a stray straw here and there.

He cried aloud and railed in his agony. He shouted through the house, and his voice came back to him from the attics. Suddenly, in a grate, he espied a printed booklet. It was an auctioneer's list. The sale had taken place that very month.

The calmness of supreme misery now stole over Harry Ringrose, and he saw that his fingers were bleeding over the auctioneer's list. He took out his handkerchief and wiped them carefully—he had no tears to staunch—and bound up the worst finger with studious deliberation. Apathy succeeded frenzy, and, utterly dazed, he sat down on the stairs, for there was nowhere else to sit, and for some minutes the only sound in the empty house was the turning of the leaves of the auctioneer's list.

Suddenly he leapt to his feet: another sound had broken the silence, and it was one that he seemed to have heard only yesterday: a sound so familiar in his home, so home-like in itself, that it seemed even now to give the lie to his wild and staring eyes.

It was the sound of wheels in the gravel drive.

CHAPTER II.

THE BREAKING OF THE NEWS.

Harry was in three minds in as many seconds: he would hide, he would rush out and learn the truth, he would first see who it was that had followed him at such an hour. The last impulse prevailed, and the study was the room from which to peep. Harry crept in on tiptoe, past the bookshelves eloquently bare, to the bow-window with the drawn Venetian blinds. Slightly raising one of the laths, he could see everything as the cab drew up at the steps.

The cab-door was flung open and out sprang an utter stranger to Harry Ringrose. This was a middle-aged man of the medium height, wearing a somewhat shabby tall hat and a frock-coat which shone unduly in the strong sunlight. He had a fresh complexion, a reddish moustache streaked with grey, a sharp-pointed nose, and a very deep chin which needed shaving; but what struck Harry first and last were the keen, decisive eyes, twinkling behind glasses with gold rims, which went straight to the broken window and surveyed it critically before their owner had set foot on the steps. It seemed that the cabman saw it too and made some remark; for the fare turned upon him, paid him and slammed his door, and ordered him off in a very peremptory voice which Harry heard distinctly. The cab turned in the sweep and disappeared among the trees. Then the stranger came slowly up the steps, with his eyes once more fixed upon the broken window. In another moment they had run like lightning over the face of the house, and, before Harry had time to move, had met his own.

The stranger raised his eyebrows, shook his head, and pointed to the front door. Harry went to it, shot the bolts back, turned the key, and flung the door wide open. He was trembling now with simple terror. His tongue would not ask what had happened. It was like standing to be shot, and having to give the signal to the firing party.

The other seemed to feel it almost equally: his fresh face was pale, and his quick eyes still with sorrow and compunction. It was evident he knew the worst. If only he would tell it unasked!

"My name is Lowndes," he began at last. "Gordon Lowndes—you must have heard of me?"

"I—I don't remember it," stammered Harry at the second attempt.

"I stayed here several times while you were in Africa. I was here in February."

"Yes, now I remember your name: it was in the last letter I had."

He could say this calmly; and yet his lips could not frame the question whose answer would indeed be life or death.

"Two years ago I did not know your people," resumed the other. "But for two years I have been their most intimate friend."

"Tell me," at length whispered Harry: "is—either of them—dead?" And he awaited the worst with a sudden fortitude.

Mr. Lowndes shook his head.

"Not that I know of," said he.

"Thank God!" the boy burst out, with the first break in his voice. "Nothing else matters—nothing—nothing! I made sure it was that! Can you swear that my father is all right?"

The other winced. "To the best of my knowledge," said he almost sharply.

"And my mother?"

"Yes, yes, I was with her three days ago."

"Where?"

"In London."

"London! And I passed through London last night! You saw her, you say, three days ago, and she was all right then?"

"I never knew her look better."

"Then tell me the worst and let us have it over! I can see that we have lost our money—but that doesn't matter. Nothing matters if they are all right; won't you come in, sir, and tell me all?"

Harry did not know it, for in his deep emotion he had lost sight of self; but there was something infinitely touching in the way the young man stood aside and ushered his senior into the hall as though it were still his home. Mr. Lowndes shook his head at the unconscious air, and he entered slowly, with it bent. Harry shut the doors behind them, and they turned into the first room. It was the room with the empty bookshelves; and it still smelt of Harry's father's cheroots.

"You may wonder at my turning up like this," said Lowndes; "but for those fools at the shipping-office I should have met you at the docks. I undertook to do so, and to break the news to you there."

"But how could you know my ship?"

The other smiled.

"Cable," said he; "that was a very simple matter. But if your shipping fellows hadn't sworn you'd be reported from the Lizard, in lots of time for me to get up from Scotland to meet you, I should never have run down there as I was induced to do on business the night before last. I should have let the business slide. As it was the telegram reached me last night in Glasgow, when I knew it was too late to keep you out of this. Still, I timed myself to get here five minutes before you, and should have done it if my train hadn't been forty minutes late. It—it must have been the devil's own quarter-of-an-hour for you, Ringrose! Have a drop of this before we go on; it'll do you good."

He took a flask from his pocket and half filled the cup with raw whisky, which Harry seized gratefully and drained at a gulp. In truth, the shock of the morning, after the night's excitement, had left him miserably faint. The spirit revived him a little.

"You are very kind to me," he said, returning the cup. "You must be a great friend of my parents for them to give you this job, and a good friend to take it on! Now, if you please, tell me every mortal thing; you will tell me nothing I cannot bear; but I am sure you are too kind to keep anything back."

Lowndes was gazing with a shrewd approval upon the plucky young fellow, in whom, indeed, disappointment and disaster had so far awakened only what was best. At the last words, however, the quick eyes fell behind the gold-rimmed glasses in a way that made Harry wonder whether he had indeed been told the worst. And yet there was already more than enough to account for the other's embarrassment; and he determined not to add to it by unnecessary or by impatient questions.

"You are doubtless aware," began Lowndes, "that the iron trade in this country has long been going from bad to worse? You have heard of the bad times, I imagine, before to-day?"

Harry nodded: he had heard of the bad times as long as he could remember. But because the happy conditions of his own boyhood had not been affected by the cry, he had believed that it was nothing else. He was punished now.

"The times," proceeded Lowndes, "have probably been bad since your childhood. How old are you now?"

"Twenty-one to-day."

"To-day!"

"Go on," said Harry, hoarsely. "Don't be sorry for me. I deserve very little sympathy." His hands were in the pockets he had wilfully emptied of every coin.

"When you were five years old," continued Lowndes, "the pig-iron your father made fetched over five pounds a ton; before you were seven it was down to two-pounds-ten; it never picked up again; and for the last ten years it hasn't averaged two pounds. Shall I tell you what that means? For these ten years your father has been losing a few shillings on every ton of pig-iron produced—a few hundred pounds every week of his life!"

"And I was enjoying myself at school, and now in Africa! Oh," groaned Harry Ringrose, "go on, go on; but don't waste any pity on me."

"You may be a very rich man, but that sort of thing can't last for ever. The end is bound to come, and in your father's case it came, practically speaking, several years ago."

"Several years? I don't follow you. He never failed?"

"It would have been better for you all if he had. You have looked upon this place as your own, I suppose, from as far back as you can remember down to this morning?"

"As my father's own—decidedly."

"It has belonged to his bankers for at least five years."

"How do you know?" cried Harry hotly.

"He told me himself, when I first came down here, now eighteen months ago. We met in London, and he asked me down. I was in hopes we might do business together; but it was no go."

"What sort of business?"

"I wanted him to turn the whole thing into a Limited Liability Company," said Gordon Lowndes, reeling off the last three words as though he knew them better than his own name; "I mean those useless blast-furnaces! What good were they doing? None at all. Three bob a ton on the wrong side! That's all the good they'd done for years, and that's all they were likely to do till times changed. Times never will change—to what they were when you were breeched—but that's a detail. Your father's name down here was as sweet as honey. All he'd got to do was to start an extra carriage or two, put up for Parliament on the winning side, and turn his works into a Limited Liability Company. I'd have promoted it. I'd have seen it through in town. The best men would have gone on the board, and we'd have done the bank so well in shares that they wouldn't have got out of it if they could. We'd have made a spanking good thing of it if only the governor would have listened to reason. He wouldn't; said he'd rather go down with the ship than let in a lot of shareholders. 'Damn the shareholders!' says I. 'Why count the odds in the day of battle?' It's the biggest mistake you can make, Ringrose, and your governor kept on making it! It was in this very room, and he was quite angry with me. He wouldn't let me say another word. And what happens? A year or so later—this last February—he wires me to come down at once. Of course I came, but it was as I thought: the bank's sick of it, and threatens to foreclose. I went to see them; not a bit of good. Roughly speaking, it was a case of either paying off half the mortgage and reconstructing the whole bag of tricks, or going through the courts to beggary. Twenty thousand was the round figure; and I said I'd raise it if it was to be raised."

This speech had barely occupied a minute, so rapidly was it spoken; and there was much of it which Harry, in his utter ignorance of all such matters, would have found difficult to follow at a much slower rate of utterance. As it was, however, it filled him with distrust of his father's friend, who, on his own showing, had made some proposal dishonourable in the eyes of a high-principled man. Moreover, it came instinctively to Harry that he had caught a first glimpse of the real Gordon Lowndes, with his cunning eyes flashing behind his *pince-nez*, the gestures of a stump orator, and this stream of unintelligible jargon gushing from his lips. The last sentences, however, were plain enough even to Harry's understanding.

"You said you'd raise it," he repeated dryly; "yet you can't have done so."

"I raised ten thousand."

"Only half; well?"

"It was no use."

"My father would refuse to touch it?"

"N-no."

"Then what did he do?"

Lowndes drew back a pace, saying nothing, but watching the boy with twitching eyelids.

"Come, sir, speak out!" cried Harry, "He will tell me himself, you know, when I get back to London."

"He is not there."

"You said he was!"

"I said your mother was."

"Where is my father, then?"

"On the Continent—we think."

"You think? And the—ten thousand pounds?"

"He has it with him," said Lowndes, in a low voice. "I'm sorry to say he—bolted with the lot!"

CHAPTER III.

THE SIN OF THE FATHER.

"It's a lie!"

The word flew through Harry's teeth as in another century his sword might have flown from its sheath; and so blind was he with rage and horror that he scarcely appreciated its effect on Gordon Lowndes. Never was gross insult more mildly taken. The elder man did certainly change colour for an instant; in another he had turned away with a shrug, and in yet another he was round again with a sad half-smile. Harry glared at him in a growing terror. He saw that he was forgiven; a blow had disconcerted him less.

"I expected you to jump down my throat," observed Lowndes, with a certain twitching of the sharp nose which came and went with the intermittent twinkle in his eyes.

"It is lucky you are not a younger man, or you would have got even more than you expected!"

"For telling you the truth? Well, well, I admire your spirit, Ringrose."

"It is not the truth," said Harry doggedly, his chest heaving, and a cold sweat starting from his skin.

"I wish to God it were not!"

"You mean to tell me my father absconded?"

"That is the word I should have used."

"With ten thousand pounds that did not belong to him?"

"Not exactly that; the money was lent to him, but for another purpose. He has misapplied rather than misappropriated it."

Harry felt his head swimming. Disaster he might bear—but disaster rooted in disgrace! He gazed in mute misery upon the stripped but still familiar room; he breathed hard, and the stale odour of his father's cheroots became a sudden agony in his dilated nostrils. Something told him that what he had heard was true. That did not make it easier to believe—on the bare word of a perfect stranger.

"Proofs!" he gasped. "What proofs have you? Have you any?"

Lowndes produced a pocket-book and extracted a number of newspaper cuttings.

"Yes," sighed he, "I have almost everything that has appeared about it in the papers. It will be cruel reading for you, Ringrose; but you may take it better so than from anybody's lips. The accounts in the local press—the creditors' meetings and so forth—are, however, rather long. Hadn't you better wait until we're on our way back to town?"

"Wait? No, show me something now! I apologise for what I said; I made use of an unpardonable word; but—I don't believe it yet!"

"Here, then," said Lowndes, "if you insist. Here's a single short paragraph from the *P.M.G.* It would appear about the last day in March."

"The day I sailed!" groaned Harry. He took the cutting and read as follows:—

THE MISSING IRONMASTER.

The Press Association states that nothing further has been ascertained with regard to the whereabouts of Mr. Henry J. Ringrose, the Westmoreland ironmaster, who was last seen on Easter Eve. He has been traced, however, as already reported in these columns, to the Café; Suisse in Dieppe, though no further. The people at the café; persist in stating that their visitor only remained a few hours, so that he would appear to have walked thence into thin air. The police, as usual, are extremely reticent; but inquiry at Scotland Yard has elicited the fact that considerable doubt exists as to whether the missing man's chief creditors will, or can, owing to the character of their claim, take further action in the matter.

"Who are the chief creditors?" asked Harry, returning the cutting with an ashy face.

"Four business friends of your father's, from whom I raised the money in his name."

"Here in the neighbourhood?"

"No, in London; they advanced two thousand five hundred each."

"It was no good, you say?"

"No; the bank was not satisfied."

"So my father ran away with their money and left the works to go to blazes—and my mother to starve?"

Lowndes shrugged his shoulders.

"I apologise again for insulting you, Mr. Lowndes," said the boy, holding out his hand. "You have been a good friend to my poor father, I can see, and I know that you firmly believe what you say. But I never will! No; not if all his friends, and every newspaper in the kingdom, told me it was true!"

"Then what are you to believe?"

"That there has been foul play!"

The elder man turned away with another shrug, and it was some moments before Harry saw his face; when he did it was grave and sympathetic as before, and exhibited no trace of the irritation which it had cost an apparent effort to suppress.

"I am not surprised at that entering your head, Ringrose."

"Has it never entered yours?"

"Everything has; but one weeds out the impossibilities."

"Why is it impossible?" Harry burst out. "It is a good deal likelier than that my father would have done what it's said he did! There's an impossibility, if you like; and you would say so, too, if you had known him better."

Mr. Lowndes shook his head, and smiled sadly as he watched the boy's flaming face through his spectacles.

"You may have known your father, Ringrose, but you don't know human nature, or you wouldn't talk like that. Nothing is impossible—no crime—not even to the best of us—when the strain becomes more than we can bear. It is a pure question of strain and strength: which is the greater of the two. Every man has his breaking-point; your father was at his for years; it's a mystery to me how he held out so long. You must look at it sensibly, Ringrose. No thinking man will blame him, for the simple reason that every man who thinks knows very well that he might have done the same thing himself under the same pressure. Besides—give him a chance! With ten thousand pounds in his pocket——"

"You're sure he had it in his pocket?" interrupted Harry. These arguments only galled his wounds.

"Or else in a bag; it comes to the same thing."

"In what shape would he have the money?"

"Big notes and some gold."

"Yet foul play's an impossibility!"

"The numbers of the notes are known. Not one of them has turned up."

"I care nothing about that," cried the boy wildly, "though it shows he hasn't spent them himself. Listen to me, Mr. Lowndes. I believe my father is dead,

I believe he has been murdered: and I would rather that than what you say! But you claim to have been his friend? You raised this money for him? Very well; take my hand—here in his room—where I can see him now, all the time I'm talking to you—and swear that you will help me to clear this mystery up! We'll inspan the best detective in town, and take him with us to Dieppe, and never leave him till we get at the truth. I mean to live for nothing else. Swear that you will help me ... swear it here ... in his own room."

The wild voice had come down to a broken whisper. Next moment it had risen again: the man hesitated.

"Swear it! Swear it! Or you may have been my father's friend, but you are none from this hour to my mother and me."

Lowndes spread his hands in an indulgent gesture.

"Very well! I swear to help you to clear up this—mystery—as long as you think it is one."

"That is all I want. Now tell me when the next train starts for town. It used to be nine-twenty?"

"It is still."

"You are returning to London yourself?"

"Yes, by that train."

"Then let us meet at the station. It is now eight. I—I want to be alone here for an hour or two. No, it will do me good, it will calm me. I feel I have been very rude to you, sir, but I have hardly known what I said. I am beside myself—beside myself!" And Harry Ringrose rushed from the room, and up the bare and sounding stairs of his empty home: it was from his own old bedroom that he heard Lowndes leave the house, and saw a dejected figure climbing the sloping drive with heavy steps.

That hour of leave-taking is not to be described. How the boy harrowed himself wilfully by going into every room and thinking of something that had happened there, and seeing it all again through scalding tears, is a thing to be understood by some, but pitied rather than commended. There was, however, another and a sounder side to Harry Ringrose, and the prayers he prayed, and the vows he vowed, these were brave, and he meant them all that bitter birthday morning, that was to have been the happiest of all his life. Then his heart was broken but still heroic: there came many a brighter day he would gladly have exchanged for that black one, for the sake of its high resolves, its pure impulses, its noble and undaunted aspirations.

He had one more rencontre before he got away: in the garden he espied their old gardener. It was impossible not to go up and speak to him; and Harry left the old man crying like a child; but he himself had no tears.

"I am glad they left you your job: you will care for things," he had said, as he was going.

"Ay, ay, for the master's sake: he was the best master a man ever had, say what they will."

"But you don't believe what they say?"

The gardener looked blank.

"Do you dare to tell me," cried Harry, "that you believe what they believe?"

It was at this the man broke down; but Harry strode away with bitter resentment in his heart, and so back to the town, with a defiant face for every passer; but this time there were none he knew. At the spot where his old companion had cut him, that affront was recalled for the first time; its meaning was plain enough now; and plain the strange conduct of the railway-porter, who kept out of his way when Harry reappeared at the station.

Lowndes was there waiting for him, and had not only taken the tickets, but also telegraphed to Mrs. Ringrose; and this moved poor Harry to a shame-faced confession of his improvidence on the way down, and its awful results, in the midst of which the other burst out laughing in his face. Harry was a boy after his own heart; it was a treat to meet anybody who declined to count the odds in the day of battle; but, in any case, Mr. Lowndes claimed the rest of the day as "his funeral." As Harry listened, and thanked his new friend, he had a keen and hostile eye for any old ones; but the train left without his seeing another.

"The works look the same as ever," groaned Harry, as he gazed out on them once more. "I thought they seemed to be doing so splendidly, with all four furnaces in blast."

"They are doing better than for some years past: iron's looking up: the creditors may get their money back yet."

"Thank God for that!"

Lowndes opened his eyes, and the sharp nose twitched amusement.

"If I were in your place that would be the worst part of all. I have no sympathy with creditors as a class."

"I want to be even with them," said Harry through his teeth. "I will be, too, before I die: with every man of them. Hallo! why, this is a first-class carriage! How does that happen? I never looked where we got in; I followed you."

"And I chose that we should travel first."

"But I can't, I won't!" cried Harry, excitedly. "It was monstrous of me last night, but it would be criminal this morning. You sit where you are. I can change into a third at the next station."

"I have a first-class ticket for you," rejoined Lowndes. "You may as well make use of it."

"But when shall I pay you back?"

"Never, my boy! I tell you this is my funeral till I deliver you over to your mother, so don't *you* begin counting the odds; you've nothing to do with them. Besides, you came up like a rocket, and I won't have you go down altogether like the stick!"

Nor did he; and Harry soon saw that his companion was not to be judged by his shabby top-hat and his shiny frock-coat; he was evidently a very rich man. Where the boy had flung half-crowns overnight—where half-a-crown was more than ample—his elder now scattered half-sovereigns, and they had an engaged carriage the whole way. At Preston an extravagant luncheon-basket was taken in, with a bottle of champagne and some of the best obtainable cigars, for the quality of both of which Gordon Lowndes made profuse apologies. But Harry felt a new being after his meal, for grief and excitement had been his bread all day, and the wine warmed his heart to the strange man with whom he had been thrown in such dramatic contact. Better company, in happier circumstances, it would have been difficult to imagine; and it was clear that, with quip and anecdote, he was doing his utmost to amuse Harry and to take him out of his trouble. But to no purpose: the boy was perforce a bad listener, and at last confessed it in as many words.

"My mind is so full of my father," added Harry, "that I have hardly given my dear mother a thought; but my life is hers from to-day. You said she was in Kensington; in lodgings, I suppose?"

"No, in a flat. It's very small, but there's a room for you, and it's been ready for weeks."

"What is she living on?"

"Less than half her private income by marriage settlement; that was all there was left, and five-eighths of it she would insist on making over to the men who advanced the ten thousand. She is paying them two-and-a-half per cent. on their money and attempting to live on a hundred and fifty a year!"

"I'll double it before long!"

"Then she'll pay them five."

"They shall have every farthing one day; and the other creditors, they shall have their twenty shillings in the pound if I live long enough. Now let me have the rest of those cuttings. I want to know just how we stand—and what they say."

Out came the pocket-book once more. They were an hour's run nearer town when Harry spoke again.

"May I keep them?" he said.

"Surely."

"Thank you. I take it the bank's all right—and thank God the other liabilities up there are not large. As to the flight with that ten thousand—I don't believe it yet. There has been foul play. You mark my words."

Lowndes looked out at the flying fields.

"Which of you saw him last?" continued Harry.

"Your mother, when he left for town."

"When was that?"

"The morning after Good Friday."

"When did he cross?"

"That night."

"Did he write to anybody?"

"Not that I know of."

"Not to my mother?"

Lowndes leant forward across the compartment: there was a shrewd look in the spectacled eyes.

"Not that I know of," he said again, but with a different intonation. "I have often wondered!"

"Did you ask her?"

"Yes; she said not."

"Then what do you mean?" cried Harry indignantly. "Do you think my mother would tell you a lie?"

"Your mother is the most loyal little woman in England," was the reply. "I certainly think that she would keep her end up in the day of battle."

Harry ground his teeth. He could have struck the florid able face whose every look showed a calm assumption of his father's infamy.

"You take it all for granted!" he fumed; "you, who say you were his friend. How am I to believe in such friendship? True friends are not so ready to believe the worst. Oh! it makes my blood boil to hear you talk; it makes me hate myself for accepting kindness at your hands. You have been very kind, I know," added Harry in a breaking voice; "but—but for God's sake don't let us speak about it any more!" And he flung up a newspaper to hide his quivering lips; for now he was hoping against hope and believing against belief.

Was it not in black and white in all the papers? How could it be otherwise than true? Rightly or wrongly, the world had found his father guilty; and was he to insult all and sundry who failed to repudiate the verdict of the world?

Harry was one who could not endure to be in the wrong with anybody: his weakness in every quarrel was an incongruous hankering for the good opinion of the enemy, and this was intensified in the case of one who was obviously anxious to be his friend. To appear ungracious or ungrateful was equally repugnant to Harry Ringrose, and no sooner was he master of his emotion than he lowered the paper in order to add a few words which should remove any such impression.

Gordon Lowndes sat dabbing his forehead with a handkerchief that he made haste to put away, as though it was his eyes he had been wiping, which indeed was Harry's first belief. But the gold-rimmed glasses were not displaced, and, so far from a tear, there was an expression behind them for which Harry could not then find the name; nevertheless, it made him hold his tongue after all.

CHAPTER IV.

THE NEW HOME.

Harry had hoped that his companion would go his own way when they got to London; but it was "his funeral," as Mr. Lowndes kept saying, and he seemed determined to conduct it to the end. Euston was crowded, where Lowndes behaved like a man in his element, dealing abuse and largesse with equal energy and freedom, and getting Harry and all his boxes off in the first cab which left the station. But he himself was at Harry's side; and there he sat until the cab stopped, half-an-hour later, beneath a many-windowed red-brick pile thrown up in the angle of two back streets.

A porter in uniform ran up to help with the luggage, and, as Harry jumped out, a voice with a glad sob in it hailed him from a first-floor window. He waved his hat, and, with a pang, saw a white head vanishing: it had not been white when he went away. Next moment he was flying up the stone stairs three at a time; and on the first landing, at an open door, there was the sweet face, all aged and lined and lighted with sorrow and shame and love; there were the softest arms in all the world, spread wide to catch and clasp him to the warmest heart.

It was a long time afterwards, in a room which made the old furniture look very big, the old pictures very sad, that Mr. Lowndes was remembered for the first time. They looked into the narrow passage: the boxes blocked it, but he was not there; they called, but there was no answer.

"Have we no servant, mother?"

"We have no room for one. The porter's wife comes up and helps me."

"I can help you! Many a meal have I cooked in Africa."

"My boy, what a home-coming!"

It was the first word about that, and with it came the first catch in Harry's mother's voice.

"No, mother, thank God I am back to take care of you; and oh! I am so thankful we are to be alone to-night."

"But I am sorry he did not come in."

"He was quite right not to."

"But he must have paid for the cab—I will look out of the window—yes, it has gone—and I had the money ready in case you forgot!"

Harry could have beaten himself, but he could not tell his mother just then that he had arrived without a penny, and that Lowndes had not only paid the cabman, but must be pounds out of pocket by him on the day.

"Don't you like him, dear?" said his mother, divining that he did not.

"I do and I don't," said Harry bluntly.

"He has been so kind to me!"

"Yes; he is kind enough."

"Did you not think it good of him to rush from Scotland to meet you and then bring you all the way to your—new—home?"

"It was almost too good. I would have been happier alone," said Harry, forgetting all else in his bitter remembrance of some speeches Lowndes had made.

"That is not very grateful, my boy. You little know what he has been to me!"

"Has he done so much?"

"Everything—all through! You see what I have saved from the wreck? It was he who went to bid for me at the sale!"

"You bought them in, mother?"

"Yes; I could accept nothing from the creditors. That is the one point on which I quarrel with Mr. Lowndes; but we have agreed to differ. Why do you dislike him, Harry?"

"Mother, don't you know?"

"I cannot imagine."

"He thinks the worst—about my father."

It was the first mention of the father's name. Mrs. Ringrose was silent for many moments.

"I know he does," she said at length.

"Then how can you bear the sight of him?" her boy burst out.

"It is no worse than all the world thinks."

And Mrs. Ringrose sighed; but now her voice was abnormally calm, as with a grief too great for tears.

The long May evening had not yet closed in, and in the ensuing silence the cries of children in the street below, and the Last Waltz of Weber from the piano of the flat above, came with equal impertinence through the open windows. Mrs. Ringrose was in the rocking-chair in which she had nursed her only child. Her back was to the light, but she was rocking slowly. Her son stood over her with horror deepening in his face, but hers he could not see, only the white head which two years ago had been hardly grey. He dropped upon his knees and seized her hands; they were cold; and he missed her rings.

"Mother—mother! You don't think it too?"

No answer.

"You do! Oh, mother, how are we to go on living after this? What makes you think it? Quick! has he written to you?"

Mrs. Ringrose started violently. "Who put that into your head?" she cried out sharply.

"Nobody. I only wondered if there had been a letter, and I asked Lowndes, but he said you said there had not."

"Was that not enough for you?"

"Oh, mother, tell me the truth!"

The poor lady groaned aloud.

"God knows I meant to keep it to myself!" she whispered. "And yet—oh, how could I destroy his letter? And I thought you ought to see it—some day—not yet."

"Mother, I must see it now."

"You will never breathe it to a soul?"

"Never without your permission."

"No one must ever dream I heard one word after he left me!"

"No one ever shall."

"I will get the letter."

His hand was trembling when he took it from her.

"It was written on the steamer, you see."

"It may be a forgery," said Harry, in a loud voice that trembled too. Yet there was a ring of real hope in it. He was thinking of Lowndes in the train. He had caught him mopping a wet brow. He had surprised a guilty look—yes, guilty was the word—he had found it at last—in those shifty eyes behind the *pince-nez*. If villainy should be at the bottom of it all, and Lowndes at the bottom of the villainy!

If the letter should prove a forgery after all!

He had it in his hand. He carried it to the failing light. He hardly dared to look at it, but when he did a cry escaped him.

It was a cry of disappointment and abandoned hope.

Minutes passed without another sound; then the letter was slowly folded up and restored to its envelope, and dropped into Harry's pocket, before his arms went round his mother's neck.

"Mother, let me burn it, so that no eyes but ours shall ever see!"

"Burn it? Burn the last letter I may ever have from him? Give it to me!" And she pressed it to her bosom.

Harry hung his head in a long and wretched silence.

"We must forget him, mother," he said at last.

"Harry, he was a good father to you, he loved you dearly. He was mad when he did what he has done. You must never say that again."

"I meant we must forget what he has done——"

"Ah God! if I could!"

"And only think of him as he used to be."

"Yes; yes; we will try."

"It would be easier—don't you think—if we never spoke of this?"

"We never will, unless we must."

"Let us think that we just failed like other people. But, mother, I will work all my life to pay off everybody! I will work for you till I drop. Goodness knows what at; but I learnt to work for fun in Africa, I am ready to work in earnest, and, thank God, I have all my life before me."

"You are twenty-one to-day!"

"Yes, I start fair in every way."

"That this should be your twenty-first birthday! My boy—my boy!"

The long May twilight deepens into night; the many windows of the red-brick block are lit up one by one; and the many lives go on. Below, at the curb, a doctor's brougham and a hansom are waiting end to end; and from that top flat a young couple come scuttling down the stone stairs, he in a crush-hat, she with a flower in her hair, and theirs is the hansom. The flat below has similar tenants, but here the doctor is, and the young man paces his desolate parlour with a ghastly face.

And in the flat below that it is Weber's Last Waltz once more, and nothing else, by the hour together. And in the flat below that—the flat that would have gone into one room of their old home—Harry Ringrose and his mother are still steeling themselves and one another to face the future and to live down the past.

The light has been lowered in their front room and transferred for a space to the tiny dining-room at the back, which looks down into the building's well, but now it is the front windows which stand out once more. Twelve o'clock comes, and there is a tinkle of homing hansoms (the brougham has gone away masterless), and the public-house at the corner empties noisily, but the light in those front windows remains the brightest in the mansions. And Weber is done with at last; but the two voices below go on and on and on into the night; nor do they cease when their light shifts yet again into the front bedroom.

It is two in the morning, and the young couple have come home crumpled from their dance, and their feet drag dreadfully on the stairs, and the doctor has taken their hansom, and the young man below them is drunk with joy, when Harry Ringrose kisses his mother for the twentieth last time and really goes. But he is too excited to sleep. In half-an-hour he creeps back into the passage. Her light is still burning. He goes in.

"You spoke of Innes, mother?"

"Yes; I feel sure he would be the first to help you."

"I cannot go to him. I can go to nobody. We must start afresh with fresh friends, and I'll begin answering advertisements to-morrow. Yet—Innes has helped me already!"

Mrs. Ringrose has been reading herself asleep, like a practical woman, out of one of the new magazines he has brought home. The sweet face on the pillow is wonderfully calm (for it is not from his mother that Harry inherits his excitability), but at this it looks puzzled.

"When has he helped you?"

"To-night, mother! There was a motto he had when I was at his school. He used to say it in his sermons, and he taught me to say it in my heart."

"Well, my boy?"

"It came back to me just now. It puts all that we have been saying in a nutshell. May I tell you, mother?"

"I am waiting to hear."

"'Money lost—little lost.'"

"It's easy to say that."

"'Honour lost—much lost.'"

"I call it everything."

"No, mother, wait! 'PLUCK lost—ALL lost!' It's only pluck that's everything. We must never lose that, mother, we must never lose that!"

"God grant we never may."

CHAPTER V.

A WET BLANKET.

The morning sun filled the front rooms of the flat, and the heavy hearts within were the lighter for its cheery rays. Sorrow may outlive the night, and small joy come in the morning; but yet, if you are young and sanguine, and the month be May, and the heavens unspotted, and the air nectar, then you may suddenly find yourself thrilling with an unwarrantable delight in mere life, and that in the very midst of life's miseries. It was so with young Harry Ringrose, on the morning following his tragic home-coming; it was even so with Harry's mother, who was as young at heart as her boy, and fully as sanguine in temperament. They had come down from the high ground of the night. The everyday mood had supervened. Harry was unpacking his ostrich eggs in the narrow passage, and thoroughly enjoying a pipe; in her own room his mother sat cleaning her silver, incredible contentment in her face, because her boy was in and out all the morning, and the little flat was going to bring them so close together.

"That's the lot," said Harry when the bed was covered with the eggs. "Now, mother, which do you think the best pair?"

"They all look the same to me."

"They are not. Look at this pair in my hands. Can't you see that they're much bigger and finer than the rest?"

"I daresay they are."

"They're for you, mother, these two."

And he set them on the table among the spoons and forks and plate-powder. She kissed him, but looked puzzled.

"What shall you do with the rest?"

"Sell them! Five shillings a pair; five tens are fifty; that's two-pound-ten straight away."

"I won't have you sell them!"

"They are mine, mother, and I must."

"You'll be sorry for it when you have a good situation."

"Ah, when!" said Harry, and he was out again with a laugh.

A noise of breaking wood came from the passage. He was opening another case. His mother frowned at her miniature in the spoon she had in hand, and when he returned, brandishing a brace of Kaffir battle-axes, she would hardly look at them.

"I feel sure Wintour Phipps would take you into his office," said Mrs. Ringrose.

"I never heard of him. Who is he?"

"A solicitor; your father paid for his stamps when he was articled."

"An old friend, then?"

"Not of mine, for I never saw him; but he was your father's godson."

"It comes to the same thing, and I can't go to him, mother. Face old friends I cannot! You and I are starting afresh, dear; I'm prepared to answer every advertisement in the papers, and to take any work I can get, but not to go begging favours of people who would probably cut us in the street. I don't expect to get a billet instantly; that's why I mean to sell all this truck—for the benefit of the firm."

"You had much better write an article about your experiences, and get it into some magazine, as you said you would last night."

Indeed, they had discussed every possible career in the night, among others that of literature, which the mother deemed her son competent to follow on the strength of certain contributions to his school magazine, and of the winning parody in some prize competition of ancient history. He now said he would try his hand on the article some day, but it would take time, and would anybody accept it when written? That was the question, said Harry, and his mother had a characteristic answer.

"If you wrote to the Editor of *Uncle Tom's Magazine*," said she, "and told him you had taken it in as long as you could remember—I bought in the bound volumes for you, my boy—I feel sure that he would accept it and pay for it too."

"Well, we'll see," said Harry, with a laugh. "Meanwhile we must find somebody to accept all these curios, and to pay for them. I see no room for them here."

"There is certainly very little."

"I wonder who would be the best people to go to?"

Mrs. Ringrose considered.

"I should try Whitbreds," said she at last, "since you are so set upon it. They sell everything; and I have had all my groceries from them for so many years that they can hardly refuse to take something from us."

To the simple-hearted lady, whom fifty years had failed to sophisticate, there seemed nothing unreasonable in the expectations which she formed of others, for they were one and all founded upon the almost fanatical loyalty which was a guiding impulse of her own warm heart. In her years of plenty it was ever the humblest friend who won her warmest welcome, and the lean years to come proved powerless to check this generous spirit. Mrs. Ringrose would be illogically staunch to tradesmen whom she had dealt with formerly, and would delight their messengers with unnecessary gratuities because she had been accustomed to give all her life; but so unconscious was she of undue liberality on her part that she was apt to credit others with her own extravagance in charity, and to feel it bitterly when not done by as perhaps she alone would have done. It simply astounded her when three of her husband's old friends, who had in no way suffered by him, successively refused her secret supplication for a desk for her boy in their offices: she would herself have slept on the floor to have given the child of any one of them a bed in her little flat.

But the treadmill round in search of work was not yet begun, though Harry was soon enough to find himself upon the wheel. Even as he unpacked his native weapons a weighty step was ascending the common stair, and the electric bell rang long and aggressively just as Mrs. Ringrose decided that it would be worth her son's while to let his trophies go for fifty pounds.

"A tall man in a topper!" whispered Harry, bursting quietly in. "I saw him through the ground glass; who can it be?"

"Your Uncle Spencer," said Mrs. Ringrose, looking straight at Harry over the wash-leather and the mustard-pot.

"Uncle Spencer!" Harry looked aghast. "What's bringing him, mother?"

"I wrote to him directly I got the telegram."

"You never said so!"

"No; I knew you wouldn't be pleased."

"Need I see him?"

"It is you he has come to see. Go, my boy; take him into the sitting-room, and I will join you when you have had your talk. Meanwhile, remember that he is your mother's brother, and will exert his influence to get you a situation; he has come so promptly, I shouldn't be surprised if he has got you one already! And you are letting him ring twice!"

Indeed, the avuncular thumb had already pressed the button longer than was either necessary or polite, and Harry went to the door with feelings which he had difficulty in concealing as he threw it open. Uncle Spencer stood without in a stiff attitude and in sombre clerical attire; he beheld his nephew without the glimmer of a smile on his funereal, bearded countenance, while his large hand was slow in joining Harry's, and its pressure perfunctory.

"So sorry to keep you waiting, but—but I forgot we hadn't a servant," fibbed Harry to be polite. "Do come in, Uncle Spencer."

"I thought nobody could be at home," was the one remark with which the clergyman entered; and Harry sighed as he heard that depressing voice again.

The Reverend Spencer Walthew was indeed the survival of a type of divine now rare in the land, but not by any means yet extinct. His waistcoat fastened behind his back in some mysterious manner, and he never smiled. He was the vicar of a semi-fashionable parish in North London, where, however, he preached in a black gown to empty pews, while a mixed choir behaved abominably behind his back. As a man he was neither fool nor hypocrite, but the natural enemy of pleasure and enthusiasm, and one who took a grim though unconscious satisfaction in disheartening his neighbour. No two proverbial opposites afford a more complete contrast than was presented by Mr. Walthew and Mrs. Ringrose; and yet at the bottom of the brother's austerity there lay one or two of the sister's qualities, for those who cared to dig deep enough in such stony and forbidding ground.

Harry had never taken to his uncle, who had frowned on Lord's and tabooed the theatre on the one occasion of his spending a part of his holidays in North London; and Mr. Walthew was certainly the last person he wanted to see that day. It made Harry Ringrose throb and tingle to look on the clergyman and to think of his father; they had never been friendly together; and if one syllable was said against the man who was down—no matter what he had done—the son of that man was prepared to make such a scene as should secure an immunity from further insult. But here Harry was indulging in fears as unworthy as his determination, and he was afterwards ashamed of both.

The clergyman began in an inevitable strain, dwelling solemnly on the blessing of adversity in general, before proceeding to point out that the particular misfortunes which had overwhelmed Harry and his mother could not, by any stretch of the imagination, be regarded as adventitious or accidental, since they were obviously the deliberate punishment of a justly irate God, and as such to be borne with patience, meekness, and humility. Harry chafed visibly, thinking of his innocent mother in the next room; but, to do the preacher justice, his sermon was a short one, and the practical issue was soon receiving the attention it deserved.

"I understand, Henry," said Mr. Walthew, "that you did obtain some useful and remunerative employment in Africa, which you threw up in order to come home and enjoy yourself. It is, of course, a great pity that you were so ill-advised and improvident; but may I ask in what capacity you were employed, and at what salary?"

"I don't admit that I was either ill-advised or improvident," cried Harry, with disrespectful warmth. "I didn't go out to work, but for my health, and I only worked for the fun of it, and am jolly glad I did come back to take care of my mother and to work for her. I was tutor in a Portuguese planter's family, and he gave me seventy pounds a year."

"And your board?"

"And my board."

"It was very good. It is a great deal better than anything you are likely to get here. How long were you with the planter?"

"Ten months."

"Only ten months! You must allow an older head than yours to continue thinking it is a pity you are not there still. Now, as to money matters, your father would doubtless cease sending you remittances once you were earning money for yourself?"

"No, he sent me fifty pounds last Christmas."

"Then, at any rate, you have brought enough home to prevent your being a burden to your mother? Between fifty and a hundred pounds, I take it?"

Harry shook his head; it was hot with a shame he would have owned to anybody in the world but Mr. Walthew.

"Not fifty pounds?"

"No."

"How much, then?"

"Not a penny!"

The clergyman opened his eyes and lifted his hands in unaffected horror. Harry could not help smiling in his face—could not have helped it if he had stood convicted of a worse crime than extravagance.

"You have spent every penny—and you smile!" the uncle cried. "You come home to find your mother at starvation's door—and you smile! You have spent her substance in—in——"

"Riot!" suggested Harry wickedly. "Sheer riot and evil living! Oh, Uncle Spencer, don't look like that; it's not exactly true; but, can't you see, I had no idea what was going to happen here at home? I thought I was coming back to live on the fat of the land, and when I'd made my miserable pile I spent it—like a man, I thought—like a criminal, if you will. Whichever it was, you must know which I feel now. And whatever I have done I am pretty badly punished. But at least I mean to take my punishment like a man, and to work like one, too, at any mortal thing I can find to do."

Mr. Walthew looked down his nose at the carpet on which he stood. He had sense enough to see that the lad was in earnest now, and that it was of no use to reproach him further with what was past.

"It seems to me, Henry," he said at length, "that it's a case of ability rather than of will. You say you are ready to do anything; the question is—what can you do?"

"Not many things," confessed Henry, in a humbler voice; "but I can learn, Uncle Spencer—I will do my best to learn."

"How old are you, Henry?"

"Twenty-one."

Harry was about to add "yesterday," but refrained from making his statement of fact an appeal for sympathy; for the man in him was coming steadily to the front.

"Then you would leave school in the Sixth Form?"

Harry had to shake his head.

"Perhaps you were on the Modern Side? All the better if you were!"

"No, I was not; I left in the form below the Sixth."

"Then you know nothing about book-keeping, for example?"

"I wish I did."

"But you are a fair mathematician?"

"It was my weakest point."

The clergyman's expression was more melancholy than ever. "It is a great pity—a very great pity, indeed," said he. "However, I see writing materials on the table, and shall be glad if you will write me down your full name, age, and address."

Harry sat down and wrote what was required of him in the pretty, rather scholarly hand which looked like and was the imitation of a prettier and more scholarly one. Then he unsuspectingly blotted the sheet and handed it to Mr. Walthew, who instantly began shaking his head in the most depressing fashion.

"It is as I feared," said he; "you do not even write a fair commercial hand. It is well enough at a distance," and he held the sheet at arm's length, "but it is not too easy to read, and I fear it would never do in an office. There are several City men among my parishioners; I had hoped to go to one or two of them with a different tale, but now I fear—I greatly fear. However, one can but try. You do not fancy any of the professions, I suppose? Not that you could afford one if you did."

"Are the fees so high?" asked poor Harry, in a broken-spirited voice.

"High enough to be prohibitive in your case, though it might not be so if you had saved your money," the clergyman took care to add. "Of which particular profession were you thinking?"

"We—we have been talking it all over, and we did speak of—the Law."

"Out of the question; it would cost hundreds, and you wouldn't make a penny for years."

"Then there is—schoolmastering."

"It leads to nothing; besides—excuse me, Henry—but do you think you are scholar enough yourself to—to presume to—teach others?"

Harry fetched a groan.

"I don't know. I managed well enough in Mozambique, but it was chiefly teaching English. I only know that I would work day and night to improve myself, if once I could get a chance."

"Well," said Uncle Spencer, "it is just possible that I may hear in my parish of some delicate or backward boy whom you would be competent to ground, and if so I shall recommend you as far as I conscientiously can. But I cannot say I am sanguine, Henry; it would be a different thing if you had worked harder at school and got into the Sixth Form. I suppose no other career has occurred to you as feasible? I confess I find the range sadly restricted by the rather discreditable limitations to which you own."

Another career had occurred to Harry, and it was the one to which he felt most drawn, but by inclination rather than by conscious aptitude, so that he would have said nothing about it had not Mrs. Ringrose joined them at this moment. Her brother greeted her with a tepid salute, then dryly indicated the drift of the conversation, enlarging upon the vista of hopeless disability which it had revealed in Henry, and concluding with a repetition of his last question.

"No," said Harry rather sullenly, "I can think of nothing else I'm fit for unless I sweep a crossing; and then you would say I hadn't money for the broom!"

"But, surely, my boy," cried his mother, "you have forgotten what you said to me last night?"

Harry frowned and glared, for it is one thing to breathe your ridiculous aspirations to the dearest of mothers in the dead of night, and quite another thing to confide them to a singularly unsympathetic uncle in broad daylight. But Mrs. Ringrose had turned to her brother, and she would go on: "There is one thing he tells me he would rather do than anything else in the world—and I am sure he could do it best."

"What is that?"

"Write!"

Harry groaned. Mr. Walthew raised his eyebrows. Mrs. Ringrose sat triumphant.

"Write what, my dear Mary?"

"Articles—poems—books."

A grim resignation was given to Harry, and he laughed aloud as the clergyman shrugged his shoulders and shook his head.

"On his own showing," said Uncle Spencer, "I should doubt whether he has—er—the education—for that."

Mrs. Ringrose looked displeased, and even dangerous, for the moment; but she controlled her feelings on perceiving that the boy himself was now genuinely amused.

"You are quite mistaken," she contented herself with saying. "Have I never shown you the parody on Gray's Elegy he won a guinea for when he was fourteen? Then I will now."

And the fond lady was on her feet, only to find her boy with his back to the door, and laughter, shame and anger fighting for his face.

"You shall do no such thing, mother," Harry said firmly. "That miserable parody!"

"It was nothing of the kind. It began, 'The schoolbell tolls the knell——'"

"Hush, mother!"

"'Of parting play'" she added wilfully.

Mr. Walthew's eyebrows had reached their apogee.

"That is quite enough, Mary," said he. "I disapprove of parodies, root and branch; they are invariably vulgar; and when the poem parodied has a distinctly religious tendency, as in this case, they are also irreverent and profane. I am only glad to see that Henry is himself ashamed of his lucubration. If he should write aught of a religious character, and get it into print—a difficult matter, Henry, for one so indifferently equipped—my satisfaction will not be lessened by my surprise. Meanwhile let him return to those classics he should never have neglected, for by the dead languages only can we hope to obtain a mastery of our own; and I, for my part, will do my best in what, after all, I regard as a much less hopeless direction. Good-bye, Mary. I trust that I shall see you both on Sunday."

But Mrs. Ringrose would not let him go without another word for her boy's parody.

"When I read it to Mr. Lowndes," said she, to Harry's horror, "he said that he thought that a lad who could write so well at fourteen should have a future before him. So you see everybody is not of your opinion, Spencer; and Mr. Lowndes saw nothing vulgar."

"Do I understand you to refer," said Mr. Walthew, bristling, "to the person who has done me the honour of calling upon me in connection with your affairs?"

"He is the only Mr. Lowndes I know."

"Then let me tell you, Mary, that his is not a name to conjure with in my hearing. I should say, however, that he is the last person to be a competent judge of vulgarity or—or other matters."

"Then you dislike him too?" cried poor Mrs. Ringrose.

"Do you?" said Mr. Walthew, turning to Harry; and uncle and nephew regarded one another for the first time with mutually interested eyes.

"Not I," said Harry stoutly. "He has been my mother's best friend."

"I am sorry to hear it," the clergyman said; "what's more, I don't believe it."

"But he has been and he is," insisted the lady; "you little know what he has done for me."

"I wouldn't trust his motives," said her brother. "I am sorry to say it, Mary; he is very glib and plausible, I know; but—he doesn't strike me as an honest man!"

Mrs. Ringrose was troubled and vexed, and took leave of the visitor with a face as sombre as his own; but as for Harry, he recalled his own feelings on the journey up, and he felt less out of sympathy with his uncle than he had ever done in his life before. But Mr. Walthew was not one to go without an irritating last word, and in the passage he had his chance. He had remarked on the packing cases, and Harry had dived into his mother's room and returned with an ostrich egg in each hand, of which he begged his uncle's acceptance, saying that he would send them by the parcels post. Mr. Walthew opened his eyes but shook his head.

"I could not dream of taking them from you," said he, "in—in your present circumstances, Henry."

"But I got them for nothing," said Harry, at once hurt and nettled. "I got a dozen of them, and any amount of assegais and things, all for love, when I was on the Zambesi. I should like you and my aunt to have something."

"Really I could not think of it; but, if I did, I certainly should not permit you to incur the expense of parcel postage."

"Pooh! uncle, it would only be sixpence or a shilling."

"*Only* sixpence *or* a shilling! As if they were one and the same thing! You talk like a millionaire, Henry, and it pains me to hear you, after the conversation we have had."

Harry wilfully observed that he never had been able to study the shillings, and his uncle stood shocked on the threshold, as indeed he was meant to be.

"Then it's about time," said he, "that you did learn to study them—and the sixpences—and the pence. You were smoking a pipe when I came. I confess I was surprised, not merely because the habit is a vile one, for it is unhappily the rule rather than the exception, but because it is also an extravagant habit. You may say—I have heard young men say—that it only costs you a few pence a week. Then, pray, study those few pence—and save them. It is your duty. And as for what you say you got for nothing, the ostrich eggs and so forth, take them and sell them at the nearest shop! That also is your bounden duty, unless you wish to be a burden to your mother in her poverty; and I am very sorry that you should compel me to tell you so by talking of not 'studying' the shillings."

He towered in the doorway, a funereal monument of righteous horror; and once more Harry held out his hand, and let his elder go with the last word. The lad realised, in the first place, that he had just heard one or two things which were perfectly true; and yet, in the second, he was certain that he could not have replied without insolence—after his own prior and virtuous resolve to sell the curios himself. Now he never would sell them—so he felt for the moment; and he found himself closing the door as though there were illness in the flat, in his anxiety to keep from banging it as he desired.

"I fear your Uncle Spencer has been vexing you too," his mother said; "and yet I know that he will do his best to secure you a post."

"Oh, that's all right, mother; he was kind enough; it's only his way," said Harry, for he could see that his mother was sufficiently put out as it was.

"It's a way that makes me miserable," said poor Mrs. Ringrose, with a tear in her voice. "Did you hear what he said to me? He said what I never shall forgive."

"Not about those rotten verses?"

"No—about Mr. Lowndes. Your uncle said he didn't think him an honest man."

CHAPTER VI.

THE GAME OF BLUFF.

An inscrutable note reached Harry by the last post that night. It was from Gordon Lowndes, and it ran:—

"Leadenhall Street, E.C.
"May 20.

"DEAR RINGROSE,—If you are still of the same mind about a matter which we need not name, let me hear from you by return, and I'll 'inspan' the best detective in the world. He is at present cooling his heels at Scotland Yard, but may be on the job again any day, so why not on ours?

"Perhaps you will kindly drop me a line in any case, as I await your instructions.

"Yours faithfully,

"GORDON LOWNDES."

"What is it, my boy?"

"A line from Lowndes."

"Am I not to see it?"

"I would rather you didn't, mother dear."

"You haven't offended him, I hope?"

"Oh, no, it's about something we spoke of in the train; it has come to nothing, that's all."

And Mrs. Ringrose gathered, as she was intended to gather, that some iron or other had already been in the fire—and come out again. She said no more. As for Harry, the final proof of his father's dishonour had put out of his mind the oath which he had made Lowndes swear in that almost happy hour when he could still refuse to believe; and the sting of the reminder, and of the contrast between his feelings then and now, was such that he was determined his mother should not bear it with him. But yet, with all the pain it gave, the note from Lowndes both puzzled and annoyed him; it was as though there were some subtle thing between the lines, a something in a cipher to which he had not the key; and he resented being forced to reply. After long deliberation, however, this was written and rewritten, and taken stealthily to the pillar in the small hours:—

"Kensington, May 21st.

"DEAR MR. LOWNDES,—I am not of the same mind about the matter which you very kindly do not name. I hope that neither you nor I will ever have occasion to name it again, and that you will forgive me for what I said yesterday before I could believe the truth. I hardly know now what I did say, but I do honestly apologise, and only beg of you never to speak, and, if possible, not to think, of it again.

"Believe me that I am grateful for your kind offer, and more than grateful for all your goodness to my mother.

"Yours sincerely,

"HARRY RINGROSE."

This had the effect of bringing Lowndes to the flat the following afternoon, in the high spirits which were characteristic of the normal man; it was only natural they should have deserted him the day before; and yet when Harry came in and found him taking tea with his mother, radiant, voluble, hilarious, the change was such that he seemed to the boy another being. Humour shone through the gold-rimmed glasses and trembled at the tip of the pointed nose. Harry had never seen a jollier face, or listened to so boisterous a laugh; and they were what he needed, for he had come in doubly embittered and depressed.

He had been to the great house which had supplied his mother with her groceries for so many years. He had seen a member of the firm, a gentleman of presence and aplomb, in whose courtly company Harry and his old clothes were painfully outclassed. The resultant and inevitable repulse was none the less galling from being couched in terms of perfectly polite condescension. Harry carried his specimen battle-axe home in the brown paper he had taken it in, and pitched it upon the sofa with a wry face before recounting his experience.

Lowndes instantly said that he would get a price for the curios if Harry would send them along to his office. Whereupon Harry thanked him, but still looked glum, for a worse experience remained untold.

The boy was in glaring need of new clothes; he could not possibly seek work in town as he was; and Mrs. Ringrose had characteristically insisted that he should go to his father's and his own old London tailors. There was, moreover, some point in such a course, since it was now known that Mr. Ringrose had settled his tailors' account, with several others of the kind, on the very eve of his flight; so that in the circumstances these people might fairly be expected to wait for their money until Harry could earn it. Elsewhere he would have to pay ready cash, a very serious matter, if not an impossibility for some time to come. So Harry was really driven to go where he was known, but yet so ashamed, that it was only the miserable interview with the well-groomed gentleman aforesaid which had brought him to the point. He had called at the tailors' on his way home, chosen his cloth and been measured, only to be confronted by the senior partner at the door.

"What do you think he wanted?" cried Harry in a blaze. "A guarantee that they would be paid! I told them they needn't trouble to make the things at all, and out I came."

Lowndes dashed down his cup and was on his legs in an instant.

"I'll give them their guarantee," said he. "You swallow your tea and get your hat; we'll take a hansom back to your tailors, and I'll give them their guarantee!"

Harry was against any such intervention, but Mrs. Ringrose was against Harry, and in less than five minutes Lowndes had carried him off. In the hansom the spirits of that mirthful man rose higher than ever; he sat rubbing his hands and chuckling with delight; but so truculent were his sentiments that Harry, who hated a row as much as his companion appeared to like one, was not a little nervous as to what would happen, and got out finally with his heart in his mouth.

What did happen need not be described. Suffice it that Mr. Lowndes talked to that master-tailor with extraordinary energy for the space of about three minutes, and that in several different strains, preparing his soil with simple reproaches, scarifying with sarcasm, and finally trampling it down with a weight of well-worded abuse the like of which Harry had never listened to off the stage. And the effect was more extraordinary than the cause: the tradesman took it like a lamb, apologised to Harry on the spot, and even solicited his friend's custom as they turned to leave the shop. The result opened Harry's mouth in sheer amazement. After a first curt refusal, Mr. Lowndes hesitated, fingered a cloth, became gradually gracious, and in the end was measured for no fewer than three suits and an Inverness cape.

"Couldn't resist it!" said he, roaring with laughter in the cab. "Trustfulness is a virtue we should all encourage, and I hope, Ringrose, that you'll continue to encourage it in these excellent fellows. I've sown the seed, it's for you to reap the flower; and recollect that they'll think much more of you when you order six suits than when you pay for one."

"It was extraordinary," said Harry, "after the dressing-down you gave them!"

"Dressing-down?" said Lowndes. "I meant to dress 'em down, and I'll dress anybody down who needs it—of that you may be sure. What's this?

Grosvenor Square? Do you see that house with the yellow balcony in the far corner? That's my Lady Banff's—I gave *her* a bit of my mind the other evening. Went to see my Lord on business. Left standing in the hall twenty minutes. Down came my Lady to dinner, so I just asked her, as a matter of curiosity, if they took me for a stick or an umbrella, to leave me there, and then I told her what I thought of the manners and customs of her house. My Lady had me shown into the library at once, and made me a handsome apology into the bargain. I guarantee friend Yellowplush to know better next time!"

Lowndes stayed to supper at the flat, and he became better and better company as Harry Ringrose gradually yielded to the contagion of his gaiety and his good-humour. He was certainly the most entertaining of men; yet for a long time Harry resented being entertained by him, and would frown one moment because he had been forced to laugh the moment before. Nor was this because of anything that had already happened; it was due entirely to the current behaviour of Gordon Lowndes. The man took unwarrantable liberties. His status at the flat was rightly that of a privileged friend, but Harry thought he presumed upon it insufferably.

Like many great talkers, Lowndes was a vile listener, who thought nothing of interrupting Mrs. Ringrose herself; while as for Harry, he tried more than once to set some African experience of his own against the visitor's endless anecdotes; but he never succeeded, and for a time the failures rankled. It was the visitor, again, who must complain of the supper: the lamb was underdone, the mint sauce too sweet for him, and the salad dressing which was on the table not to be compared with the oil and vinegar which were not. These were the things that made Harry hate himself when he laughed; yet laugh he must; the other's intentions were so obviously good; and he did not offend Mrs. Ringrose. She encouraged him to monopolise the conversation, but that without appearing to attach too much importance to everything he said. And once when Harry caught her eye, himself raging inwardly, there was an indulgent twinkle in it which mollified him wonderfully, for it seemed to say: "These are his little peculiarities; you should not take them seriously; they do not make him any the less my friend—and yours." It was this glance which undermined Harry's hostility and prepared his heart for eventual surrender to the spell of which Gordon Lowndes was undoubted master.

"I tell you what, Ringrose," said he, as they rose from the table, "if you don't get a billet within the next month, I'll give you one myself."

"You won't!" cried Harry, incredulously enough, for the promise had been made without preliminary, and it seemed too good to be possible.

"Won't I?" laughed Lowndes; "you'll see if I won't! What's more, it'll be a billet worth half-a-dozen such as that uncle of yours is likely to get you. What would you say to three hundred for a start?"

"I knew you were joking," was what Harry said, with a sigh; and his mother turned away as though she had known it too.

"I was never more serious in my life," retorted Lowndes. "I'm up to my chin in the biggest scheme of the century—bar none—though I'm not entitled to tell you what it is at this stage. It's a critical stage, Ringrose, but this week will settle things one way or the other. It's simply a question whether the Earl of Banff will or whether the Earl of Banff won't, and he's going to answer definitely this week. If he will—and I haven't the slightest doubt of it in my own mind—the Company will be out before you know where you are—and you shall be Secretary———"

"Secretary!"

"Be good enough not to interrupt me, Ringrose. You shall be Secretary with three hundred a year. Not competent? Nonsense; I'll undertake to make you competent in a couple of hours; but if I say more, you'll know too much before the time, and I'm pledged to secrecy till we land the noble Earl. He's a pretty big fish, but I've as good as got him. However, he's to let us know this week, and perhaps it would be as well not to raise the wind on that three hundred meanwhile; but it's as good as in your pocket, Ringrose, for all that!"

Mrs. Ringrose sat in her chair, without a sound save that of her knitting needles; and Harry formed the impression that she was already in the secret of the unmentionable scheme, but that she disapproved of it. He remarked, however, that he only wished he had known of such a prospect in time to have mentioned it to his uncle at their interview.

"Your uncle!" cried Lowndes. "I should like to have seen his face if you had! I asked him to take shares the other day—told him I could put him on the best thing of the reign—and it was as good as a pantomime to see his face. Apart from his religious scruples, which make him regard the City of London as the capital of a warmer place than England, he's not what you would call one of Nature's sportsmen, that holy uncle of yours. He's a gentleman who counts the odds. I wouldn't trust him in the day of battle. Never till my dying day shall I forget our first meeting!"

And Lowndes let out a roar of laughter that might have been heard throughout the mansions; but Harry looked at his mother, who was smiling over her knitting, before he allowed himself to smile and to ask what had happened.

"Your mother had written to tell him I was going to call," said Lowndes, wiping the tears from his eyes, "and when I did go he wanted proof of my identity because I didn't happen to have a card on me. I suppose he thought I looked a shady cuss, so he took it into his head I wasn't the real Simon Pure. You see, there's nothing rash about your uncle; as for me, I burst out laughing in his face, and that made matters worse. He said he'd want a witness then—a witness to my identity before he'd discuss his sister's affairs with me. 'All right,' says I, 'you shall have half a dozen witnesses, for I'll call my underclothes! There's "Gordon Lowndes" on my shirt and collar—there's "Gordon Lowndes" on my pants and vest—and if there isn't "Gordon Lowndes" on both my socks there'll be trouble when I get home,' I told him; and I was out of my coat and waistcoat before he could stop me. I'd have gone on, too, but that was enough for your uncle! I can see him now—it was on his doorstep—but he let me in after that!"

Harry had a hearty, boyish laugh which it was a pleasure to hear, and Mrs. Ringrose heard it now as she had not heard it for two years; for she had shown that the story did not offend her by laughing herself; and besides, the boy also could see his uncle, with sable arms uplifted, and this impudent Bohemian coolly stripping on the doorstep. His innate impudence was brought home to Harry in different fashion a moment later, when the visitor suddenly complained of the light, and asked why on earth there was only one gas-bracket in a room of that size.

"Because I could not afford more," replied Mrs. Ringrose.

"Afford them, my dear madam? There should have been no question of affording them!" cried Gordon Lowndes. "You should have brought what you wanted from your own house."

"But it wasn't our own," sighed Mrs. Ringrose; "it belonged to—our creditors."

"Your creditors!" echoed Lowndes, with scathing scorn. "It makes me positively ill to hear an otherwise sensible lady speak of creditors in that submissive tone! I regard it as a sacred obligation on all of us to get to windward of our creditors, by fair means or foul. We owe it to our fellow-creatures who may find themselves similarly situated to-morrow or next day. If we don't get to windward of our creditors, be very sure they'll get to windward of us. But to pamper and pet the enemy—as though they'd dare to say a word about a petty gas-bracket!—was a perfect crime, my dear Mrs. Ringrose, and one that showed a most deplorable lack of public spirit. I only wish I'd thought of your gas-brackets when I was down there the day before yesterday!"

"Why? What would you have done?" demanded Harry with some heat.

"Come away with one in my hat!" roared Lowndes. "Come away with the chandelier next my skin!"

And he broke into a great guffaw in which Harry Ringrose joined in his own despite. It was absurd to apply conventional standards to this sworn enemy of convention. It was impossible to be angry with Gordon Lowndes. Harry determined to take no further offence at anything he might say or do, but to follow his mother's tacit example and to accept her singular friend on her own tolerant terms. Nor was it hard to see when the lad made amiable resolutions; they flew like flags upon his face; and Mrs. Ringrose was able to go to bed and to leave the pair together with an easy mind.

Whereupon they sat up till long after midnight, and Harry, having relinquished all thought of entertaining Gordon Lowndes, was himself undeniably entertained. He had seen something of the world (less than he thought, but still something), yet he had never met with anybody half so interesting as Lowndes, who had been everywhere, seen everything, and done most things, in his time. He had made and lost a fortune in different companies, the names of which Harry hardly caught, for they set him speculating upon the new Company which was to make his own small fortune too. Lowndes, however, refused to be drawn back to that momentous subject. Nor were all the exploits he recounted of a financial cast; there were some which Harry would have flatly disbelieved the day before; but one and all were consistent with the character of the man as he had seen it since.

Great names seemed as familiar to him as his own, and, after the scene at the tailors', Harry could well believe that Mr. Lowndes had heckled a very eminent politician to his inconvenience, if not to the alleged extent of altering the entire course of a General Election. He was also the very man to have defended in person an action for libel, and to have lost it by the little error of requesting the judge to "be good enough to hold his tongue." The consequences had been serious indeed, but Lowndes described them with considerable relish. His frankness was not the least of his charms as a raconteur. Before he went he had confessed to one crime at least—that of blackmailing a surgeon-baronet for a thousand pounds in his own consulting-room.

"He got a hold of the bell-rope," said Lowndes, "but it was no use his playing the game of bluff with *me*. I simply laughed in his face. He'd murdered a poor man's wife—vivisected her, Ringrose—taken her to pieces like a watch—and he'd got to pay up or be exposed."

For it was disinterested blackmail, so that even this story was characteristic if incredible. It illustrated what may be termed an officious altruism—which Harry had seen operating in his own behalf—side by side with a perfectly piratical want of principle which Lowndes took no pains to conceal. It was impossible for an impressionable young fellow, needing a friend, not to be struck by one so bluff, so masterful, so kind-hearted, and probably much less unscrupulous than it pleased him to appear; and it was impossible for Harry Ringrose not to put the kind heart first, as he came upstairs after seeing Lowndes into a hansom, and thought how joyfully he would come up them if he were sure of earning even one hundred a year.

And Lowndes said three!

"I am thankful you like him," said Mrs. Ringrose, who was still awake. "But—we all can see the faults of those we really like—and there's one fault I do see in Mr. Lowndes. He is so sanguine!" Mrs. Ringrose might have added that we see those faults the plainest when they are also our own.

"Sanguine!" said Harry. "How?"

"He expects Lord Banff to make up his mind this week."

"Well?"

"It has been 'this week' all this year!"

Harry looked very sad.

"Then you don't think much of my chances of that—three hundred? I might have seen you didn't at the time."

"No, my boy, I do not. Of his will to help you there can be no question; his ability is another matter; and we must not rely on him."

"But you say he has helped you so much?"

"In a different way."

"Well," said Harry after a pause, "in spite of what you say, he seems quite sure himself that everything will be settled to-morrow. He has an appointment with Lord Banff in the afternoon. He wants to see me afterwards, and has asked me to go down and spend the evening with them at Richmond."

Mrs. Ringrose lay conspicuously silent.

"Who are 'they,' mother?" continued her son. "Somehow or other he is a man you never associate with a family, he's so complete in himself. Is he married?"

"His wife is dead."

"Then there are children?"

"One daughter, I believe."

"Don't you know her?"

"No; and I don't want to!" cried Mrs. Ringrose. So broke the small storm which had been brewing in her grave face and altered voice.

"Why not, mother?"

"She has never been near me! Here I have been nearly two months, and she has never called. I shall refuse to see her when she does. The father can come, but we are beneath the daughter. We are in trouble, you see! I only hope you'll have very little to say to her."

"I won't go at all if you'd rather I didn't."

"No, you must go; but be prepared for a snub—and to snub her!"

The bitterness of a sweet woman is always startling, and Harry had never heard his mother speak so bitterly. Her spirit infected him, and he left her with grim promises. Yet he went to bed more interested than ever in Gordon Lowndes.

CHAPTER VII.

ON RICHMOND HILL.

It was the hour before sunset when Harry Ringrose took the train from Earl's Court to Richmond, and, referring to an envelope which Lowndes had given him overnight, inquired his way to Sandringham, Greville Road, Richmond Hill. Having no experience of suburban London, he was prepared to find a mansion not absolutely unworthy of its name, and was rather astonished at having to give that of the road to the policeman who directed him. He had half expected that officer to look impressed and say, "Oh, yes, Mr. Lowndes's; the large house on the hill; you can't mistake it." For though he gathered that Lowndes was only about to become a millionaire, and that his contempt for creditors was founded upon some former personal experience of that obnoxious class, it nevertheless appeared to Harry that his friend must be pretty well off as it was. At all events, he thought nothing of losing the last train and driving all this way home.

Harry had never been in Richmond before, and the picturesque features with which its narrow streets still abound were by no means lost upon him. Here a quaint gable, and there a tile roof, sunken and discoloured with sheer age, reminded him that he was indeed in the old country once more; and he rejoiced in the fact with a blessed surcease of the pain and shame with which his home-coming had been fraught. May was in his blood; and as he climbed the hill the words of the old song, that another Richmond claims, rang so loud in his head that he had a work to keep them back from his lips:—

"On Richmond Hill there lives a lass,

More bright than May-day morn;

Whose charms all other maids' surpass—

A rose without a thorn.

This lass so neat, with smiles so sweet,

Has won my right good will.

I'd crowns resign to call her mine,

Sweet lass of Richmond Hill!"

The young fellow could not help thinking that it was a lass of Richmond Hill he was about to meet, and wondering whether her smiles would prove sweet, and her charms superior to those of all other maids. Harry Ringrose had never been in love. He had been duly foolish in his callow day, but that was nothing. From the firm pedestal of one-and-twenty he could look back, and lay his hand upon his heart, and aver with truth that it had never been irretrievably lost. Nevertheless, Harry was quite prepared to lose his heart as soon as ever he realised the ideal which was graven upon it; or he had been so prepared until the revelation of these last days had hurled such idle aspirations to the winds. But, for some reason, the memory of that revelation did not haunt him this evening; and, accordingly, he was so prepared once more.

One of the many inconveniences of preconceiving your fate lies in the nervous feeling that it may be lurking round every corner in the shape of every woman you are about to meet. Even when he met them Harry was not always sure. His ideal was apt to be elastic in the face of obvious charms. It was only the impossibles that he knew at sight, such as the girl who was climbing the hill ahead of him at this moment. Harry would not have looked twice at her but for one circumstance.

She was tall and well-built, on a far larger scale than Harry cared about, and yet she was continually changing a bag which she carried from one hand to the other. It was a leather travelling-bag, of no excessive size, but as she carried it in one hand her body bent itself the other way; and she never had it in the same hand long.

The hill was steep and seemed interminable; it was the warm evening of a hot day; and Harry, slowly overhauling the young woman, might have seen that she had pretty hair and ears, but he could think of nothing but her burden and her fatigue. He could not even think of himself and his ideals, and had so ceased committing his besetting sin. What he did see, however, was that the girl was a lady, and he heartily wished that she were not. He longed to carry that bag for her, but he could not bring himself to offer to do so. He had too much delicacy or too little courage.

Irresolutely he slackened his pace; he was ashamed, despite his scruples, to pass her callously without a word. He was close behind her now. He heard her breathing heavily. Was there nothing he could say? Was there no way of putting it without offence? Harry was still thinking when the knot untied itself. The girl had stopped dead, and put the bag down with a deep sigh, and Harry had caught it up without thinking any more.

"What are you doing?" cried the girl. "Give that back to me at once."

Her voice was very indignant, but also a little faint; and the note of alarm with which it began changed to one of authority as she saw that, at any rate, she was not dealing with a thief.

"I beg your pardon," said Harry, very red, as he raised his hat with his unoccupied hand; "but—but you really must let me carry it a little way for you."

"I could not dream of it. Will you kindly give it me back this instant?"

The girl was now good-humoured but very firm. She also had coloured, but her lips remained pale with fatigue. And she had very fine, fearless, grey eyes; but Harry found he could defy them in such a cause, so that they flashed with anger, and a foot—no very small one—stamped heartily on the pavement.

"Did you hear what I said?"

"I did; but——"

"Give it to me!"

"It's so heavy."

"Give it to me!"

He was wondering whether the bag was full of jewels, that she was in such a state about it, when all at once she grabbed at the handle he still hesitated to relinquish. The bag came open between them—and to his amazement he saw what it contained.

Coals!

A few fell out upon the pavement. Harry stooped, put them in again, and shut the bag. The young lady had moved away. She was walking on slowly ahead, and from her shoulders Harry feared that she was crying. He followed miserably but doggedly with the bag.

She never looked round, and he never took his eyes from those broad, quivering shoulders. He felt an officious brute, but he had a certain fierce consolation too: he had got his way—he had not been beaten by a woman. And the heaviness of the bag, no longer to be wondered at, was in itself a justification; he also had changed it from hand to hand, and that more than once, before they came to the top of the hill.

Here he followed his leader down a broad turning to the left, and thence along a smaller road until she stopped before the low wooden gate of a shabby little semi-detached house. Evidently this was her destination, and she was waiting for her bag. And now Harry lost confidence with every step he took, for the girl stood squarely with her back to the gate, and her eyes were dry but very bright, as though she meant to give him a bit of her mind before she let him go.

"You may put it down here."

Harry did so without a word.

"Thank you. You are a stranger to Richmond, I think?"

The thanks had sounded ironical, and the question took Harry aback. The grey eyes looked amused, and it was the last expression he had expected in them.

"How did you know that?" he simply asked.

"You are too sunburnt for Richmond, and—perhaps—too gallant!"

"Or officious?"

Her pleasant tone put him at his ease.

"No; it was very kind of you, and one good turn deserves another. Were you looking for any particular road or house?"

"Yes, for Sandringham, in the Greville Road."

She stood aside and pointed to the name on the little wooden gate.

"Why, this is it!" gasped Harry Ringrose.

"Yes; this is Sandringham," said the girl, with a sort of shamefaced humour. "No wonder you are disappointed!"

His eyes came guiltily from the little house with the big name. "Then are you Miss Lowndes?" he inquired aghast.

"That is my name—Mr. Ringrose."

Spoken with the broadest smile, this was the last straw so far as Harry's manners were concerned.

"How on earth do you know mine?" cried he.

"I guessed it in the road."

"How could you?"

"How did I know you were a stranger to Richmond?" rejoined Miss Lowndes. "Anybody could see that you have come from foreign parts; and I had heard all about you from my father. Besides, I expected you. I only hoped to get home first with my coals. And to be caught like this—it's really too bad!"

"I am awfully sorry," murmured Harry, and with such obvious sincerity that Miss Lowndes smiled again.

"I think you may be!" said she. "One may find that stupidity in the kitchen has run one short of coals at the very moment when they are wanted most, and the quickest thing may be for one to go oneself and borrow a few from a friend. But it's hard lines to be caught doing so, Mr. Ringrose, for all that!"

So this was the explanation. To Harry Ringrose it was both simple and satisfying; but before he could say a word Miss Lowndes had changed the subject abruptly by again pointing to the grand name on the gate.

"This is another thing I may as well explain for your benefit, Mr. Ringrose; it is one of my father's little jokes. When he came here he was so tickled by the small houses with the large names that he determined to beat his neighbours at their own game. It was all I could do to prevent him from having 'Buckingham Palace' painted on the gate. So you are quite forgiven for finding it difficult to believe that this was the house, and also for upsetting my coals. And now I think we may shake hands and go in."

He took with alacrity the fine firm hand which was held out to him, and felt already at his ease as he followed Miss Lowndes to the steps, again carrying the bag. By this time, moreover, he had noted and admired her pretty hair, which was fair with a warm tinge in it, her rather deep but very pleasant voice, and the clear and healthy skin which had her father's freshness in finer shades. She was obviously older than Harry, and stronger-minded as well as less beautiful than his ideal type. But he had a feeling, even after these few minutes, which had not come to him in all the hours that he had spent with Gordon Lowndes. It was the feeling that he had found a real friend.

But the surprises of the evening were only beginning, for while Harry contemplated a warped and blistered front door, in thorough keeping with the poverty-stricken appearance of the house, it was opened by a man-servant not unworthy of the millionaire of the immediate future. And yet next moment he found himself in a sitting-room as sordid as the exterior. The visitor was still trying to reconcile these contradictions when Miss Lowndes followed him slowly into the room, reading a telegram as she came.

"Are you very hungry, Mr. Ringrose?" said she, looking up in evident anxiety.

"Not a bit."

"Because I am afraid my father will not be home for another hour. This is a telegram from him. He has been detained. But it doesn't seem fair to ask you to wait so long!"

"I should prefer it. I shall do myself much better justice in an hour's time," said Harry, laughing; but Miss Lowndes still appeared to take the situation seriously, though she also seemed relieved. And her embarrassment was notable after the way in which she had carried off the much more trying contretemps in the road. It was as though there were something dispiriting in the atmosphere of the poky and ill-favoured house, something which especially distressed its young mistress; for they sat for some time without a word, while dusk deepened in the shabby little room; and it was much to Harry's relief when he was suddenly asked if he had ever seen the view from Richmond Hill.

"Never," he replied; "will you show it to me, Miss Lowndes? I have often heard of it, and I wish you would."

"It would be better than sitting here," said his companion, "though I'm afraid you won't see much in this light. However, it's quite close, and we can try."

It was good to be in the open air again, but, as Miss Lowndes observed, it was a pity she had not thought of it before. In the park the shadows were already deep, and the deer straggling across the broad paths as they never do till nightfall. A warm glow still suffused the west, and was reflected in the river beneath, where pleasure-boats looked black as colliers on the belt of pink. It was the hour when it is dark indoors but light without, and yellow windows studded the woody levels while the contour of the trees was yet distinct. Even where the river coiled from pink to grey the eye could still follow it almost to Twickenham, a leaden track between the leaves.

"I only wish it were an hour earlier," added Miss Lowndes when she had pointed out her favourite landmarks. "Still, it's a good deal pleasanter here than indoors." She seemed a different being when she was out of that house; she had been talkative enough since they started, but now she turned to Harry.

"Tell me about Africa, Mr. Ringrose. Tell me all the interesting things you saw and did and heard about while you were out there!"

Harry caught his breath with pleasure. It was the unconscious fault of his adolescence that he was more eager to convey than receive; it was the complementary defect of the quality of enthusiasm which was Harry's strongest point. He had landed from his travels loaded like a gun with reminiscence and adventure, but the terrible return to the old home had damped his priming, and at the new home the future was the one affair of his own of which he had had time or heart to think. But now the things came back to him which he had come home longing to relate. He needed no second bidding from the sympathetic companion at his side, but began telling her, diffidently at first, then with all his boyish gusto as he caught and held her interest, the dozen and one experiences that had been on his tongue three days (that seemed three weeks) ago.

To talk and be understood—to talk and be appreciated—it was half the battle of life with Harry Ringrose at this stage of his career. It is true that he had seen but little, and true that he had done still less, even in these two last errant years of his. But whatsoever he had seen or done, that had interested him in the least, he could bring home vividly enough to anybody who would give him a sympathetic hearing. And to do so was a deep and a strange delight to him; not, perhaps, altogether unconnected with mere vanity; but ministering also to a subtler sense of which the possessor was as yet unconscious.

And Miss Lowndes listened to her young Othello, an older and more critical Desdemona, who liked him less for the dangers he had passed than for his ingenuous delight in recounting them. The talk indeed interested, but the talker charmed her, so that she was content to listen for the most part without a word. Meanwhile they were sauntering farther and farther afield, and at length the new Desdemona was compelled to tell Othello they must turn. He complied without pausing in the story. Her next interruption was more serious.

"Don't you write?" she suddenly exclaimed.

"Write what?"

"Things for magazines."

"I wish I did! The magazine at school was the only one I ever tried my hand for. Who told you I wrote?"

"Mrs. Ringrose has shown things to my father, and he thought them very good. It only just struck me that what you are telling me would make such a capital magazine sketch. But it was very rude of me to interrupt. Please go on."

"No, Miss Lowndes, I've gone on too long as it is! Here have I been talking away about Africa as though nothing had happened while I was there; and it's only three days since I landed and found out—everything!"

His voice was strangely altered: the shame of forgetting, the pain of remembering, saddened and embittered every accent. Miss Lowndes, however, who had so plainly shared his enthusiasm, as plainly shrank from him in his depression. Harry was too taken up with his own feelings to notice this. Nor did he feel his companion's silence; for what was there to be said?

"You should take to writing," was what she did say, presently. "You have a splendid capital to draw upon."

"Do you write?"

"No."

"It is odd you should speak of it. There's nothing I would sooner do for a living—and something I've got to do—only I doubt if I have it in me to do any good with my pen. I may have the capital, but I couldn't lay it out to save my life."

He spoke wistfully, however, as though he were not sure. And now Miss Lowndes seemed the more sympathethic for her momentary lapse. She was very sure indeed.

"You have only to write those things down as you tell them, and I'm certain they would take!"

"Very well," laughed Harry, "I'll have a try—when I have time. I suppose you know what your father promises me?"

"No, indeed I don't," cried Miss Lowndes.

"The Secretaryship of this new Company when it comes out!"

For some moments the girl was silent, and then: "I'd rather see you writing," she said.

"But this would mean three hundred a year."

"I would rather make one hundred by my pen!"

Harry said that he would, too, as far as liking was concerned, but that there were other considerations. He added that of course he did not count upon the Secretaryship, which seemed far too good a thing to be really within his reach, for it would be many a day before he was worth three hundred a year in any capacity. Nevertheless, it was very kind of Mr. Lowndes to have thought of such a thing at all.

"He is kind," murmured the girl, breaking a silence which had influenced Harry's tone. And it was a something in her tone that made him exclaim:

"He is the kindest man I have ever met!"

"You really think so?" she cried, wistfully.

"I know it," said Harry, at once touched and interested by her manner. "It isn't as if he'd only been kind to me. He was more than kind three days ago, and—and I didn't take it very well from him at first; but I shall never forget it now! It isn't only that, however; it's his kindness to my dear mother that I feel much more; and then—he was my father's friend!"

They walked on without a word—they were nearly home now—and this time Harry thought less of his companion's silence, for what could she say? But already he felt that he could say anything to her, and "You knew my father?" broke from him in a low voice.

"Oh, yes; I knew him very well."

"He has been here?" said Harry, looking at the semi-detached house with a new and painful interest as they stopped at the gate.

"Yes; two or three times."

"When was the last?"

But the latch clicked with his words, and Miss Lowndes was hastening up the path.

CHAPTER VIII.

A MILLIONAIRE IN THE MAKING.

There was a bright light in the little drawing-room, and Harry made sure that the master of the house had returned from town. Miss Lowndes put the question as soon as the door was opened, however, and he heard the reply as he followed her within.

"No, miss, not yet."

"Then who is here?"

"Mr. Huxtable."

"Mr. Huxtable—in the drawing-room?"

"He insisted on waiting, and I thought he might as well wait there as anywhere."

Harry thought the man's manner presumptuous, and, looking at him severely, was actually answered with a wink. Before he had time to think twice about that, however, Miss Lowndes marched erect into the drawing-room, and the visitor at her heels became the unwilling witness of a scene which he never forgot.

A little bald man had planted himself on the hearthrug, where he stood trembling like a terrier on the leash, in an attitude of indescribable truculence and determination.

"Good evening, young lady!" cried he, in a tone so insolent that Harry longed to assault him on the spot.

"Good evening, Mr. Huxtable. Do you wish to speak to me?"

"No, thank you, miss. Not this time. I've spoken to you often enough and nothing's come of it. To-night I mean to see your pa. 'E's not come 'ome yet, 'asn't 'e? Then 'ere I stick till 'e does."

"May I ask what you want with him?"

"May you arst?" roared Mr. Huxtable. "I like that, I'm blessed if I don't! Oh, yes, you may arst, young lady, and you may pretend you don't know; and much good it'll do you! I want my money; that's what *I* want. Thirty-eight pound seventeen shillings and fourpence for butcher-meat delivered at this 'ere 'ouse—that's all *I* want! If you've got it 'andy, well and good; and if 'e's got it 'andy when 'e comes in, well and good again, for 'ere I wait; but if not, I'll county-court 'im to-morrow, and there's plenty more'll follow my example. It's a perfect scandal the way this 'ouse is conducted. Not a coal or a spud, let alone a bit o' meat, are you known to 'ave paid for this blessed year. It's all over Richmond, and for my part I'm sick of it. I've been put off and put off but I won't be put off no more. 'Ere I stick till 'is nibs comes in."

During the first half of this harangue—considerably lengthened by pauses during which the tradesman gasped for breath and seemed once or twice on the verge of apoplexy—Harry Ringrose was on the horns of a dilemma in the hall. One moment he was within an ace of rushing in and ejecting the fellow on his own responsibility, and the next he felt it better to spare his new friend's feelings by making his own escape. But the butcher had only partly said his say when a latch-key grated in the door, and Gordon Lowndes entered in time to overhear the most impertinent part. Shutting the door softly behind him, he stood listening on the mat, with his head on one side and a very comical expression on his face. Harry had been tremulous with indignation. Lowndes merely shook with suppressed amusement; and, handing a heavy parcel to Harry, entered the room, as the tradesman ceased, in a perfect glow of good-humour and geniality.

"Ah! my dear Huxtable, how are you?" cried he. "Delighted to see you; only hope I haven't kept you very long. You must blame the Earl of Banff, not me; he kept me with him until after eight o'clock. Not a word, my dear sir—not one syllable! I know exactly what you are going to say, and don't wonder at your wishing to see me personally. My dear Huxtable, I sympathise with you from my soul! How much is it? Thirty or forty pounds, eh? Upon my word it's too bad! But there again the Earl of Banff's to blame, and I've a very good mind to let you send in your account to him. His Lordship has been standing between me and a million of money all this year, but he won't do so much longer. I think I've brought him to reason at last. My good Mr. Huxtable, we're on the eve of the greatest success in modern finance. The papers will be full of it in about a week's time, and I shall be a rich man. But meanwhile I'm a poor one—I've put my all on it—I've put my shirt on it—and I'm a much poorer man than ever you were, Huxtable. Poor men should hang together, shouldn't they? Then stand by me another week, and I give you my word I'll stand by you. I'll pay you thirty shillings in the pound! Fanny, my dear, write Mr. Huxtable an IOU for half as much again as we owe him; and let him county-court me for *that* if he doesn't get it before he's many days older!"

Mr. Huxtable had made several ineffectual attempts to speak; now he was left without a word. Less satisfied than bewildered, he put the IOU in his pocket and was easily induced to accept a couple of the Earl of Banff's cigars before he went. Lowndes shook hands with him on the steps, and returned rubbing his own.

"My dear Ringrose," said he, "I'm truly sorry you should have come in for this little revelation of our *res angusta*, but I hope you will lay to heart the object-lesson I have given you in the treatment of that harmful and unnecessary class known as creditors. There are but two ways of treating them. One is to kick them out neck-and-crop, and the other you have just seen for yourself. But don't misunderstand me, Ringrose! I meant every word I said, and he shall have his thirty shillings in the pound. The noble Earl has been a difficult fish to play, but I think I've landed him this time. Yes, my boy, you'll be drawing your three hundred a year, and I my thirty thousand, before midsummer; but I'll tell you all about it after supper. Why, bless my soul, that's the supper you've got in your hands, Ringrose! Take it from him, Fanny, and dish it up, for I'm as hungry as a coach-load of hunters, and I've no doubt Ringrose is the same."

And now Harry understood the trepidation with which Miss Lowndes had consulted him as to whether they should wait supper for her father, and her relief on hearing his opinion on the point: there had been no supper in the house. Lowndes, however, had brought home material for an excellent meal, of which caviare, a raised pie, French rolls, camembert, peaches and a pineapple, and a bottle of Heidsieck, were conspicuous elements. Black coffee followed, rather clumsily served by the man-servant, who waited in a dress suit some sizes too small for him. And after supper Harry Ringrose at last heard something definite concerning the Company from which he was still assured that he might count on a certain income of three hundred pounds a year.

"Last night my tongue was tied," said Lowndes; "but to-night the matter is as good as settled; and I may now speak without indiscretion. I must tell you first of all that the Company is entirely my own idea—and a better one I never had in my life. It is founded on the elementary principle that the average man gives more freely to a good cause than to a bad one, but most freely to the good cause out of which he's likely to get some change. He enjoys doing good, but he enjoys it most when it pays him best, and there you have the root of the whole matter. Only hit upon the scheme which is both lucrative and meritorious, which gives the philanthropist the consolation of reward, and the money-grubber the kudos of philanthropy, and your fortune's made. You may spread the Gospel or the Empire, and do yourself well out of either; but, for my part, I wanted something nearer home—where charity begins, Ringrose—and it took me years to hit upon the right thing. Ireland has been my snare: to ameliorate the Irish peasant and the English shareholder at the same swoop: it can't be done. I wasted whole months over the Irish Peasants' Potato Produce Company, but it wouldn't pan out. Nobody will put money into Ireland, and potatoes are cheap already as the dirt they grow in. But I was working in the right direction, and the crofter grievances came as a godsend to me about a year ago. The very thing! I won't trouble you with the intermediate stages; the Highland Crofters' Salmon and Trout Supply Association, Limited, will be registered this week; and the greatest of Scottish landlords, my good old Earl of Banff, is to be Chairman of Directors and rope in all the rest."

Harry asked how it was to be made to pay. Lowndes had every detail at his finger-ends, and sketched out an amazing programme with bewildering volubility. The price of salmon would be reduced a hundred per cent. The London shops would take none but the Company's fish. Fresh trout would sell like herrings in the street, and the Company would buy up the fishmongers' shops all over the country, just as brewers bought up public-houses. As soon as possible they would have their own line to the North, and expresses full of nothing but fish would do the distance without stopping in time hitherto unprecedented in railway annals.

"But," said Harry, "there are plenty of fish in the sea, and in other places besides the Highlands."

"So there are, but in ten years' time we shall own every river in the kingdom, and every cod-bank round the coast."

"And where will the crofters come in then?"

Lowndes roared with laughter.

"They won't come in at all. It will be forgotten that they ever were in: the original Company will probably be incorporated with the British Fresh Water and Deep Sea Fishing Company, Limited. Capital ten millions. General Manager, Sir Gordon Lowndes, Bart., Park Lane, W. Secretary, H. Ringrose, Esq., at the Company's Offices, Trafalgar Square. We shall buy up the Grand Hotel and have them there. As for the crofters, they'll be our Empire and our Gospel; we'll play them for all they're worth in the first year or two, and then we'll let them slide."

Miss Lowndes had been present all this time, and Harry had stolen more than one anxious glance in her direction. She never put in a word, nor could she be said to wear her thoughts upon her face, as she bent it over some needlework in the corner where she sat. Yet it was the daughter's silent presence which kept Harry himself proof for once against the always contagious enthusiasm of the father. He could not help coupling it with other silences of the early evening, and the Highland Crofters' Salmon and Trout Supply Association, Limited, left him as cold as he felt certain it left Miss Lowndes. It was now after eleven, however, and he rose to bid her good-night, while Lowndes went to get his hat in order to escort him to the station.

"And I shall never forget our walk," added Harry, and unconsciously wrung her hand as though it were that of some new-found friend of his own sex.

"Then don't forget my advice," said Miss Lowndes, "but write—write—write—and come and tell me how you get on!"

It was her last word to him, and for days to come it stimulated Harry Ringrose, like many another remembered saying of this new friend, whenever he thought of it. But at the time he was most struck by her tacit dismissal of the more brilliant prospects which had been discussed in her hearing.

"A fine creature, my daughter," said Lowndes, on the way to the station. "She's one to stand by a fellow in the day of battle—she's as staunch as steel."

"I can see it," Harry answered, with enthusiasm.

"Yes, yes; you have seen how it is with us, Ringrose. There's no use making a secret of it with you, but I should be sorry for your mother to know the hole we've been in, especially as we're practically out of it. Yet you may tell her what you like; she may wonder Fanny has never been to see her, but she wouldn't if she knew what a time the poor girl has had of it! You've no conception what it has been, Ringrose. I couldn't bear to speak of it if it wasn't all over but the shouting. To-night there was oil in the lamps, but I shouldn't like to tell you how many times we've gone to bed in the dark since they stopped our gas. You may keep your end up in the City, because if you don't you're done for, but it's the very devil at home. We drank cold water with our breakfast this morning, and I can't conceive how Fanny got in coals to make the coffee to-night."

Harry could have told him, but he held his tongue. He was trying to reconcile the present tone of Lowndes, which had in it a strong dash of remorse, with the countless extravagances he had already seen him commit. Lowndes seemed to divine his thoughts.

"You may wonder," said he, "how I managed to raise wind enough for the provender I had undertaken to bring home. I wonder if I dare tell you? I called at your tailors' on my way to the noble Earl's, and—and I struck them for a fiver! There, there, Ringrose, they'll get it back next week. I've lived on odd fivers all this year, and I simply didn't know where else to turn for one to-day. Yet they want me to pay an income tax! I sent in my return the other day, and they sent it back with 'unsatisfactory' written across my writing. So *I* sent it back with 'I entirely agree with you' written across theirs, and that seems to have shut them up. One of the most pestilent forms of creditor is the tax gatherer, and the income tax is the most iniquitous of all. Never you fill one in correctly, Ringrose, if you wish me to remain your friend."

"But," said Harry, as they reached the station and were waiting for the train, "you not only keep servants——"

"Servants?" cried Lowndes. "We have only one, and she's away at the seaside. I send her there for a change whenever she gets grumpy for want of wages. I tell her she looks seedy, and I give her a sovereign to go. It has the air of something thrown in, and it comes a good deal cheaper than paying them their wages, Ringrose. I make you a present of the tip for what it's worth."

"But you have a man-servant, too?"

"A man-servant! My good fellow, that's no servant of mine. I only make it worth his while to lend a hand."

"Who is he, then?"

"This is your train; jump in and I'll tell you."

The spectacled eyes were twinkling, and the sharp nose twitching, when Harry leant out of the third-class carriage window.

"Well, who is it?"

"The old dodge, Ringrose, the old dodge."

"What's that?"

"The Man in Possession!"

And Gordon Lowndes was left roaring with laughter on the platform.

CHAPTER IX.

THE CITY OF LONDON.

It was a considerably abridged version of his visit to Richmond which Mrs. Ringrose received from her son. Gordon Lowndes had indeed given Harry free leave to tell his mother what he liked, but not even to her could the boy bring himself to repeat all that he had seen and heard. He preferred to quote the frank admissions of Lowndes himself, and that with reticence and a definite object. It was Harry's ambition to remove his mother's bitterness against the young woman who had never been to see her; and, by explaining the matter as it had been explained to him, he easily succeeded, since Mrs. Ringrose would have sympathised and sorrowed with her worst enemy when that enemy was in distress. In uprooting one prejudice, however, her son went near to planting another in its stead.

"I only hope, my boy, that you are not going to fall in love with her."

"Mother!"

"She seems to have made a deep impression on you."

"But not that sort of impression! She is a fine creature, I can see, and we got on capitally together. We shall probably become the best of friends. But you need have no fears on any other score. Why, she must be ever so much older than I am."

"She is twenty-seven. He told me so."

"There you are! Twenty-seven!" cried Harry, triumphantly.

But it was not a triumph he enjoyed. Twenty-seven seemed a great age to him, and six years an impassable gulf. Doubtless it was just as well, especially when a person did not in the least resemble another person's ideal; still, he had not supposed she was so old as that. He wished he had not been told her age. Certainly it gave him a sense of safety, just as he was beginning to wonder what the view would be like from Richmond Hill to-day. But it was a little dull to feel so safe as all that.

This was the day on which Harry Ringrose had intended to pack up his African curios and send them off to Lowndes's office. But, after the conversation of which the above was a snatch, his mother charged him to do nothing of the kind. If Mr. Lowndes was in such difficulties, it was certainly not their place to add to them by claiming further favours at his hands. Harry agreed, but said the idea had originated with Lowndes himself. His mother was firm on the point, and counselled him either to sell his own wares or to listen to her and give up the idea.

So Harry haunted the Kensington Public Library, and patiently waited his turn for such journals as the *Exchange and Mart*. But it was in an evening paper that he came across the advertisement which brought the first grist to his mill. A lady in a suburb guaranteed good prices for secondhand books, left-off jewellery, and all kinds of bric-á;-brac and "articles of vertu," and inserted her advertisement in places as original as itself. It caught Harry's eye more than once before the idea occurred to him; but at length he made his way to that suburb with a pair of ostrich eggs, an assegai, and a battle-axe studded with brass-headed nails. He came back with a basket of strawberries, a pot of cream, and several shillings in his pocket. Next evening a post-office order to the amount of that first-class fare to London was remitted to Gordon Lowndes, while a new silk hat hung on the pegs, to give the boy a chance in the City. All that now remained of the curios were one pair of ostrich eggs and a particularly murderous tomahawk, with which Harry himself chopped up the empty packing-cases to save in firewood.

So a few days passed, and the new clothes came home, and Harry Ringrose was externally smart enough for the Stock Exchange itself, before the first letter came from Uncle Spencer. He had spoken to several of the business men among his congregation, but, he regretted to say, with but little result so far. Not that this had surprised him, as conscience had of course forbidden him to represent his nephew as other than he was in respect of that training and those qualifications in which Harry was so lamentably deficient. He understood that for every vacant post there were some hundreds of applicants, all of whom could write shorthand and keep books, while the majority had taken the trouble to master at least one foreign language. Harry had probably learned French at school, but doubtless he had wasted his opportunities in that as in other branches. Shorthand, however, appeared to be the most essential requirement, and, as it was unfortunately omitted from the public-school curriculum, Mr. Walthew was sending Harry a "Pitman's Guide," in the earnest hope that he would immediately apply himself to the mastery of this first step to employment and independence. Meanwhile, one gentleman, whose name and address were given, had said that he would be glad to see Henry if he cared to call, and of course it was just possible that something might come of it. Henry would naturally leave no stone unturned, and would call on this gentleman without delay. Uncle Spencer, however, did not fail to add that he was not himself sanguine of the result.

"He never is," said Harry. "What's the good of going?"

"You must do what your uncle says," replied Mrs. Ringrose, to whom the letter had been written.

"But what's the good if he's given me away beforehand? He will have told the fellow I can't even write an office fist, and am generally no use, so why should he take me on? And if the fellow isn't going to take me on, why on earth should I go and see him?"

Mrs. Ringrose pointed out that this was begging the question, and reminded Harry that his Uncle Spencer took a pessimistic view of everything. She herself then went to the opposite extreme.

"I think it an excellent sign that he should want to see you at all, and I feel sure that when he does see you he will want to snap you up. What a good thing you have your new clothes to go in! Your uncle doesn't say what the business is, but I am quite convinced it has something to do with Africa, and that your experience out there is the very thing they want. So be sure that you agree to nothing until we have talked it over."

Harry spent a few minutes in somewhat pusillanimous contemplation of the Pitman hieroglyphs, wondering if he should ever master them, and whether it would help him so very much if he did. It was not that he was afraid of work, for he only asked to be put into harness at once and driven as hard as they pleased. But it was a different matter to be told first to break oneself in; and to begin instantly and in earnest and alone required a higher order of moral courage than Harry could command just then.

But he went into the City that same forenoon, and he saw the gentleman referred to in his uncle's letter. The interview was not more humiliating than many another to which Harry submitted at the same bidding; but it was the first, and it hurt most at the time. No sooner had it begun than Harry realised that he had no clue as to the relations subsisting between Mr. Walthew and the man of business, nor yet as to what had passed between them on the subject of himself, and he saw too late that he had allowed himself to be placed in a thoroughly false position. It looked, however, as though the clergyman had been less frank than he professed, for Harry was put through a second examination, and his admissions received with the most painful tokens of surprise. He was even asked for a specimen of his handwriting, which self-consciousness made less legible than ever; in the end his name was taken, "in case we should hear of anything," and he was bowed out with broken words of gratitude on his lips and bitter curses in his heart.

He went home vowing that he never would submit to that indignity again: yet again and again he did.

Mr. Walthew was informed of the result of the interview which he had instigated, and wrote back to say how little it surprised him. But he mentioned another name and another address, and, in short, sent his nephew hat-in-hand to some half-dozen of his friends and acquaintances, none of whom showed even a momentary inclination to give the lad a trial. Harry did not blame them, but he did blame his uncle for making him a suppliant in one unlikely quarter after another. Yet he never refused to go when it came to the point; for, though a week slipped by without his learning to write a line of shorthand, Harry Ringrose had character enough not to neglect a chance—no matter how slight—for fear of a rebuff—no matter how brutal.

Yet he never forgot the exquisite misery of those unwarrantable begging interviews: the excitement of seeking for the office in the swarming, heated labyrinth of the City—the depression of the long walk home with another blank drawn from the bag. How he used to envy the smart youths in the short black jackets and the shiny hats—all doing something—all earning something! And how stolidly he looked the other way when in one or two of those youths he recognised a schoolfellow. How could he face anybody he had ever known before?—an idler, a pauper, and disgraced. They would only cut him as he had been cut that first morning on his way to the old home; therefore he cut them.

But one day he was forced to break this sullen rule: his arm was grabbed by the man he had all but passed, and a sallow London face compelled his recognition.

"You're a nice one, Ringrose!" said a voice with the London twang. "Is it so many years since you shared a cabin on a ship called the *Sobraon*, with a chap of the name of Barker?"

"I'm awfully sorry," cried Harry with a blush. "You—I wasn't looking for any one I knew. How are you, Barker?"

"Oh, as well as a Johnny can be in this hole of a City. Thinking of knocking up again and getting the gov'nor to send me another long voyage. I'm not a man of leisure like you, Ringrose. What brings *you* here?"

"Oh, I've only been to see a man," said Harry, without technical untruth.

"I pictured you loafin' about that rippin' old place in the photos you used to have up in our cabin. Not gone to Oxford yet, then?"

"No—the term doesn't begin till October. But——" Harry tried to tell the truth here, but the words choked him, and the moment passed.

"Not till October! Four clear months! What a chap you are, Ringrose; it makes me want to do you an injury, upon my Sam it does. Look at me! At it from the blessed week after I landed—at it from half-past nine to six, and all for a measly thirty-five bob a week. How would you like that, eh? How would you like that?"

Harry's mouth watered, but he said he didn't know, and contrived to force another smile as he held out a trembling hand.

"Got to be going, have you?" said the City youth. "I thought you bloated Johnnies were never in a hurry? Well, well, give a poor devil a thought sometimes, cooped up at a desk all day long. Good-bye—you lucky dog!"

The tears were in Harry's eyes as he went his way, yet the smile was still upon his lips, and it was grimly genuine now. If only the envious Barker knew where the envy really lay! How was it he did not? To the conscious wretch it was a revelation that all the world was not conversant with his disappointment and his disgrace.

To think that he had talked of going up to Oxford next term! It had never been quite decided, and he blushed to think how he must have spoken of it at sea. Still more was he ashamed of his want of common pluck in pretending for a moment that he was going up still.

"'Pluck lost, all lost,'" he thought, remorsefully; "and I've lost it already! Oh, what would Innes think of me, for carrying his motto in my heart when I don't need it, and never acting on it when I do!"

That night he wrote it out on the back of a visiting card, and tacked the tiny text to the wall above his bed:—

"MONEY LOST—LITTLE LOST
HONOUR LOST—MUCH LOST
PLUCK LOST—ALL LOST."

And his old master's motto sent Harry Ringrose with a stout heart on many another errand to the City, and steeled and strengthened him when he came home hopeless in the evening. Yet it was very, very hard to live up to; and many also were the unworthy reactions which afflicted him in those dark summer days, that he had expected to be so free from care, and so full of happiness.

One afternoon he crept down from a stockbroker's office, feeling smaller than ever (for that stockbroker had made the shortest work yet of him), to see a man selling halfpenny papers over a placard that proclaimed "extraordinary scoring at Lord's." A spirit of recklessness came over Harry, and buying a paper was but the thin end of his extravagance. A minute later he had counted his money and found enough to take him to St. John's Wood and into the ground; and it was still the money that he had obtained for his curios; and town was intolerable with that sinister London heat which none feel more than your seasoned salamander from the tropics. Harry's new clothes were sticking to him, and he thought how delicious it would be at Lord's. To think was to argue. What was sixpence after all? He had had no lunch, and that would have cost him sixpence more or less; he would do without any lunch, and go to Lord's instead.

It was delicious there, and Harry was so lucky as to squeeze into a seat. Quite a breeze, undreamt of in the City, blew across the ground, blowing the flannels of the players against their bodies and fetching little puffs of dust from the pitch. The wicket was crumbling, the long scores of the morning were at an end. It was only the tail of the Middlesex team that Harry was in time to see batting, but they were good enough for him. All his life he had nourished a hopeless passion for the game, and every care was forgotten until the last man was out.

"Why—Harry?"

He had been looking at the pitch, and he spun round like an arrested criminal. Yet the strong hand on his shoulder was also delicate and full of kindness, and he was gazing into the best face he had ever seen. His ideal woman he was still to find, but his ideal man he had loved and worshipped from his twelfth year; and here he stood, supple and athletic as ever, only slimmer and graver; and their hands were locked.

"Mr. Innes!"

"I had no idea you were in England, Harry."

"I have been back three weeks."

"Why didn't you write?"

He knew everything. Harry saw it in the kind, strong face, and heard it in a voice rich with sympathy and reproach.

"I was too ashamed," he murmured—and he hung his head.

"You might have trusted me, old fellow," said Mr. Innes. "Come and sit on top of the pavilion and tell me all about yourself."

At any other time it would have been a sufficient joy to Harry Ringrose to set foot in that classic temple of the sacred game; now he had eyes for nothing and nobody but the man who led him up the steps, through the cricketing throng, up the stairs. And when they sat together on top, and the ground was cleared, and play resumed, not another ball did Harry watch with intelligent eyes. He was sitting with the man to whom he had been too proud to write, but whose disciple he had been at heart for many a year. He was talking to the object of his early hero-worship, and he found him his hero still.

Mr. Innes listened attentively, gravely, but said very little himself. He appreciated the difficulty of starting in life without money or influence, and was too true a friend to make light of it. He thought that business would be best if only an opening could be found. Schoolmastering led to nothing unless one had money or a degree. Still they must think and talk it over, and Harry must come down to Guildford and see the new chapel and the swimming-bath. Could he come for a day or two before the end of the term? Was he sure he could leave his mother? Harry was quite sure, but would write when he got home.

Then it was time for Mr. Innes to go, but first he gave Harry tea in the members' dining-room, and after that a lift in his hansom as far as Piccadilly. So that Harry reached home both earlier and in better case than he might have done; whereupon Mrs. Ringrose, hearing his key in the latch, came out to meet him with a face of mystery which contrasted oddly with his radiance.

"Oh, mother," he cried, "whom do you think I've seen! Innes! Innes! and he's the same as ever, and wants me to go and stay with him, so you were right, and I was wrong! What is it then? Who's here?" His voice sank in obedience to her gestures.

"Your Uncle Spencer," she whispered, tragically.

"Delighted to see him," cried Harry, who had been made much too happy by one man to be readily depressed by any other.

"He has been waiting to see you since five o'clock, my boy."

"Has he? Very sorry to hear that, uncle," said Harry, bursting into the sitting-room and greeting the clergyman with the heartiness he was feeling for all the world. Mr. Walthew looked at his watch.

"Since a quarter before five, Mary," said he, "and now it wants seven minutes to six. Not that I shall grudge the delay if it be attributable to the only cause I can imagine to account for it. The circumstances, Henry, are hardly those which warrant levity; if you have indeed been successful at last, as I hope to hear——"

"Successful, uncle?"

"I understand that you have been to see the gentleman on the Stock Exchange, who was kind enough to say that he would see you, and of whom I wrote to you yesterday?"

"So I have! I had quite forgotten that."

"Forgotten it?" cried Mr. Walthew.

"I beg your pardon, Uncle Spencer," said Harry, respectfully enough; "but since I saw your friend I have been with Mr. Innes my old schoolmaster, the best man in the whole world, and I am afraid it has put the other interview right out of my head."

"He did give you an interview, however?"

"Yes, for about a minute."

"And nothing came of it, as usual?" sneered the clergyman.

"And nothing came of it—as usual—I am very sorry to say, Uncle Spencer."

"And what time was this?"

"Between two and three."

"You must excuse me, Henry, but I am doing my best to obtain employment for you—I cannot say I have much hope now—still, I am doing my best, and I am naturally interested in the use you make of your time. May I ask—as I think I have a right to ask—where you have spent the afternoon?"

"Certainly, Uncle Spencer; at Lord's Cricket-ground."

Harry was well aware that he had delivered a bombshell, and he quite expected to receive a broadside in return. But he had forgotten Uncle Spencer's mode of expressing superlative displeasure. It has been said that Mr. Walthew never smiled, but there were occasions when a weird grin shed a sort of storm-light on his habitual gloom. That was when indignation baffled invective, and righteous anger fell back on holy scorn. The present was an occasion in point.

Mr. Walthew stared at Harry without a word, but gradually this unlovely look broke out upon him, and at last he positively chuckled in his beard.

"You are out of work, and too incompetent to obtain any," said he, "and yet you can waste your own time and your mother's money in watching a cricket-match!"

"I went without my lunch in order to do so," was Harry's defence. "And besides, it was my money—I got it for my spears and things."

"And you call that your money?" cried Uncle Spencer. "I would not talk about my money until I was paying for my board and residence under this roof!"

"Now, that will do!" cried Mrs. Ringrose. "That is my business, Spencer, and I will not allow you to speak so to my boy."

"Come, come, mother," Harry interrupted, "my uncle is quite right from his point of view. I admit I had qualms about going to Lord's myself. But I think I must have been meant to go—I know there was some meaning in my meeting Innes."

"If anything could surprise me in you, Henry," resumed Mr. Walthew, "it would be the Pagan sentiments which you have just pained me by uttering. May you live to pray forgiveness for your heresy, as also for your extravagance! But of the latter I will say no more, though I certainly think, Mary, that where my assistance has been invoked I have a right to speak my mind. The waste of money is, however, even less flagrant, in my opinion, than the waste of time. It is now several days, Henry, since I sent you a guide to shorthand. An energetic and conscientious fellow, as anxious as you say you are to work for his daily bread, could have mastered at least the rudiments in the time. Have you?"

"I told you he had not!" cried Mrs. Ringrose. "How can you expect it, when every day he has been seeking work in the City? And he comes in so tired!"

"Not too tired to go to Lord's Cricket-ground, however," was the not unjust rejoinder. "But perhaps his energy has found another outlet? Last time I was here he was going to write articles and poems for the magazines—so I understood. How many have you written, Henry?"

Harry scorned to point out that it was his mother's words which were being quoted against him, not his own; yet ever since his evening at Richmond he had been meaning to try his hand at something, and he felt guilty as he now confessed that he had not written a line.

"I was sure of it!" cried the clergyman. "You talk of getting employment, but you will not take the trouble to qualify yourself for the humblest post; you talk of writing, but you will not take the trouble even to write! Not that I suppose for a moment anything would come of it if you did! The magazines, Henry, do not open their columns to young fellows without literary training, any more than houses of business engage clerks without commercial education or knowledge. Yet it would be something even if you tried to write! It would be something if you wrote—as probably you would write—for the waste-paper basket and the dust-bin. But no, you seem to have no application, no energy, no sense of duty; and what more I can do for you I fail to see. I have written several letters on your account; I have risked offending several friends. Nothing has come of it, and nothing is likely to come of it until you put your own shoulder to the wheel. I have put mine. I have done *my* best. My conscience is an easy one, at any rate."

Mr. Walthew caught up his hat and brought these painful proceedings to a close by rising abruptly, as though his feelings were too much for him. Mrs. Ringrose took his hand without a word, and without a word Harry showed him out.

"So his conscience is easy!" cried the boy, bitterly. "He talks as if that had been his object—to ease his conscience—not to get me work. He has sent me round the City like a beggar, and he calls that doing his best! I had a good mind to tell him what I call it."

"I almost wish you had," said Mrs. Ringrose, shedding tears.

"No, mother, there was too much truth in what he says. I have been indolent. Nevertheless, I believe Innes will get me something to do. And meanwhile I intend to have my revenge on Uncle Spencer."

"How, my boy?"

Harry had never looked so dogged.

"By getting something into a magazine within a week."

CHAPTER X.

A FIRST OFFENCE.

When Harry Ringrose vowed that he would get something into a magazine within a week, he simply meant that he would write something and get it taken by some editor. But even so he had no conception of the odds against him. Few beginners can turn out acceptable matter at a day's notice, and fewer editors accept within the week. Fortune, however, often favours the fool who rushes in.

Harry began wisely by deciding to make his first offering poetical, for verses of kinds he had written for years, and besides, they would come quicker if they came at all. Undoubted indolence is also discernible in this choice, but on the whole it was the sound one, and that very evening saw Harry set to work in a spirit worthy of a much older literary hand.

He found among the books the selected poems of Shelley which he had brought home some mid-summers before as a prize for his English examination. His own language was indeed the only one for which poor Harry had shown much aptitude, though for a youth who had scribbled for his school magazine, and formed the habit of shedding verses in his thirteenth year, he was wofully ill-read even in that. Let it be confessed that he took down his Shelley with the cynical and shameless intention of seeking what he might imitate in those immortal pages. The redeeming fact remains that he read in them for hours without once recalling his impious and immoral scheme.

It was years since he had dipped into the book, and its contents caused him naive astonishment. He had read a little poetry in his desultory way. Tennyson he loved, and Byron he had imitated at school But in all his adventurings on the Ægean seas of song, he had never chanced upon such a cluster of golden islets as the lyrics in this selection. The epic mainland had always less attraction for him. He found it demand a concentrative effort, and Harry was very sorry and even ashamed, but he loved least to read that way. So he left "Alastor" and "The Witch of Atlas" untouched and untried, and spent half the night in ecstasies over such discoveries as the "Indian Serenade" and "Love's Philosophy." These were the things for him; the things that could be written out on half a sheet of notepaper or learnt in five minutes; the things he loved to read, and would have died to write.

He forgot his proposed revenge; he forgot his uttered vow. He forgot the sinister design with which he had taken up his Shelley, and it was pure love of the lines that left him, when he had blown out his candle, saying his last-learnt over to himself:

"Rarely, rarely, comest thou,

Spirit of Delight!

Wherefore hast thou left me now

Many a day and night?

Many a weary night and day

'Tis since thou art fled away.

How shall ever one like me

Win thee back again?

With the joyous and the free

Thou wilt scoff at pain.

Spirit false! thou hast forgot

All but those who need thee not.

As a lizard with the shade

Of a trembling leaf,

Thou with sorrow art dismayed——"

Here he stuck fast and presently fell asleep, to think no more of it till he was getting up next morning. He was invaded with a dim recollection of this poem while the water was running into his bath. As he took his plunge, the lines sprang out clear as sunshine after rain, and the man in the bath made a discovery.

They were not Shelley's lines at all. They were his own.

At breakfast he was distraught. Mrs. Ringrose complained. Harry pulled out an envelope, made a note first, and then his apology. Mrs. Ringrose returned as usual to her room, but Harry did not follow her with his pipe. He went to his own room instead, and sat down on the unmade bed, with a pencil, a bit of paper, and a frightful furrow between his downcast eyes. In less than half-an-hour, however, the thing was done: a highly imitative effort in the manner of those verses which he had been saying to himself last thing the night before.

The matter was slightly different: the subject was dreams, not delight, and instead of "Spirit of Delight," the dreams were apostrophised as "Spirits of the Night." Then the form of the stanza was freshened up a little: the new poet added a seventh line, rhyming with the second and fourth, while the last word of the fifth was common to all the stanzas, and necessitated a new and original double-rhyme in the sixth line of each verse. Harry found a rhyming dictionary (purchased in his school-days for the benefit of the school magazine) very handy in this connection. It was thus he made such short work of his rough draft. But the fair copy was turned out (in the sitting-room) in even quicker time, and a somewhat indiscreet note written to the Editor of *Uncle Tom's Magazine*, though not on the lines which Mrs. Ringrose had once suggested. A "stamped directed envelope" was also prepared, and enclosed in compliance with *Uncle Tom's* very explicit "Notice to Contributors." Then Harry stole down and out, and posted his missive with a kind of guilty pride: after all, the deed itself had been a good deal less cold-blooded than the original intention.

Mrs. Ringrose knew nothing. She had seen Harry scribble on an envelope, and that was all. She knew how the boy blew hot and cold, and she did him the injustice of concluding he had renounced his vow, but the kindness of never voicing her conclusion. Yet his restless idleness, and a something secretive in his manner, troubled her greatly during the next few days, and never more than on the Saturday morning, when Harry came in late for breakfast and there was a letter lying on his plate.

"You seem to have been writing to yourself," said Mrs. Ringrose, as she looked suspiciously from Harry to the letter.

"To myself?" he echoed, and without kissing her he squeezed round the table to his place.

"Yes; that's your writing, isn't it? And it looks like one of my envelopes!"

It was both. Harry stood gazing at his own superscription, and weighing the envelope with his eye. He was afraid to feel it. It looked too thin to contain his verses. It was too thin! Between finger and thumb it felt absolutely empty. He tore it open, and read on a printed slip the sweetest words his eyes had ever seen.

"The Editor of *Uncle Tom's Magazine* has great pleasure in accepting for publication———"

The title of the verses (a very bad one) was filled in below, the date below that, and that was all.

"Oh, mother, they've accepted my verses!"

"Who?"

"*Uncle Tom's Magazine.*"

"Did you actually send some verses to *Uncle Tom*?"

"Yes, on Tuesday, the day after Uncle Spencer was here. I've done what I said I'd do. He'll see I'm not such an utter waster after all."

"And you—never—told—me!"

His mother's eyes were swimming. He kissed them dry, and began to make light of his achievement.

"Mother, I couldn't. I didn't know what you would think of them. I didn't think much of them myself, nor do I now. The verses in *Uncle Tom* are not much. And then—I thought it would be a surprise."

"Well, it wouldn't have been one if I had known you had sent them," said Mrs. Ringrose; and now she was herself again. "I only hope, my boy," she added, "that they will pay you something."

"Of course they will. *Uncle Tom* must have an excellent circulation."

"Then I hope they'll pay you something handsome. Did you tell the Editor how long we have taken him in?"

"Mother!"

"Then I've a great mind to write and tell him myself. I am sure it would make a difference."

"Yes; it would make the difference of my getting the verses back by return of post," said Harry, grimly.

Mrs. Ringrose looked hurt, but gave way on the point, and bade him go on with his breakfast. Harry did so with the *Uncle Tom* acceptance spread out and stuck up against the marmalade dish, and one eye was on it all the time. Afterwards he went to his room and read over the rough draft of his verses, which he had not looked at since he sent them away. He could not help thinking a little more of them than he had thought then. He wondered how they would look in print, and referred to one of the bound *Uncle Toms* to see.

"Well, have you brought them?" said Mrs. Ringrose when he could keep away from her no longer.

"The verses? No, dear, I have only a very rough draft of them, which you couldn't possibly read; and I could never read them to you—I really couldn't."

"Not to your own mother?"

He shook his head. He was also blushing; and his diffidence in the matter was not the less genuine because he was swelling all the time with private pride. Mrs. Ringrose did not press the point. The pecuniary side of the affair continued to interest her very much.

"Do you think fifty?" she said at length, with considerable obscurity; but her son knew what she was talking about.

"Fifty what?"

"Pounds!"

"For my poor little verses? You little know their length! They are only forty-two lines in all."

"Well, what of that? I am sure I have heard of such sums being given for a short poem."

"Well, they wouldn't give it for mine. Fifty shillings, more like."

"No, no. Say twenty pounds. They could never give you less."

Harry shook his head and smiled.

"A five-pound note, at the very outside," said he, oracularly. "But whatever it is, it'll be one in the eye for the other uncle! Upon my word, I think we must go to his church to-morrow evening."

"It will mean going in to supper afterwards, and you know you didn't like it last time."

"I can lump it for the sake of scoring off Uncle Spencer!"

But that was more easily said than done, especially, so to speak, on the "home ground," where a small but exclusively feminine and entirely spiritless family sang a chorus of meek approval to the reverend gentleman's every utterance. When, therefore, Mr. Walthew added to his melancholy congratulations a solemn disparagement of all the lighter magazines (which he boasted were never to be seen in his house), the echo from those timid throats was more galling than the speech itself. But when poor Mrs. Ringrose ventured only to hint at her innocent expectations as to the honorarium, and her brother actually laughed outright, and his family made equally merry, then indeed was Harry punished for the ignoble motives with which he had attended his uncle's church.

"My good boy," cried Uncle Spencer, with extraordinary geniality, "you will be lucky if you get a sixpence! I say again that I congratulate you on the prospect of getting into print at all. I say again that even that is not less a pleasure than a surprise to me. But I would not delude myself with pecuniary visions until I could write serious articles for the high-class magazines!"

Between his mother's presentiments and his uncle's prognostications, the contributor himself endeavoured to strike a happy medium; but even he was disappointed when an afternoon post brought a proof of the verses, together with a postal order for ten-and-sixpence. Harry showed it to his mother without a word, and for the moment they both looked glum. Then the boy burst out laughing, and the lady followed suit.

"And I had visions of a fiver," said Harry.

"Nay, but I was the worst," said his mother, who was laughing and crying at the same time. "I said twenty!"

"It only shows how much the public know about such things. Ten-and-six!"

"Well, my boy, that's better than what your uncle said. How long did it take you to write?"

"Oh, not more than half an hour. If it comes to that, the money was quickly earned."

For a minute and more Mrs. Ringrose gazed steadily at an upper sash, which was one's only chance of seeing the sky through the windows of the flat. Her lips were tightly pursed; they always were when she was in the toils of a calculation.

"A thousand a year!" she exclaimed at length.

"What do you mean, mother?"

"Well, if this poem only took you half an hour, you might easily turn out half a dozen a day. That would be three guineas. Three guineas a day would come to over a thousand a year."

Harry laughed and kissed her.

"I'll see what I can do," he said; "but I'm very much afraid half a dozen a week will be more than I can manage. Three guineas a week would be splendid. I shouldn't have to go round begging for work any more; they would never give me half as much in an office. Heigho! Here are the verses for you to read."

He put on his hat, and went into the High Street to cash his order. It was the first money his pen had ever earned him in the open market, and, since the sum seemed to Harry too small to make much difference, he determined to lay out the whole of it in festive and appropriate, if unjustifiable fashion. The High Street shops met all his wants. At one he bought a ninepenny tin of mulligatawny, and a five-and-ninepenny bottle of Perrier Jouet; at another, some oyster patties and meringues and half a pound of pressed beef (cut in slices), which came to half-a-crown between them. The remaining shilling he spent on strawberries and the odd sixpence on cream. He would have nothing sent, so we may picture a triumphant, but rather laborious return to the flat.

He found his mother in tears over the proofs of his first verses; she shed more when he showed her how he had spent his first honorarium. Yet she was delighted; there had been very little in the house, but now they would be able to do without the porter's wife to cook, and would be all by themselves for their little treat. No one enjoyed what she loved to call a "treat" more than Mrs. Ringrose; and perhaps even in the best of days she had never had a greater one than that now given her by her extravagant son. It was unexpected, and, indeed, unpremeditated; it had all the elements of success; and for one short evening it made Harry's mother almost forget that she was also the wife of a fraudulent and missing bankrupt.

Harry, too, was happier than he had been for many a day. In the course of the evening he stole innumerable glances at his proof, wondering what this friend or that would think of the verses when they came out in *Uncle Tom*. Once it was through Lowndes's spectacles that he tried to look at them, more than once from Mr. Innes's point of view, but most often with the sterling grey eyes of the girl on Richmond Hill, who had so earnestly begged him to write. He had heard nothing of her from that evening to this; her father had not mentioned her in the one letter Harry had received from him, and neither of them had been near the flat. But he believed that Fanny Lowndes would like the verses; he knew that she would encourage him to go on.

And go on he did, with feverish energy, for the next few days. But the good luck did not repeat itself too soon; for though the first taste of printer's ink gave the lad energy, so that within a week he had showered verses upon half the magazines in London, all those verses returned like the dove to the ark, because it did not also bring him good ideas, and his first success had spoilt him a little by costing no effort. Even *Uncle Tom* would have no more of him; and the unhappy Harry began to look upon his imitation of Shelley as the mere fluke it seemed to have been.

CHAPTER XI.

BEGGAR AND CHOOSER.

The one communication which Harry Ringrose had received from Gordon Lowndes was little more than a humorous acknowledgment of the sum refunded to him after the sale of the trophies. The writer warmly protested against the payment of a debt which he himself had never regarded in that light. The worst of it was that he was not in a position to refuse such payment. The prospects of the Highland Crofters' Salmon and Trout Supply Association, Limited, were if anything rosier than ever. But it was an axiom that the more gigantic the concern, the longer and more irritating the initial delay, and no news of the Company would be good news for some time to come.

"Meanwhile I am here every day of my life," concluded Lowndes, "and pretty nearly all day. Why the devil don't you look me up?"

Indeed, Harry might have done so on any or all of those dreadful days which took him a beggar to the City of London. His reason for not doing so was, however, a very simple one. He did not want Lowndes to think that he disbelieved in the H.C.S. & T.S.A., as he must if he knew that Harry was assiduously seeking work elsewhere. Harry was not altogether sure that he did utterly disbelieve in that colossal project. But it was difficult to put much confidence in it after the revelations at Richmond, and when it was obvious that the promoter's own daughter lacked confidence in his schemes. Certainly it was impossible to feel faith enough in the Highland Crofters' to leave lesser stones unturned. And yet to let Lowndes know what he was doing might be to throw away three hundred a year.

So Harry had avoided Leadenhall Street on days when the company-promoter's boisterous spirits and exuberant good-humour would have been particularly grateful to him. But this was before he became a successful literary man. He wanted Lowndes to hear of his success; he particularly wanted him to tell his daughter. He was not sure that he should avoid Leadenhall Street another time, nor did he when it came.

This was after the successful effort had realised only half-a-guinea, and when some subsequent attempt was coming back in disgrace by every post. Mrs. Ringrose had taken a leaf out of Harry's book, and committed a letter to the post without even letting him know that she had written one. An answer came by return, and this she showed to Harry in considerable trepidation. It was from the solicitor whom she had mentioned on the day after Harry's arrival. In it Mr. Wintour Phipps presented his compliments to Mrs.

Ringrose, and stated that he would be pleased to see her son any afternoon between three and four o'clock.

"I thought old friends were barred?" Harry said, reproachfully. "I thought we were agreed about that, mother?"

"But this is not an old friend of yours or mine, my dear. I never knew him; I only know what your father did for him. He paid eighty pounds for his stamps, so I think he might do something for you! And so does he, you may depend, or he would not write that you are to go and see him."

"He doesn't insist upon it," said Harry, glancing again at the solicitor's reply. "He puts it pretty formally, too!"

"Have I not told you that I never met him? It was your father and his father who were such old friends."

"So he writes to you through a clerk!"

"How do you know?"

"It's the very hand they all tell me I ought to cultivate."

"I have no doubt he is a very busy man. I have often heard your father say so. Yet he can spare time to see you! You will go to him, my boy—to please your mother?"

"I will think about it, dear."

The mid-day post brought back another set of rejected verses. Harry swallowed his pride.

"It's all right, mother; I'll go and see that fellow this afternoon."

And there followed the last of the begging interviews, which in character and result had little to differentiate it from all the rest. Harry did indeed feel less compunction in bearding his father's god-son than in asking favours of complete strangers. He also fancied that he was better fitted for the law than for business, and, when he came to Bedford Row, he could picture himself going there quite happily every day. The knowledge, too, that this Wintour Phipps was under obligations to his father, sent the young fellow up a pair of dingy stairs with a confidence which had not attended him on any former errand of the kind. And yet in less than ten minutes he was coming down again, with his beating heart turned to lead, but with a livelier contempt for his own innocence than for the hardness of the world as most lately exemplified by Wintour Phipps. Nor would the last of these interviews be worth mentioning but for what followed; for it was on this occasion that Harry went on to Leadenhall Street to get what comfort he could from the one kind heart he knew of in the City of London.

But there an unexpected difficulty awaited him. He remembered the number, but he looked in vain for the name of Gordon Lowndes among the others that were painted on the passage wall as you went in. So he doubted his memory and tried other numbers; but results brought him back to the first, and he climbed upstairs in quest of the name that was not in the hall. He never found it; but as he reached the fourth landing a peal of unmistakable laughter came through a half-open door. And Harry took breath, for he had found his friend.

"Very well," he heard a thin voice saying quietly, "since you refuse me the slightest satisfaction, Mr. Lowndes, I shall at once take steps."

"Steps—steps, do you say?" roared Lowndes himself. "All right, take steps to the devil!"

And a small dark man came flying through the door, which was instantly banged behind him. Harry caught him in his arms, and then handed him his hat, which was rolling along the stone landing. The poor man thanked him in an agitated voice, and was tottering down the stairs, when he turned, and with sudden fury shook his umbrella at the shut door.

"The dirty scamp!" he cried. "The bankrupt blackguard!"

Harry never forgot the words, nor the working, whiskered face of the man who uttered them. He stood where he was until the trembling footfalls came up to him no more. Then he knocked at the door. Lowndes himself flung it open, and the frown of a bully changed like lightning to the most benevolent and genial smile.

"You!" he cried. "Come in, Ringrose—come in; I'm delighted to see you."

"Yes, it's me," said Harry, letting drop the hearty hand which he felt to be a savage fist unclenched to greet him. "Who did you think it was?"

"Why, the man you must have met upon the stairs! A little rat of a creditor I've chucked out this time, but will throw over the banisters if he dares to show his nose up here again."

Harry was forcibly reminded of the butcher at Richmond.

"So this is the other way of treating them?" said he.

"This is the other way. Ha! ha! I recollect what you mean. Well, I have some sympathy with a small tradesman whom the fortune of war has kept out of his money for weeks and months; not a particle for a little Jew who has the insolence to come up here and browbeat and threaten me in my own office for a few paltry pounds! If he had written me a civil note, reminding me of the debt, which was really so small that I'd forgotten all about it, he should have had his money in time. Now he may whistle for it till he's black in the face!"

Lowndes's indignation was so much more impressive than that of the little dark man on the stairs, that Harry's sympathies changed sides without his knowledge. He merely felt his heart warm to Lowndes as the latter took him by the arm and led him through the outer office (in which an undersized urchin was mastheaded on an abnormally high stool) into an inner one, where a red-nosed man sat at the far side of a large double desk.

"My friend Mr. Backhouse," said Lowndes, introducing the red-nosed man. "We're not partners; not even in the same line of business; but we share the office between us, and the clerks, too—don't we, Bacchus?"

The red-nosed man grinned at his blotting-pad, and Harry perceived that the "clerks" consisted of the small child in the outer office.

"I noticed your name down below in the passage," said Harry to Mr. Backhouse, "but I couldn't see yours, Mr. Lowndes. I nearly went away again."

"Ah! it's in Backhouse's name we have the office; it suits my hand to keep mine out of it. I'm playing a deep game, Ringrose—one of the deepest that ever was played in the City of London. I stand to win a million of money!"

Lowndes had assumed an air of suitable subtlety and mystery; his eyes were half-closed behind their gold-rimmed lenses, and he nodded his head slowly and impressively as he stood with his back to the fireplace. Harry noticed that he still wore the shabby frock-coat, and that his trousers were as baggy as ever at the knees. He could not help asking how the deep game was progressing.

"Slowly, Ringrose, slowly, but as surely as the stride of time itself. My noble Earl is up in the Highlands with his yacht. Insisted on looking into the thing with his own eyes. That's what's keeping us all, but I expect him back in another week, and then, Ringrose, you may throw up your hat; for I have not the slightest shadow of a doubt as to the result of the old chap's investigations."

Here the clock struck four, and the red-nosed man, who had also a stiff leg, put on his hat, and stumped out of the office.

"Now we can talk," said Lowndes, shutting the door, giving Harry a chair, and sitting down himself. "He'll be gone ten minutes. It's his whisky-time; he has a Scotch whisky every hour as regularly as the clock strikes. Wonderful man, Bacchus, for I never saw him a penn'orth the worse. Some day he'll go pop. But never mind him, Ringrose, and never mind the Company; tell us how the world's been using you, my boy; that's more to the point."

So Harry told him about the accepted verses, and Gordon Lowndes not only promised to tell his daughter, but was himself most emphatic in encouraging Harry to go on as he had begun. It might be his true vocation after all. If he wrote a book and made a hit it would be a better thing even than the Secretaryship of the H.C.S. & T.S.A. The delay there was particularly hard lines on Harry. Lowndes only hoped he was letting no chances slip meanwhile.

"It is always conceivable," said he, "that my aristocratic directors may each have a loafing younger son whom they may want to shove into the billet. You may depend upon me, Ringrose, to resist such jobbery tooth-and-nail; but, if I were you, I wouldn't refuse the substance for the shadow; you could always chuck it up, you know, and join us just the same."

"Then you won't be offended," said Harry, greatly relieved, "if I tell you that I have had one or two other irons in the fire?"

"Offended, my boy? I should think you a duffer if you had not."

In another minute Harry had made a clean breast of his other journeys to the City, and was recounting the latest of those miserable experiences when Lowndes cut him short.

"What!" cried he, "your father paid for the fellow's stamps, and he refused to pay for yours?"

"We never got so far as that," said Harry bitterly. "He wanted a premium with me, and that settled it. He said three hundred guineas was the usual thing, but in consideration of certain obligations he had once been under to my father (he wasn't such a fool as to go into particulars), he would take me for a hundred and fifty. And he made a tremendous favour of that. He expected me to go down on my knees with gratitude, I daresay, but I just told him that a hundred and fifty was as far beyond me as three hundred, and said good afternoon and came away. Mind you, I don't blame him. Why should I expect so much for so little? He's no worse than any of the rest; they're all the same, and I don't blame any of them. Who am I that I should go asking favours of any one of them? My God, I've asked my last!"

"You're your father's son, that's who you are," said Gordon Lowndes. "What your father did for this skunk of a solicitor, he should be the first man to do for you. What's his name, by the way?"

"Phipps."

"Not Wintour Phipps?"

Harry nodded; and his nod turned up every light in the other's expressive face. Gordon Lowndes seized his hat and was on his legs in an instant, as radiant and as eager as when he set out to chasten and correct Harry's tailors. Such little punitive crusades were in fact the salt and pepper of his existence.

"My boy," he cried, "I've known Wintour Phipps for years. I know enough to strike Wintour Phipps off the rolls to-morrow. I guess he'll do anything for me, will Wintour Phipps! So you sit just as tight as wax till I come back. I shan't be long." And he was gone before Harry grasped his meaning sufficiently to interfere. For the young fellow was apt to be slow-witted when taken by surprise: and though he ran headlong down the stairs a minute later, he was only in time to see Lowndes dive into a hansom on the other side of the crowded street, and be driven away.

He could do nothing now. He was annoyed with Lowndes, and yet the man meant well—by Harry, at all events Others might take him as they found him, and call him a scamp if they chose. Very possibly he was one; indeed, on his own showing, in his own stories, he was nothing else. But he had a kind heart, and Harry's needs and rebuffs inclined him to rate a sympathetic rogue far higher in the moral scale than a callous paragon. Whatever else might be said of Lowndes, there was no end to the trouble he would take for another. Even when he insisted on doing what the person most concerned would have had him leave undone (as in this instance), it was impossible not to feel grateful to him for doing anything at all. His unselfish enthusiasm in other people's causes was beyond all praise. He might not be a good man, but that was a virtue which many a good man had not.

Still Harry was annoyed. What Gordon Lowndes had gone to say to Wintour Phipps he could only conjecture; but the object was plainly intercessory, and Harry hated the thought of such intercession on his behalf. There was nothing for it, however, but to climb upstairs again (he had done so), and patiently to await the return of Lowndes. So the afternoon passed. Mr. Backhouse stumped in, took his hat off, wrote letters, reached his hat, and stumped out again. But still no Lowndes.

"Good-night," said Harry to the retreating Bacchus.

"Oh, I'm not going—I shall be back directly," replied that methodical man. "I have a little business down below." And he was back in ten minutes, sucking his moustache, and followed almost immediately by Gordon Lowndes, who stalked into the room with an air which Harry had not before seen him affect. His triumph was self-evident, but it was beautifully suppressed. He put down his hat with exasperating deliberation, and then stood beaming at Harry through his glasses.

"Well?" said Harry.

"It's all right," said Lowndes, very quietly, as of a foregone conclusion: "you may start work to-morrow, Ringrose. Our friend Phipps will be only too glad to have you. He will pay for the stamps for your articles, and, so far from charging you a premium, he will give you a small salary from the beginning. It won't be much, but then articled clerks as a rule get nothing. Our friend Phipps is going to make an exception in your case—and just you let me know when he treats you again as he did this afternoon. He never will! You'll find him tame enough now. You're to go to him again to-morrow morning; and you see if he don't receive you with open arms!"

"But why?" cried Harry. "What have you said?"

"What have I said? Well, I reminded him of a trifling incident which there was no need to remind him of at all, for the mere thought of it turned him pale the moment he saw me. So I took the liberty of showing him what might still happen if he didn't do exactly what I wanted about you. My boy, the thing was settled in two minutes. A rising young fellow like Wintour Phipps is not the man to be struck off the rolls if he knows it! But I wasn't coming away without having the whole thing down in black and white, and here it is."

From his inner pocket he took out a long blue envelope and slapped it down on the desk.

"May I see?" said Harry in a throbbing voice.

"Certainly; it's your business now, not mine."

Harry ran his eye over the brief document. Then he looked up.

"It's my business now—not yours?"

"To be sure."

"Then I'm very much obliged to you, Mr. Lowndes, but here's an end of it."

He tore the paper twice across, and carefully dropped it into the waste-paper basket. Then he looked up again. And he had never seen Lowndes really pale until that moment, nor really red until the next. Yet the storm passed over after all.

"Well—upon—my—soul!" said Gordon Lowndes, very slowly, but with more humour and less wrath in each successive word. "And you're the man who wanted a billet!"

"I want one still, but not on such terms. I'd rather starve."

"There's no accounting for taste."

"But I'm very sorry, I am indeed, that you should have troubled yourself to no purpose," continued Harry, holding out his hand with genuine emotion. "It was awfully good of you, and I shall never forget it."

"Nonsense—nonsense!" said Lowndes sharply. "Don't name it, my good fellow. We all look at these things differently—don't we, Bacchus? You wouldn't have had any scruples, would you? No more would I, my boy, I tell you frankly. But don't name it again. It was no trouble at all, and, even if it had been, there's nothing I wouldn't do for any of you, Ringrose, and now you know it. Hurt my feelings? Not a bit of it, my dear boy, I'm only frightened I hurt yours. Good night, good night, and my love to the old lady. Cut away home and tell her I've no more principles than Bacchus has brains!"

But Harry thought the matter over in the Underground; and it was many a day before he mentioned it at the flat.

CHAPTER XII.

THE CHAMPION OF THE GODS.

Harry had gathered that another week would decide the fate of the H.C.S. & T.S.A., Ltd., and he could not help feeling anxious as that week drew to its close. Not that he himself had gained much confidence in the mighty scheme in question, for he found it more and more impossible to believe very deeply in Gordon Lowndes or any of his works. Yet he knew now that Lowndes would help him if he could, by fair means or by foul, and he could say the same of no other man. Lowndes was not merely his friend, but his only friend in London, and you cannot afford to be hypercritical of an only friend. He might be unscrupulous, he might be unreliable, but he stood by himself for staunchness and the will to help. He might be a straw for sinking hopes, but there was no spar in sight.

So Harry searched the papers at the Public Library, not only for likely advertisements (which he would answer to the tune of several stamps a day), but also for the announcement of the return from Scotland of the Earl of Banff, K.G. When that announcement appeared, and two or three days slipped by without a line from Lowndes, though the week was more than up, then, and not until then, did Harry Ringrose abandon his last hope of getting anything to do in London. His one friend there had failed him, and was very likely himself in prison for debt. He had, it is true, an infinitely better friend at Guildford, whom he was on the eve of visiting, and who might help him to some junior mastership, but this was the most that he could hope for now. Such a post would in all probability separate him from his mother, but even that would be better than living upon her as he was now doing. And in London he seemed to stand no chance at all.

To this melancholy conclusion had Harry come on the day before he was to go to Guildford, when the electric bell began ringing as though it was never going to stop, and there stood Lowndes himself at ten o'clock in the morning. Harry instantly demanded to be told the worst or the best. The other held up his finger and shook his head. His face seemed wilfully inscrutable, but it was also full of humour and encouragement.

"The fact is, Ringrose," said Lowndes, "I have heard so much of that blessed Company every day for so many months, that I mean to give myself one day without thinking or speaking about it at all. Come to me to-morrow and you shall know everything. Meanwhile you and your mother must dine with me this evening to celebrate the occasion. Let us say the Grand Hotel and seven o'clock. Then we can all go to some theatre afterwards."

Harry ran to tell his mother he felt certain the Company was coming out at last, and to repeat this invitation word for word; but he had great difficulty in getting her to accept it. How could she go out again? She might be seen; it would look so bad; and she did not want to enjoy herself. Then, said Harry, neither did he; and so gained his point by rather doubtful means. Lowndes, who was on his way to the City, and would not come in, whispered to Harry that a little outing would do his mother all the good in the world; then his eyes fell, and he stood quizzically contemplating the shiny suit which he still seemed to prefer to all the new ones he had ordered from Harry's tailors.

"I think, Ringrose," said he, "that you and I had better dress. I keep some war-paint in the City, so it will be no trouble to either of us. Tell your mother not to bother, however, as my daughter will not be in evening dress. I forgot to mention, by the way, that she is coming in to pay her belated respects to Mrs. Ringrose this afternoon, and I want you to be so good as to bring her along with you to the Grand Hotel. Seven o'clock, recollect, and you and I will dress."

With that he ran down the stone stairs, and the swing doors closed behind him with a thud while Harry Ringrose still loitered on the landing outside the flat. Delighted as he was at the unwonted prospect of a little gaiety, and more than thankful for all that it implied, those emotions were nothing to the sudden satisfaction with which he found himself looking forward to seeing Miss Lowndes again and at the flat. It is true that the keener pleasure was also the less perfect. It was mingled with a personal anxiety which it was annoying to feel, but which Harry could not shake off. He was unreasonably anxious that his mother should like Miss Lowndes, and that Miss Lowndes should like his mother. And yet he told himself it was a natural feeling enough; he recalled its counterpart in old days when he had taken some schoolfellow home for the holidays.

As for Mrs. Ringrose, she was not only pleased to hear the girl was coming, but regarded that unprecedented fact as a happier augury than any other circumstance.

"I really think you must be right," said she, "and that the ship he has always talked about is coming in at last. I am sure I hope it is true, for I know of nobody who would make a better millionaire than Mr. Lowndes. He is generous with his money when it seems that he has less than I should have believed possible, so what will he be when he is really rich! But he never would tell me what his great scheme was; and I am not sure that I altogether care for it from your description, my boy. I like Mr. Lowndes immensely, but I am not sure that I want to see you concerned in a pure speculation. However, let us hope for the best, and let neither of them suppose that we do not believe the best. Yes, of course, I shall be glad to see the daughter. Go down, my boy, and tell the porter's wife to come up and speak to me."

When in the fulness of time Miss Lowndes arrived, the door was opened by neither Harry nor Mrs. Ringrose, and the flat was brightened by a few fresh flowers which the former had brought in without exciting his mother's suspicions. Mrs. Ringrose, indeed, had an inveterate love of entertaining, which all her troubles had not killed in her, and she received the visitor in a way that made Harry draw a very long breath. Palpably and indeed inexplicably nervous as she came in, so genial was the welcome that the girl recovered herself in a moment, and in another Harry's anxieties were at an end. Once she had mastered her momentary embarrassment, it was obvious that Miss Lowndes was in infinitely better spirits than when he had seen her last at Richmond. She looked younger; there was a warmer tinge upon her cheek, her eyes were brighter, her dress less demure. Harry had only to look at her to feel assured that fortune was smiling after all upon the H.C.S. & T.S.A.; and he had only to hear the two women talking to know that they would be friends.

Miss Lowndes explained why she had never been to call before. She said frankly that they had been terribly poor, and she herself greatly tied in consequence. She spoke of the poverty in the perfect tense, with the freedom and nonchalance with which one can afford to treat what is passed and over. Nothing could have been more reassuring than her tone, nothing pleasanter than the way in which she and Mrs. Ringrose took to one another. Harry was so pleased that he was quite contented to sit by and listen, and to wait upon Miss Lowndes when the tea came in, and only put in his word here and there. It was his mother who would speak about the accepted verses, and when Harry fled to dress he left her ransacking the escritoire for his notorious outrage on Gray's Elegy. Nor was this the final mark of favour. When they started for Charing Cross, it was Mrs. Ringrose who insisted that they should take an omnibus, and Mrs. Ringrose who presently suggested that the young people would be cooler outside. It was as though Fanny Lowndes had made a deeper impression on Harry's mother than on Harry himself.

Now, there is no more delightful drive than that from Kensington to the Strand, at the golden end of a summer's afternoon and on the top of a Hammersmith omnibus. If you are so fortunate as to get a front seat where nobody can smoke in your face and the view is unimpeded, it is just possible that your coppers may buy you as much of colour and beauty and life and interest as Harry Ringrose obtained for his; but certainly Harry was very young and much addicted to enthusiasm over small things; and perhaps nobody else is likely to breast the first green corner of the Gardens with the thrill it gave him, or to covet a certain small house in Kensington Gore as he coveted it, or to see with his eyes through the railings and the thick leaves of the Park, or to read as much romance upon the crowded flagstones of Piccadilly. Already he knew and loved every furlong of the route; but Fanny Lowndes was the first companion who had been with him over the ground; and afterwards, when he came to know every yard, every yard was associated with her. The beginning of the Gardens henceforth reminded Harry of his first direct question about the Company, and her assurances ever afterwards accompanied him to the Memorial. That maligned monument he never passed again without thinking of the argument it had led to, without deploring his companion's views as to gilt and gay colours, without remembering sadly that it was the one subject on which they disagreed that happy summer evening. He found her more sympathetic even than he had been imagining her since their first meeting. They touched a score of topics on which their spirits jumped as one: in after days he would recall them in their order when he came that way alone, and see summer sunshine through the dripping fogs, and green leaves on the black branches in the Park.

Their last words he remembered oftenest, because even the Underground leads to Trafalgar Square, and it was there that they were spoken. The shadows of the column lay sharp and black across the Square; that of the Admiral was being run over by innumerable wheels in the road beyond, and the low sun flashed in every window of the Grand Hotel.

"Our future offices!" laughed Harry, pointing to the pile.

"I don't think I want them to be yours," said Fanny Lowndes.

"Why not?"

"I want you to go on with your writing."

"But you see how little good I am. One thing accepted out of seven written! I should never make bread and butter at it."

"You have not done what I told you to do at Richmond. You should try prose, and draw on your own experiences."

"Would you be my critic?"

"If I had the qualifications."

"Well, will you read me and say what you think?"

"With all my heart."

"Then I'll set to work as soon as ever I get back from Guildford. You would put pluck into a mouse, Miss Lowndes, and I'll try to deserve the interest you take in me."

The omnibus stopped, and their eyes met with a mutual regret as they rose. Harry could not have believed that a change of fortune would so change a face; that of Miss Lowndes was always lighted by intelligence and kindness, but with the light of happiness added it was almost beautiful. And yet, the fine eyes fell before Harry's, and fell again as he handed her to the curb with a cordial clasp, so that the boy was thoughtful as they crossed to the hotel, thinking of her nervousness at the flat.

A few hours later he could understand the daughter of Gordon Lowndes feeling nervous in accompanying comparative strangers to public places under the wing of that extraordinary man.

It was evident from the first that Lowndes was in a highly excitable state. Harry overheard him telling his daughter she was five minutes late in a tone which made his young blood boil. But it was the hotel officials who had the chief benefit of the company-promoter's mood. Something was wrong with the soup—Harry was talking to Miss Lowndes and never knew what. All he heard was Lowndes sending for the head waiter, and the harangue that followed. The head waiter ventured to answer; he was instantly told to fetch the general manager. A painful scene seemed inevitable, but the worst was over. In making two officials miserable, and in greatly embarrassing his daughter and his guests, it suddenly appeared that Lowndes had quite recovered his own spirits, and the manager found a boisterous humourist instead of the swashbuckler for whom he had come prepared. The complaint was waived with dexterous good-nature; but care seemed to be taken that no loophole should be given for a second. The remainder of the repast was unexceptionable (as, indeed, the soup had seemed to Harry), and Lowndes, who drank a good deal of champagne, continued uproariously mirthful almost to the end. He told them the name of the piece for which he had taken stalls. It had only been produced the previous evening, so none of them could say that they had seen it before.

"I don't know what it's like," added Lowndes. "I never read criticisms. Have you seen anything about it, Ringrose?"

"Why, yes," said Harry; "I looked in at the library this morning, and I saw two or three notices. They say it is a good enough play; but there was a bit of a row last night. The papers are full of it. In fact that's how I came to read the criticisms."

"A row in the theatre?" said Lowndes. "What about?"

"Fees," said Harry. "You know there are no fees at the Lyceum and the Savoy, and three or four more of the best theatres, so they want to abolish them there also."

"Who do?"

"The public."

"But it's a question for the management entirely. The public have nothing to do with it."

"I don't know about that," argued Harry. "The public pay, and they think they shouldn't."

"Why?" snapped Lowndes; and it became disagreeably apparent that his lust for combat had revived.

"Well, they think they pay quite enough for their places without any extras afterwards, such as a fee for programmes. They say you might as well be charged for the bill-of-fare when you dine at a restaurant. But their great point seems to be that if half-a-dozen good theatres can do without fees all good theatres can. They call them an imposition."

"Rubbish," snorted Lowndes, in so offensive a manner that Harry could say no more; he was therefore surprised when, after a little general conversation in which Lowndes had not joined, the latter leant across to him with all the twinkling symptoms of his liveliest moments.

"I presume," said he, "that all the row last night was kicked up by the pit and gallery?"

"So I gathered."

"Ah! What they want is a remonstrance from the stalls. There would be some sense in that."

There were no more disagreeables at the hotel, and none with either of the cabmen outside the theatre. All at once Lowndes seemed to have grown unnaturally calm and sedate, Harry could not imagine why. But only too soon he knew.

They had four stalls in the centre of the third row. Harry sat on the extreme left of the party, with Fanny Lowndes on his right, to whom he was talking as he tucked his twelve-shilling "topper" as carefully as possible under the seat, when his companion suddenly looked round and up with a startled expression. Harry followed her example, and there was Gordon Lowndes standing up in his place and laughing in the reddening face of the pretty white-capped attendant. In his hand were four programmes.

"Certainly not," he was saying. "The system of fees, in a theatre like this, is an outrage on the audience, and I don't intend to submit to it."

"I can't help the system, sir."

"I know you can't, my good girl. I don't blame you. Go about your business."

"But I must fetch the manager."

"Oh, fetch the police if you like. Not a penny-piece do I pay."

And Gordon Lowndes stood erect in his place, fanning himself with the unpaid-for programmes, and beaming upon all the house. Already all eyes were upon him; it was amusing to note with what different glances. The stalls took care to look suitably contumelious, and the dress-circle were in proper sympathy with the stalls. But the front row of the pit were leaning across the barrier, and the gallery was a fringe of horizontal faces and hats.

"We're behind you," said a deep voice in the pit.

"Good old four-eyes!" piped another from aloft.

The gods had recognised their champion: he gave them a magnificent wave of the programmes, and stood there with swelling shirt-front, every inch the demagogue.

"Now, sir, now!"

The manager was a smart-looking man with a pointed beard, and a crush-hat on the back of his head. He spoke even more sharply than was necessary.

"Now, sir, to you," replied Lowndes suavely, and with an admirable inclination of his head.

"Well, what's the matter? Why won't you pay?"

"I never encourage fees," replied Lowndes, shaking his twinkling face in the most fatherly fashion. He articulated his words with the utmost deliberation, however, and there was a yell of approval from the gods above. A ripple of amusement was also going round the house; for Mrs. Ringrose was holding up half-a-crown and making treacherous signs to the manager, which, however, he would not see. It seemed he was a fighting man himself, and his eyes were locked in a tussle with Lowndes's spectacles.

"You must leave the theatre, that's all."

"Nonsense," retorted Lowndes, with his indulgent smile.

"We shall see about that. May I trouble you, ladies and gentlemen, to leave your places for one moment?"

Lowndes's incomparable guffaw resounded through the auditorium. It was receiving a hearty echo in pit and gallery, when he held up his programmes, and the gods were still. The ladies and gentlemen had kept their seats.

"My dear sir, why give yourself away?" said Gordon Lowndes, still chuckling, to the manager. "You daren't touch me, and you know you daren't. A pretty figure you'd cut at Bow Street to-morrow morning! Now kindly listen to me—" and he tapped the programmes authoritatively with his forefinger.

"You know as well as I do that there was trouble last night in this theatre about this very thing; my dear sir, I can promise you there'll be trouble every night until you discontinue your present obsolete and short-sighted policy. How I wish you were a sensible man! Then you would think twice before attempting to force a barefaced imposition of this sort down the throats of your audience; an imposition that every theatre of repute has recognised as such and thrown overboard long and long ago. You don't force it down *my* throat, I can tell you that. You don't bluff or bully *me*. As if we didn't pay enough for our seats without any such exorbitant extras! Why, they might as well charge us for the bill-of-fare at a first-class restaurant. Besides, what a charge! Sixpence for these—sixpence for this!" And he spun one of his programmes into the pit, and waved another towards the gallery.

But that cool quick tongue was no sooner silent than the house was in a hubbub. Here and there arose a thin, peevish cry of "Turn him out," but on the whole the sympathy of the house was with Lowndes. The stalls were no longer visibly ashamed of him; the dress-circle jumped with the stalls; but the pit clapped its ungloved hands and stamped with its out-of-door boots, while every species of whistle, cheer and cat-call came hurtling from the gallery. This went on for some three minutes, which is a long time thus filled. There was no stopping it. The manager retreated unheard and impotent. A minute later the curtain went up, only to give the tumult a new impetus. The hapless actors looked at one another and at the front of the house. The curtain came down, and the popular and talented lessee himself stepped in front of it, dressed in his stage costume. But even him they would not hear. Then arose the unknown, middle-aged gentleman in the stalls, with the splendid temper and the gold eye-glasses—and him they would.

"Come, come, ladies and gentlemen," cried he, "haven't we done enough for one night? We have all paid our money, are we not to see the piece? As for that other matter, I think it may safely be left in the hands of yonder wise man who stands before us."

And it was—with a result you may remember. Meantime the curtain was up for good and the play proceeding after a very short interval indeed, during which Gordon Lowndes bore himself with startling modesty, sitting quietly in his place and doing nothing but apologise to Mrs. Ringrose for having caused such a scene on an occasion when she was his guest. He should have thought only of his guests; but his sense of public duty, combined with his bitter and inveterate intolerance of anything in the shape of an imposition, had run away with him, and on Mrs. Ringrose's account he was humbly sorry for it. That lady forgave him, however. Through a perfect agony of shame and indignation she had come to a new and not unnatural pride in her eccentric friend.

As for Harry, there was no measure to his enthusiasm: the tears had been in his eyes from sheer excitement.

"A wonderful man, your father!" he whispered again and again to the pale girl on his right.

"He is," she answered, with a smile and a sigh. And the smile was the sadder of the two.

Between the acts Harry visited the foyer with Lowndes, who was complimented by several strangers on his spirited and public-spirited behaviour.

"But do you know," said Harry, when they were alone, "from the way you spoke at dinner I fancied you took quite an opposite view of the whole question of fees?"

"So I did," whispered Lowndes, with his tremulous grin, "but I saw my way to some sport, and that was enough for me. I was spoiling for some sport to-night, and a bit of bluff from the stalls was obviously what was wanted. You must excuse my using your arguments, but the fact is I very seldom set foot inside a theatre, and they were the only ones I'd ever heard."

"At dinner you said they were nonsense!"

The other winked as he lowered his voice.

"So they were, my dear Ringrose. That was exactly where the sport came in."

CHAPTER XIII.

THE DAY OF BATTLE.

It was the following morning that Harry Ringrose received a first return for the many letters he had written in answer to advertisements seen in the Public Library. The advertisement had been for an articled clerk. The clerk was to be articled on really "exceptional terms" (duly specified), and a "public-school boy" was "preferred." It was, in fact, the likeliest advertisement Harry had seen, and its possibilities were not altogether dissipated by the communication now received:—

"DEAR SIR,—We beg to acknowledge your letter of the 19th instant, and to say that this is an increasing business, and that we require further assistance in it. You would have an opportunity of thoroughly learning the whole business under the supervision of Mr. Shuttleworth himself; would accompany him to the various courts, and eventually other arrangements might be made. You will notice that the premium is only fifty guineas, which will be returned in salary—a very unusual thing.

"Perhaps you will give me a call at your early convenience, of which we shall be glad to have notice, as we must take someone at once.

"Yours faithfully,

"WALTER SHUTTLEWORTH & CO."

Like most of his correspondence, this letter was read by Harry to his mother, who looked up at him as though his fortune were already made. She had been in favour of the Law all along, and she was prepared to break into her capital for the fifty guineas' premium and for the eighty pounds for stamps. It would decrease their income by a few pounds, but if Harry were getting a good salary they would be the gainers by the difference. In any case he must telegraph to these people without a moment's loss of time—he must see Mr. Shuttleworth before starting for Guildford that afternoon. His bag should be ready immediately, and, as he also wanted to see Mr. Lowndes, he could leave it in Leadenhall Street and pop in for it afterwards on his way to Waterloo.

Such was his mother's advice, and Harry took it to the letter. The bag was his father's dressing-bag, which Mrs. Ringrose said would make a good appearance at Mr. Innes's. It was heavy with silver-mounted fittings, but there was just room for Harry's dress suit, which made it heavier still. Consequently the way from Aldgate to Leadenhall Street had never seemed so long before, and Harry was thankful when he and the bag were at last aloft in Lowndes's office. Here he instantly forgot his wet forehead and his aching arm. He had dropped in upon the queerest scene.

Gordon Lowndes was in the inner office. Harry saw him through the open door, and his first impression was that Lowndes had been up all night. He was still in evening dress. The very hat and Inverness, in which Harry had seen the last of him at eleven the night before, completed his attire at eleven this morning. There was one quaint difference: instead of a white bow he wore a blue scarf tied in an ordinary knot, which stultified the whole costume. Harry looked hard. Lowndes was looking even harder at him, with a kind of what-do-*you*-want glare. But he was palpably sober; he wore every sign of the man who had slept heartily and risen in his vigour, and in an instant his features had relaxed and his hands lay affectionately on Harry's shoulders.

"Well, Ringrose, my boy, what brought you along so early? And what have you got there?"

"It's my bag," said Harry. "I'm going down to Guildford for a day or two, but I've got to see a man this morning, and I thought I might leave it here in the meantime. May I?"

"Surely, Ringrose, surely. Come inside; I've got my daughter here. My dear, here's Harry Ringrose, and this is his bag. Gad! but it's heavy!"

Miss Lowndes blushed painfully as she shook hands with Harry. Her other arm was held behind her back with incriminating care.

"Now, my dear," said Lowndes, briskly, "since we are bowled out let's be bowled out. Ringrose is bound to know the truth sooner or later, so he may as well know it now." And with a rough laugh he snatched from behind his daughter's back the shiny old clothes in which he had called at the flat the previous morning.

Harry thought that the best thing he could do was to join in the laugh. Next moment his heart smote him, for Miss Lowndes had turned her back and stood looking at the window: not through it: it was opaque with grime.

"Fact is, Ringrose." continued Lowndes, "the noble Earl is trying to play me false. He won't keep it up, mind you; he's in too deep with me to dare; but he's trying it on. Yesterday was the day we were to fix things up for good and all. I wasn't sure of him, Ringrose; he's shown himself a slippery old cuss too often. However, I had raised a breath of wind since I saw you last, and I had a fiver left, so I thought we'd make sure of our little spree. Blue your last fiver—that's my rule. Never count the odds in the day of battle, and blue your last fiver for luck! If you don't blue that fiver you may never have another to blue, and I'm hanged if you deserve one! Well, that was my last fiver we blued last night. Don't look like that, man—I tell you I blued it for luck. The luck hasn't come yet, but you may bet your shirt it's on the way. You'll see the noble Earl trot back to heel when I threaten to expose him if he doesn't! Why, I've got letters from him that would make him the laughing-stock of the Lords; yet he leaves me one crying off in so many words, and has cleared for the Mediterranean in his yacht. Either he'll come back within a week, Ringrose, and go through with the Company, or by God he shall pay through the nose for breaking his word and wasting my time! But I see you looking at my toilet. It is a bit of an anachronism, I confess."

"I suppose you have been sitting up all night," said Harry. "I'm not surprised after what you tell me."

Lowndes guffawed.

"You'll never find me doing that!" he cried. "I leave the sitting up to my creditors! They'll sit up pretty slick before I've done with 'em—so will the noble Earl. Now let me enlighten you. You remember all those clothes I ordered from your trustful tailors, and how I told you never to neglect a good credit? Well, to give you a practical illustration of the merits of my advice, I've been living on those clothes ever since. I have so! Yesterday this time the whole boiling were up the spout. I just got out the dress-suit and this Inverness for one night only, and changed into them up here. Now I've got to put them in pop again, and that's why you find me with them on. Do you follow me, Ringrose? Those good old duds are the only garments I've got in the world—thanks to the so-called Right Honourable the Earl of Banff."

Harry could not smile. He was thinking of his tailors, and he shuddered to remember that Lowndes had also borrowed five pounds in hard cash from the accommodating firm. Harry had dazzling visions of eventual trouble and responsibility; then his eyes stole over to the forlorn figure by the window; and it was quivering in a way that cut him to the heart.

"You may like to blue your last fiver," he turned to Lowndes and cried; "but I wish to heaven you hadn't blued it on us! As for my mother, when she hears——"

"Don't tell her, Mr. Ringrose!" cried a breaking voice. "I shall die of shame if she ever knows."

Fanny Lowndes had turned about with her fine eyes drowned in tears, her strong hands clutched together in an agony of entreaty; and just then Harry felt that he could forgive her father much, but never for the grief and shame which he first heaped upon the girl, and then forced her to display.

"It's a queer thing, Ringrose," observed Lowndes, "that women never can be got to take a sensible view of these matters. Your mother—my daughter—they're every one of them alike."

He swung on his heel with a shrug, and went into the outer office to meet his friend Backhouse, who here returned from the usual errand. A trembling hand fell on Harry's arm.

"Do not think the worst of him!" whispered Fanny.

"It is only on your account," was his reply.

"But he is so good to me!"

"Yet yesterday he let you think that all was well."

"He wanted to give me a pleasure while he could."

Harry looked in the brave wet eyes, and his heart gave a sudden bound.

"How staunch you are!" he murmured. "He is a lucky man who has you at his back!"

Then he followed her father into the outer office, saying he must go, but that he would be back in an hour for his bag.

He was back in less.

His interview with Messrs. Walter Shuttleworth (one gentleman) had proved but little more satisfactory than any of his other interviews. Still, here was a man who had need of Harry, and that was something. He was the first. Harry rather took to him. He was a dashing young fellow, a public-school man; and it was a public-school man such as Harry that he wanted in his office. At present he appeared to keep but one juvenile clerk, a size larger than Lowndes's—and he had no partner. This was the opening which was dimly and dexterously held out to Harry as an ultimate probability. And for one dazzling moment Harry felt that here was his chance in life at last. But when he came to ask questions, the fabric fell to pieces like all the rest, and he knew that he was sitting in Mr. Shuttleworth's office for the last time as well as for the first. For, though the premium was to be returned "in salary," it would only be returned during the last twelvemonth of Harry's articles, and for four weary years he must work for nothing. He shook his head; he was bitterly disappointed. He was then told that the proposed arrangement was an offer in a thousand; but that he knew. He took his hat, simply saying he could never afford it. But he was asked to think it over and to write again, for he was just the sort of fellow for the place; and this he promised to do, because it seemed just the sort of place for him.

Mr. Backhouse had stumped into the office as Harry was leaving, and now Harry met him stumping out. It was this that showed him that he had been less than an hour away. But Lowndes had found time to array himself once more in his "good old duds," to put his dress-suit back into pawn, and to run through Leadenhall Market with Fanny before packing her back to

Richmond. And now he was ready to listen to Harry, and very anxious to know how he had got on, and with whom, and where, and what it had all been about.

Harry told him everything. He was only too glad to do so, since however Lowndes might misuse his wits and talents in his own affairs, they were ever at the service of his friends, and it seemed but right that someone should have the benefit of those capital parts. The boy had felt differently an hour before, but now he needed advice, and here was Lowndes as eager as ever to advise. As usual, he saw to the heart of the matter long ere the whole had been laid before him. Ten to one, he said, the thing was past praying for now; it depended, however, on how strong a fancy this lawyer had taken to Ringrose, for he was by no means the only public-school boy to be had in London. His best policy now was to write a letter which should heighten that fancy, while it set forth his own circumstances and needs more explicitly than Harry appeared to have done in the interview. That would get at the man's heart, if he had one, and if not there was no further chance. Such a letter was eventually written at Lowndes's dictation; but Harry never felt comfortable about it; and it was only the sore necessity of employment that prevailed upon him to let Lowndes post it as they were both on their way out to luncheon.

They lunched at Crosby Hall. Harry took little because he meant to pay. Lowndes, however, would not hear of that, and Harry had to give way on the point, little as he liked doing so in the circumstances. They then left the place arm-in-arm, but in the street Lowndes withdrew his hand and held it out.

"I won't drag you out of your way again," said he, "especially as I have a lot of letters to write this afternoon. Good-day to you, Ringrose."

"You forget my bag," said Harry, smiling.

"What about it?"

"I left it in your office."

"In my office? To be sure, so you did. And now I think of it, I've got something to say to you about your bag."

Harry wondered what. Evidently it was something he preferred not to say in the street, for Lowndes strode along with a square jaw and a face frowning with thought. Backhouse was at the desk. Lowndes put down sixpence and told him to buy himself an irregular. Backhouse limped out, shutting the door, and they were alone. Harry could not see his bag.

"Ringrose," said Lowndes, "I've stood by you and yours in the day of battle, and now it's your turn to stand by me and mine. You can't conceive what a hole we've been in. Not a penny piece in the house down yonder—not a crust—not a bone. I came in this morning to raise a few shillings by hook or crook, and I brought in my daughter so as to send her back with enough to buy the bare necessary. I tried Bacchus, but he swears he's getting his drinks on tick. I tried the caretaker, but I've stuck her so often that she wouldn't be stuck again. I knew it was no use trying you, Ringrose, yet I knew you would want to help me, so I'll tell you what I've done. I've run in that bag of yours along with my dress-suit."

"You didn't pawn it?"

"Certainly I did."

"You mean to tell me———"

"Kindly lower your voice. If you want the office-boy to hear what you're saying, I don't. I mean to tell you that the situation was desperate, and your bag has saved it for the time being. I mean to tell you that I'd pawn the shirt off my back to get you out of half as bad a hole as I've been in this morning. Come, Ringrose, I thought you were sportsman enough to stand by the man who has stood by you?"

Harry's indignation knew no bounds, and yet the plausibility of the older man told upon him even in his heat.

"I am ready enough to stand by you," he cried, "but this is a different thing. I freely acknowledge your kindness to my mother and myself, but it doesn't give you the right to put my things in pawn, and you must get them out again at once."

"My good fellow," said Lowndes, "I fully intend to do so. I have sent an urgent letter to the noble Earl's solicitors this very morning, telling them of the straits to which the old villain has reduced me, and of the steps I intend to take failing a proper and immediate indemnification. I haven't the least doubt that they will send me a cheque on account before the day's out, and then I shall instantly send round for your bag."

Harry shook off the hand that had been laid upon his arm, and pulled out his watch.

"It's twenty to three," said he quietly. "I leave Waterloo by the five-forty, and my bag leaves with me. Let there be no misunderstanding about that, Mr. Lowndes. I must have it by five o'clock—not a minute later."

"Why must you? Surely they could fix you up for one night? I guarantee it won't be longer."

"They dress for dinner down at Guildford," said Harry; "it isn't the fixing up for the night."

"Well, why not lose your bag on the way? Nothing more natural in a young fellow of your age."

Harry lost his temper instead.

"Look here, Mr. Lowndes, you have been a good friend to us, as you say. You were a good friend to us last night. You've been a good friend to me this very day. But I simply can't conceive how you could go and do a thing like this; and I must have my bag by five o'clock, or we shall be friends no longer."

There was heat enough and fire enough in the young fellow's tone to bring blood to the cheek of an older man so spoken to. Lowndes looked delighted; he even clapped his hands.

"Well said, Ringrose; said like a sportsman!" he cried. "I like to hear a young chap talk out straight from the chest like that. I think all the more of you, my son, and you shall have your old bag by five o'clock if I bust for it. Only look here: don't you be angry with your grandfather!"

Harry burst out laughing in his own despite.

"It's impossible to be angry with you," he said. "Still, I must——"

"I see you must. So I'll jump into a hansom and I'll raise the fiver to redeem your bag if I have to drive all over the City of London for it!"

Harry laughed again, and sat down to wait as Lowndes went clattering down the stone stair-case. And as he sat there alone he suddenly grew pale. In his rage with Lowndes he had forgotten Lowndes's daughter, and now the thought of her turned his heart sick. He found it possible to forgive the father for an indictable offence. It should have been comparatively easy to forgive the daughter for receiving in her sore need the virtual proceeds of that crime. Yet the thought that she had done so was intolerable to him, and his heart began a sudden tattoo as a stiff step was heard ascending the stairs.

"Mr. Backhouse," said Harry, as that worthy reappeared, "I want a plain answer to a plain question."

"I shall be delighted to give you one," said Mr. Backhouse, "if it is in my power, sir."

"Do you know where my bag is?"

Mr. Backhouse said nothing.

"Then I see you do," cried Harry; "and so do I; and that was not my question at all. Did Miss Lowndes know about it?"

"No, sir."

"You are sure?"

"Certain! She never saw him take it out; he took jolly good care she shouldn't; and he came back with a yarn as long as your leg to account for the money."

Harry's feelings were a revelation to himself; they were the beginning of the greatest revelation of his life. But he cloaked them carefully and passed the better part of an hour reading the newspaper and exchanging an occasional remark with the lessee of the office. And no later than a quarter to four, which was long before Harry expected him, Lowndes was back. But he looked baffled, and there was no bag in his hand.

"Will either of you fellows lend me five bob for the cab?" he panted. "I've been all over the City of London."

Mr. Backhouse shook his head.

"And I can't," said Harry, "for I have barely enough to take me down to Guildford and back."

"Then we must keep him waiting too. Here, Jimmy"—to the office-child—"you stand by to take a telegram. Now, Ringrose, you're going to see me play trumps. Old Bacchus has seen 'em before." Indeed, that specimen's unwholesome face was already wreathed in dissipated grins.

Lowndes seized a telegram form, sat down with his hat on the back of his head, and began writing and talking at the same time.

"Like you, Ringrose, I have a near relative in the Church. An own brother, my boy, who cut me off with a text more years ago than I care to count, and hasn't spoken to me since. He's about as High as that uncle of yours is Low, but luckily there's one point on which even the parsons think alike. They funk a family scandal even more than other folks, and they funk it most when they have episcopal aspirations like my precious brother. What d'ye think of this for him, boys? 'Wire solicitors pay me fiver by five o'clock or I shall never see six.—Gordon Lowndes.' What price that for an ace of trumps? Not many parsons would care to go into the witness-box and read that out at their own brother's inquest—eh, Ringrose?"

Harry only stared.

"Too many fives," objected Mr. Backhouse, with an air of literary censorship. "Make it a tenner."

"Most noble Bacchus! For every reason, a tenner it is."

"And it's too obscure, that about never seeing six. Six what? I know what you mean, but trust a parson to miss the point. Your last was much better—that about the police in the outer office."

"We can't play the police twice. It's suicide or nothing this time—but hold on!" He seized another form and scribbled furiously. "How about this, then? 'Wire solicitors pay me ten pounds immediately or I am a dead man by 5.15.—Gordon.' That'll give you time to do it, Ringrose, with a good hansom."

"Oh, I daresay there's another train," said Harry. "And candidly, Mr. Lowndes, rather than drive you to this sort of thing, I should prefer to say I've lost my luggage and be done with it."

"Not a bit of it, my good fellow. I've got you into this mess, and I'll get you out again or know the reason why. I assure you, Ringrose, I'm quite enjoying it. Besides, there'll be a fiver over, thanks to old Bacchus here. Jimmy, run like sin with this telegram. Don't say you haven't a bob, Bacchus? Good man, you shall reap your reward when we've got this boy his blessed bag."

Lowndes waited until half-past four, talking boisterously the whole time. Harry had never heard him tell more engaging stories, nor come out with better phrases. At the half-hour, however, he drove off in his long-suffering hansom to his brother's solicitors. And by a quarter-past five he was back, in the same hansom, with the bag on top.

Harry met him down below.

"Here you are, my son!" cried Gordon Lowndes, jumping out with his face all flushed with triumph and twitching with glee. "That reverend brother of mine has never been known to fail when approached in a diplomatic manner—no more will your reverend uncle, if you try my tip on him! No, boy, it shall never happen again: jump in, and you've heaps of time. Cabby, take this gentleman on to Waterloo main line, and I'll pay for the lot. Will fifteen bob do you?"

"Thank'ee, sir, it'll do very well."

And Harry drove off with his hand aching from a pressure which he had, indeed, returned; almost forgetting the enormity of the other's offence in the zest, humour, and promptitude of the amend; and actually feeling, for the moment, under a fresh obligation to Gordon Lowndes.

CHAPTER XIV.

A CHANGE OF LUCK.

Quite apart from all that came of it, this visit to Guildford was something of a psychological experience at the time. The devotion of Harry Ringrose to his first school had been for years second only to his love for his old home, and now that the old home was his no longer, the old school was the place he loved best on earth. He knew it when he saw the well-remembered building once more in the golden light of that summer's evening. He knew it when he knelt in the school chapel and heard the most winning of human voices reading the school prayers. The chapel was new since Harry's day, but the prayers were not, and they reminded him of his own worst acts since he had heard them last. Mr. Innes sang tenor in the hymn, as he had always done, and Harry kept his ear on the voice he so loved; but the hymn itself was one of his old favourites, associated for ever with his first school, and it reminded him too. He looked about him, among the broad white collars, the innocent pink faces, and the open, singing mouths. He wondered which of the boys were leaving this term, and if one of them would leave with better resolutions than he had taken away with him seven years before ... and yet.... He had not been worse than others, but better perhaps than many; and yet there seemed no measure to his vileness, there certainly was none to his remorse, as he knelt again and prayed as he seemed never to have prayed since he was himself a little boy there at school. Then the organ pealed, and Mr. Innes went down the aisle with his grave fine face and his swinging stride. Mrs. Innes and Harry went next; the masters followed in their black gowns; and they all formed line in the passage outside, and the boys filed past and shook hands and said good-night on their way up to the dormitories.

Harry's visit extended over some days, and afterwards he used sometimes to wish that he had cut it short after the first delightful night. He was a creature of moods, and only a few minutes of each day were spent in chapel. It was a novel satisfaction to him to smoke his pipe with his old schoolmaster, to talk to him as man to man, and he knew too late that he had talked too much. He did not mean to be bombastic about his African adventures, but he was anxious that Mr. Innes should realise how much he had seen. Harry was in fact a little self-conscious with the man he had worn in his heart so many years, a little disappointed at being treated as an old boy rather than as a young man, and more eager to be entertaining than entertained. So when he came to the end of his own repertoire he related with enthusiasm some of the exploits of Gordon Lowndes. But the enthusiasm evaporated in the process, for Mr. Innes did not disguise his disapproval of the type of man described. And Harry himself saw Lowndes in a different light henceforth;

for this is what it is to be so young and impressionable, and so keenly alive to the influence of others.

The best as well as the strongest influence Harry had ever known was that of Mr. Innes himself. He felt it as much now as ever he had done—and in old days it had been of Innes that he would think in his remorse for wrongdoing, and how it would hurt Innes that a boy of his should fall so far short of his teaching. It never occurred to him then that his hero was probably a man of the world after all, capable of human sympathy with human weakness, and even liable to human error on his own account. Nor did this strike him now—for Harry Ringrose was as yet too far from being a man of the world himself. The old idolatry was as strong in him as ever. And the old taint of personal emulation still took a little from its worth.

"If only I could be more like you!" he broke out when Mr. Innes had spoken a kind, strong word or two as Harry was going. "I used to try so hard—I will again!"

"What, to get like me?" said Innes with a laugh. "I hope you'll be a much better man than I am, Harry. But it's time you gave up trying to be like anybody."

"How do you mean?" asked Harry, his enthusiasm rather damped.

"Be yourself, old fellow."

"But myself is such a poor sort of thing!"

"Never mind. Try to make yourself strong; but don't think about yourself. Don't you see the distinction? Only think about doing your duty and helping others; the less you dwell upon yourself, the easier that will be. Good-bye, old fellow. Let me know how you get on."

"Good-bye, sir," said Harry. "You don't know how you help me! You are sending me away with a new thought altogether. I will do my best. I will indeed."

"I know you will," said Mr. Innes.

So ended the visit.

The new thought made its mark on Harry's character, but it was not all that he brought away with him from Guildford. The visit fired a train of sufficiently important material results, though the fuse burnt slowly, and for weeks did not seem to be burning at all. Harry came away with the match in his pocket, in the shape of a letter of introduction to a firm of scholastic agents.

Mr. Innes had by no means encouraged his old boy to try to become a schoolmaster; he feared that the two years in Africa would tell against Harry rather than in his favour, and then without a degree there was absolutely no future. He thought better of Harry's chances in literature. It was he who had encouraged the boy's very earliest literary leanings and attempts, and he took the kindest view of the accepted verses, of which he was shown a copy; but when he heard of the many failures which had followed that one exceeding small success, and of all the repulses which Harry had met with in the City, his old master was silent for some minutes, after which he sat down at his desk and wrote the introduction there and then.

"These fellows will get you something if anybody can," he had said; and, indeed, the gentlemen in question, on whom Harry called on his way back to Kensington, seemed confident of getting him something without delay. He had come to them in the very nick of time for next term's vacancies. They would send him immediately, and from day to day, particulars of posts for which he could apply; they had the filling of so many, there was little doubt but that he would obtain what he wanted before long. Their charge would be simply five per cent. on the first year's salary, which would probably be fifty pounds, or sixty if they were lucky.

Harry went home jubilant. The agents had taken down his name and his father's name without question or comment. They declined to regard the years in Africa as a serious disqualification, much less since he had been a tutor there; and Harry began to think that Mr. Innes had taken an unnecessarily black view of his chances. He knew better in a few weeks' time.

It is true that at first he had a thick letter every day, containing the promised particulars of several posts. How used he grew to the clerk's mauve round hand, to the thin sheets of paper damp from the gelatine that laid each opening before Heaven knew how many applicants—to the unvarying formula employed! The Reverend So-and-So, of Dashton, Blankshire, would require in September the services of a junior master, possessing qualifications thereupon stated with the salary offered. The vacant posts were in all parts of the country, and the sanguine Harry pictured himself in almost every county in England while awaiting his fate in one quarter after another. In few cases were the qualifications more than he actually possessed, for he was at least capable of taking the lowest form in a preparatory school, while he could truthfully describe himself as being "fond of games." But the agents' clients would have none of him, and as time went on the agents' envelopes grew thin with single enclosures, and came to hand only once in a way.

And yet several head-masters wrote kindly answers to Harry's application, and two or three seemed on the verge of engaging him. Some interviewed him at the agents' offices, and one had him down to luncheon at his school, paying Harry's fare all the way into Hertfordshire and back. Another only rejected him because Harry was not a fast round-hand bowler, and a fast round-hand bowler was essential—not for the school matches, in which the masters took no part, but for the town, for which they played regularly every Saturday: the music-master bowled slow left, and fast right was indispensable at the other end. But the failures that were all but successes were only the harder to bear, and the bitter fact remained that the lad was no more wanted in the schoolroom than in the office. It struck him sometimes as a grim commentary on the education he had himself received. A thousand or two had been spent upon it, and he had not left school a dunce. He knew as much, perhaps, as the average boy on going up to the university from a public school, and of what use was it to him? It did not enable him to earn his bread. He felt some bitterness against the system which had taught him to swim only with the life-belt of influence and money. It had been his fate to be pitched overboard without one.

Not that he was idle all this time. In the dreadful dog-days, when none but the poor were left in London, and the heat in the little flat became well-nigh insupportable, so that poor Mrs. Ringrose was quite prostrate from its effects, her son sat in his shirt and trousers and plied his pen again in sheer desperation. He wrote out the true incident which he had been advised would make a capital magazine article if written down just as he told it. So he tried to do so; and sent the result to *Uncle Tom*. It came back almost by return of post, with a civil note from the Editor, saying that he could not use the story as the end was so unsatisfactory. It was unsatisfactory because the story happened to be true, and the author never thought of meddling with the facts, though he weighted his work with several immaterial points which he had forgotten when telling the tale verbally. He now flew to the opposite extreme, and dashed off a brief romance unadulterated by a solitary fact or a single instance of original observation. This was begun with ambitious ideas of a match with some shilling monthly, but it was only offered to the penny weeklies, and was burnt unprinted some few months later.

One day, however, the day on which Harry went down to Hertfordshire at a pedagogue's expense, and was coming back heavy with the knowledge that he would not do, the spirit moved him to invest a penny in a comic paper with a considerable vogue. He needed something to cheer him up, and for all he knew this sheet might be good or bad enough to make him smile; it was neither, but it proved to be the best investment he had ever made. It contained a conspicuous notice to contributors, and a number of sets of intentionally droll verses on topics of the week. Before Harry got out at King's Cross he had the rough draft of such a production on his shirtcuff; he wrote it out and sent it off that night; and it appeared in the very next issue of that comic pennyworth.

And this time Harry felt that he had done something that he could do again; but days passed without a word from the Editor, and it looked very much as though the one thing he could do would prove to be unpaid work. At length he determined to find out. The paper's strange name was *Tommy Tiddler* ("St. Thomas must be your patron saint," said Mrs. Ringrose), and its funereal offices were in a court off the Strand. Harry blundered into the counting-house and asked to see the Editor, at which an elderly gentleman turned round on a high stool and viewed him with suspicion. What did he want with the Editor?

"I had a contribution in the last issue," said Harry, nervously, "and—and I wanted to know if there would be any payment."

"But that has nothing to do with the Editor," said the old gentleman. "That is my business."

He got down from his stool and produced a file of the paper, in which the price of every contribution was marked across it, with the writer's name in red ink. Harry was asked to point out his verses, and with a thrill he saw that they were priced at half-a-sovereign. In another minute the coin was in his purse and he was signing the receipt with a hand that shook.

"Monday is our day for paying contributors," the old gentleman said. "In future you must make it convenient to call or apply in writing on that day."

In future!

On his way out he had to pass through the publishing department, where stacks of the new issue were being carried in warm from the machines. It was not on sale until the following day, but Harry could not resist asking to look at a copy, for he had sent in a second set of verses on the appearance of the first. And there they were! He found them instantly and could have cried for joy.

The Inner Circle was never a slower or more stifling route than on that August afternoon; neither was Harry Ringrose ever happier in his life than when he alighted before the train stopped at High Street, Kensington. He had done it two weeks running. He knew that he could go on doing it. He was earning twenty-six pounds a year, and earning it in an hour a week! He almost ran along the hot street, and he took the stairs three at a time. As he fumbled with his latch-key in his excitement, he heard talking within and had momentary misgivings; but his lucky day had dawned at last: the visitor was Fanny Lowndes.

CHAPTER XV.

IT NEVER RAINS BUT IT POURS.

Not since the incident of the dressing-bag had Harry heard a word of Lowndes. He had no idea what had become of that erratic financier or of his daughter, and as to the former he no longer greatly cared. You may have the knack of carrying others with you, but it is dangerous so to carry them against their own convictions; a reaction is inevitable, and Harry had undergone one against Gordon Lowndes. In the warmth of the moment he had freely forgiven the pawning of his bag, but he found it harder to confirm that forgiveness on subsequent and cool reflection. And the visit to Guildford had something to do with this. It had replaced old standards, it had brightened old ideals; and the influence of Mr. Innes was directly antagonistic to that of Lowndes. Add the scholastic disappointments and the literary attempts, and it will be obvious that in the lad's life there had been little room of late for the promoter of the H.C.S. & T.S.A.

But of the promoter's daughter Harry Ringrose had thought often enough. His mind had flown to her in many a difficulty, and it was only his revised view of Lowndes which had kept him from going down to Richmond for her sympathy upon the fate of the manuscript for which she was responsible. Even this afternoon he had thought of her in the Underground, side by side with his mother, as the one other person whom he longed to tell of his success. So that it seemed little short of a miracle to find these two together.

Fanny had already been shown the first *Tiddler* verses, and she now shared Mrs. Ringrose's joy over the half-sovereign and the news of a second accepted contribution. It was delightful to Harry to see her kind face again, to see it happy, and to remember (as he suddenly did) in what trouble he had seen it last. And now he noticed that the girl was brightly dressed, with new gloves and a brilliant sunshade, and he could not but ask after her father and his affairs.

It appeared that the Highland Crofters' Salmon and Trout Supply Association, Limited, was still on the tapis, but under another name and other patronage. The Earl of Banff was no longer connected with the enterprise, but in his stead Lowndes had secured the co-operation of one the Hon. Pelham Tankervell, a personage who appeared to be on a friendly footing with the light and leading of both Houses of Parliament. This Harry gathered from a sheaf of most interesting letters which Fanny Lowndes had brought with her at her father's request. These letters were addressed to Mr. Tankervell by the most illustrious persons, nearly all of whom gave that gentleman permission to use their distinguished names as patrons of the

Crofter Fisheries, Limited, which was the old Company's new name. It was difficult to glance over the letters without imbibing some degree of confidence, and it was plain to Harry that Miss Lowndes herself had more than of old. She told him that the Earl's solicitors had compounded with her father for a substantial sum, and she pointed to her gorgeous parasol as one of the cab-load of purchases with which her father had driven home after cashing the lawyers' cheque. It was plain that the little house on Richmond Hill was in much better case than heretofore; indeed, Fanny Lowndes told Harry as much, though she did add that she no more wished to see him Secretary of the Crofter Fisheries than of the H.C.S. & T.S.A.

"But you believe in it now?" he could not help saying.

"More than I did—decidedly."

"Then why should you dislike to see me in it?"

"You are fit for something better; and—and I think that after this Mr. Tankervell will expect to be made Secretary."

Harry was neither surprised nor vexed to hear it; but he was thinking less of this last sentence than of the last but one.

"You call writing for the *Tiddler* something better?"

"For you—I do. It is a beginning, at any rate."

Until her train went he was telling her of his prose flights and failures, and she was bemoaning her share in one of them. The High Street seemed a lonely place as he walked home to the flat. Yet the day was still the happiest that he had spent in London.

The third week he sent a couple of offerings to *Tommy Tiddler*, but only one of them got in. He tried them with two again. Meanwhile there was an unexpected development in an almost forgotten quarter.

After nearly a month's interval, there came one more thin envelope from the scholastic agents; and this time it was a Mrs. Bickersteth, of the Hollies, Teddington, who required a resident master immediately, to teach very little boys. Very little also was the salary offered. It was thirty pounds; and Harry was for tossing the letter into the first fire they had sat over in the flat, when his mother looked up from the socks which she was knitting for him, and took an unexpected line.

"I wish you to apply for it," said she.

"What, leave you for thirty pounds, when I can make twenty-six at home?"

"That will make fifty-six; for you would be sure to have some time to yourself, and you say the verses only take you an hour on the average. At any rate I wish you to apply, my boy. I will tell you why if they take you."

"Well, they won't; so here goes—to please you."

He sat down and dashed off an answer there and then, but with none of the care which he had formerly expended on such compositions. And instead of the old unrest until he knew his fate, he forthwith thought no more about the matter. So the telegram took him all aback next morning. He was to meet Mrs. Bickersteth at three o'clock at the agents'. By four he had the offer of the vacant mastership in her school.

It was the irony of Harry's fate that a month ago he would have jumped at the chance and flown home on the wings of ecstasy; now he asked for grace to consult his mother, but promised to wire his decision that evening, and went home very sorry that he had applied.

Mrs. Ringrose sighed to see his troubled face.

"Do you mean to tell me it has come to nothing?"

"No; the billet's mine if I want it."

"And you actually hesitated?"

"Yes, mother, because I do not want it. That's the fact of the matter."

Mrs. Ringrose sat silent and looked displeased.

"Is the woman not nice?" she asked presently.

"She seemed all right; rather distinguished in her way; but the hours are atrocious, and I made that my excuse for thinking twice about accepting such a salary. I have promised to send a telegram this evening. But, oh, mother, I don't want to leave you; not to go to a dame's school and thirty pounds a year!"

"You would get your board as well."

"But you would be all alone."

"I could go away for a little. Your Uncle Spencer has asked me to go to the seaside next month with your aunt and the girls. I—I think it would do me good."

"You could leave me in charge, and I would write verses all the time."

"It would be much cheaper to shut up the flat. Then we should be really saving. And—Harry—it is necessary!"

Then the truth came out, and with it the real reason why Mrs. Ringrose wished him to accept the cheap mastership at Teddington. She was trying to keep house upon a hundred and fifty a year; so far she was failing terribly. The rent of the flat was sixty-five; that left eighty-five pounds a year, or but little over thirty shillings a week for all expenses. It was true they kept no servant, but the porter's wife charged five shillings a week, and when the washing was paid there was seldom more than a pound over, even when the stockings and the handkerchiefs were done at home. A pound a week to feed and clothe the two of them! It sounded ample—the tailors had not even sent in their bill yet—and yet somehow it was lamentably insufficient. Mrs. Ringrose had been a rich woman all her life until now; that was the whole secret of the matter. Even Harry, ready as he still was for an extravagance, was in everyday minutiæ more practical than his dear mother. She never called in the porter without giving him a shilling. She seldom paid for anything at the door without slipping an additional trifle into the recipient's hand. And once when some Highlanders played their bagpipes and danced their sword-dances in the back street below, she flung a florin through the window because she had no smaller silver, and to give coppers she was ashamed.

Harry was the last to take exception to traits which he had himself inherited, but he had long foreseen that disaster must come unless he could earn something to add to their income, and so balance the bread he ate and the tea he swallowed. And now disaster had come, insomuch that the next quarter's money was condemned, and Harry's duty was clear. Yet still he temporised.

"A month ago it would have been bad enough," said he; "but surely we might hang together now that I have got a start. Ten bob a week! You shall see me creep up to a pound and then to two!"

"You must first make sure of the ten bob," said Mrs. Ringrose, who had a quaint way of echoing her son's slang, and whose sanguine temperament had been somewhat damped by late experience.

"I am sure of it. Are not three weeks running good enough?"

"But you say they only take you an hour, and that you could spare at the school, even though you had to do it in your own bedroom. Besides, it need only be for one term if you didn't like it; to economise till Christmas, that is all I ask."

Harry knew what he ought to say. He was troubled and vexed at his own perverseness. Yet all his instincts told him that he was finding a footing at last—humble enough, Heaven knew!—on the ladder to which he felt most drawn. And a man does not go against his instincts in a moment.

"Come, my boy," urged Mrs. Ringrose. "Send the telegram and be done with it."

"Wait!" cried Harry, as the bell rang. "There's the post. It may be that my story is accepted."

He meant the story which never was accepted, but whose fitness for the flames he had yet to realise. The letter, however, did not refer to either of his prose attempts. It was from the Editor of *Tommy Tiddler*, enclosing both sets of verses which Harry had sent him that week, and very civilly stating that they were not quite up to his contributor's "usual mark."

Harry went straight out of the flat and was gone some minutes.

"I've sent that telegram," said he when he came back. "I should have told you that the term begins this next Saturday, and I've got to be there on Friday evening."

CHAPTER XVI.

A DAME'S SCHOOL.

The Hollies, Teddington, was situated in a quiet road off the main street. A wooden gate, varnished and grained, displayed a brass plate with Mrs. Bickersteth's name engraved upon it, while that of the house was lettered in black on one of the stucco gate-posts, and perhaps justified by the few evergreens which grew within. A low wall was topped by a sort of balustrade, likewise stuccoed, and behind this wall stood half-a-dozen cropped and yellowing limes.

The house itself was hardly what Harry had expected so far from town. He seemed to have passed it daily for the last four months, for it was the plain, tall, semi-detached, "desirable" and even "commodious residence," which abounds both in Kensington and Camden Town, in the groves of St. John's Wood and on the heights of Notting Hill. A flight of exceedingly clean steps led up to a ponderous front door with a mighty knocker; on the right were two long windows which evidently stretched to the floor, for a wire screen protected the lower part of each; and above these screens, late on the Friday afternoon, some eight or nine rather dismal little faces were pressed to watch the arrival of the new master.

The cabman carried the luggage up the steps and was duly overpaid. The servant shut the great door with a bang—it was a door that would not shut without one—and Harry Ringrose had gone to school again at one-and-twenty.

He was shown into a very nice drawing-room—the kind of drawing-room to reassure an anxious parent—and here for a minute he was alone. Through a thin wall came a youthful buzz, and Harry distinctly heard, "I wonder if he's strict?" He also heard an irritable, weak, feminine voice exclaiming: "Be silent—be silent—or you shall all have fifty lines!" Then the door opened, and he was shaking hands with Mrs. Bickersteth.

The lady was short, stout, and rather more than elderly, yet with a fresh-coloured face as free from wrinkles as it was full of character, and yellow hair which age seemed powerless to bleach. Her manner was not without kindness or distinction, but neither quality was quite so noticeable as when Harry had seen her at the agents' in her mantle and bonnet. Indeed the fresh cheeks had a heightened tinge, and the light eyes a brightness, which Harry Ringrose was destined to know better as the visible signs of Mrs. Bickersteth's displeasure.

"We are a little late," began the schoolmistress (who had this way of speaking to the boys, and who early discovered a propensity to treat Harry as one of them): "we are a little later than I expected, Mr. Ringrose. Now that we have come, however, we will say no more about it."

And the lady gave a perfunctory little laugh, meant to sound indulgent, but Harry had a true ear for such things, and he made his apologies a little stiffly. If Mrs. Bickersteth had named an hour he would have made it his business to be there by that hour; as she had but said the afternoon, he had presumed that five o'clock would be time enough. Mrs. Bickersteth replied that she called five o'clock the evening, with a playfully magnanimous smile which convinced Harry even less than her laugh: he had a presentiment of the temper which it masked.

"But pray let us say no more about it," cried the lady once more. "I only thought that it would be a good opportunity for you to get to know the little men. I am glad to say that all the boarders have arrived; they are now, as I daresay you hear, in the next room with the other governess. Dear me, what am I saying! You see, Mr. Ringrose, I have always had two governesses in the house hitherto. Mr. Scrafton, who comes every morning (except Saturday) to teach the elder boys, has been our only regular master for many years, though a drill-sergeant also comes twice a week from the barracks at Hampton Court. But in taking a master into my house, in place of one of the governesses, I am trying an experiment which I feel sure we will do our best to justify."

Harry replied as suitably as possible, but made more than one mental note. His engagement had not been termed an experiment at their previous interview. Neither had he heard the name of Mr. Scrafton until this moment.

"I hear the servant taking your portmanteau upstairs," continued Mrs. Bickersteth, "and presently I shall show you your room, as I am going to ask you to oblige me by always wearing slippers in the house. The day-boys change their boots the moment they arrive. Before we go upstairs, however, there is one matter about which I should like to speak. We have a delicate little fellow here whose name is Woodman, and whose parents—very superior, rich people—live down in Devonshire, and trust the little man entirely to my care. He is really much better here than he is at home; still he has to have a fire in his room throughout the winter, and consequently he cannot sleep with the other boys. Hitherto one of the governesses has slept in his room, but now I am going to take the opportunity of putting you there, as I am sorry to say he is a boy who requires firmness as well as care. If you will accompany me upstairs I will now show you the room."

It was at the end of a passage at the top of the house, and a very nice room Harry thought it. The beds were in opposite corners, a screen round the smaller one, and the space between at present taken up with Harry's portmanteau and the boy's boxes, which were already partially unpacked. A fire burnt in the grate; a number of texts were tacked to the walls. Harry was still looking about him when Mrs. Bickersteth made a dive into one of the little boy's open boxes and came up with a gaily-bound volume in each hand.

"More story-books!" cried she. "I have a good mind to confiscate them. I do not approve of the number of books his parents encourage him to read. If you ever catch him reading up here, Mr. Ringrose, I must ask you to report the matter instantly to me, as I regret to say that he has given trouble of that kind before."

Harry bowed obedience.

"Little Woodman," continued the schoolmistress, "though sharp enough when he likes, is, I am sorry to say, one of our most indolent boys. He would read all day if we would let him. However, he is going to Mr. Scrafton this term, so he will have to exert himself at last! And now, if you like your room, Mr. Ringrose, I will leave you to put on your slippers, and will take you into the schoolroom when you come downstairs."

The schoolroom was long and bare, but unconventional in that a long dining-table did away with desks, and the boys appeared to be shaking off their depression when Harry and his employer entered five minutes later. They were making a noise through which the same angry but ineffectual voice could be heard threatening a hundred lines all round as the door was thrown open. The noise ceased that moment. The governess rose in an apologetic manner; while all the boys wore guilty faces, but one who was buried in a book, sitting hunched up on the floor. Like most irascible persons, however, the schoolmistress had her moments of conspicuous good-temper, and this was one.

"These are the little men," said she. "Children, this is your new master. Miss Maudsley—Mr. Ringrose."

And Harry found himself bowing to the lady with the voice, a lady of any age, but no outward individuality; even as he did so, however, Mrs. Bickersteth beckoned to the governess; and in another moment Harry was alone with the boys.

The new master had never felt quite so shy or so self-conscious as he did during the next few minutes; it was ten times worse than going to school as a new boy. The fellows stood about him, staring frankly, and one in the background whispered something to another, who told him to shut up in a loud voice. Harry seated himself on the edge of the table, swung a leg, stuck his hands in his pockets (where they twitched) and asked the other boys their names.

"James Wren," said the biggest, who looked twelve or thirteen, and was thickly freckled.

"Ernest Wren," said a smaller boy with more freckles.

"Robertson."

"Murray."

"Gifford."

"Simes."

"Perkins."

"Stanley."

"And that fellow on the floor?"

"Woodman," said James Wren. "I say, Woodman, don't you hear? Can't you get up when you're spoken to?"

Woodman shut his book, keeping, however, a finger in the place, and got up awkwardly. He was one of the smallest of the boys, but he wore long trousers, and beneath them irons which jingled as he came forward with a shambling waddle. He had a queer little face, dark eyes and the lightest of hair; and he blushed a little as, alone among the boys, but clearly unconscious of the fact, he proceeded to shake hands with the new master.

"So you are Woodman?" said Harry.

"Yes, sir," said the boy. "Have you come instead of Mr. Scrafton, sir?"

"No, I have come as well."

At this there were groans, of which Harry thought it best to take no notice. He observed, however, that Woodman was not among the groaners, and to get upon safe ground he asked him what the book was.

"One of Ballantyne's, sir. It's magnificent!" And the dark eyes glowed like coals in what was again a very pale face.

"*The Red Eric*," said Harry, glancing at the book. "I remember it well. You're in an exciting place, eh?"

"Yes, sir: the mutiny, sir."

"Then don't let me stop you—run along!" said Harry, smiling; and Woodman was back on the floor and aboard his whaler before the new master realised that this was hardly the way in which he had been instructed to treat the boy who was always reading.

But he went on chatting with the others, and in quite a few minutes he felt that, as between the boys and himself, all would be plain sailing. They were nice enough boys—one or two a little awkward—one or two vocally unacquainted with the first vowel—but all of them disposed to welcome a man (Harry thought) after the exclusive authority of resident ladies. Traces of a demoralising rule were not long in asserting themselves, as when Robertson gave Simes a sly kick, and Simes started off roaring to tell Mrs. Bickersteth, only to be hauled back by Harry and given to understand (evidently for the first time) that only little girls told tales. The bigger boys seemed to breathe again when he said so. Then they all stood at one of the windows in the failing light, and Harry talked cricket to them, and even mentioned his travels, whereat they clamoured for adventures; but the new master was not such a fool as to play all his best cards first. They were still at the window when the gate opened and in walked a squat silk-hatted gentleman with a yellow beard and an evening paper.

"Here comes old Lennie!" exclaimed Gifford, who was the one with the most to say for himself.

"Who?" said Harry.

"Lennie Bickersteth, sir—short for Leonard," replied Gifford, while the other boys laughed.

"But you mustn't speak of him like that," said Harry severely.

"Oh, yes, I must!" cried Gifford, excited by the laughter. "We all call him Lennie, and Reggie Reggie, and Baby Baby; don't we, you fellows? Bicky likes us to—it makes it more like home."

"Well," said Harry, "I know what Mrs. Bickersteth would *not* like, and if you say *that* again I shall smack your head."

Which so discomfited and subdued the excitable Gifford that Harry liked him immensely from that moment, and not the less when he discovered that the boy's incredible information was perfectly correct.

Mrs. Bickersteth was a widow lady with three grown-up children, whom she insisted on the boys addressing, not merely by their Christian names, but by familiar abbreviations of the same. Leonard and Reginald were City men who went out every morning with a bang of the big front door, and came home in the evening with a rattle of their latch-keys. Both were short and stout like their mother, with beards as yellow as her hair, while Leonard, the elder, was really middle-aged; but it was against the rules for the boys to address or refer to them as anything but Lennie and Reggie, and only the governess and Harry were permitted to say "Mr. Bickersteth." As for the baby of the family, who was Baby still to all her world, she was certainly some years younger; and the name was more appropriate in her case, since she wore the family hair down to eyes of infantile blue, and had the kind of giggle which seldom survives the nursery. She knew no more about boys than any other lady in the house, but was a patently genuine and good-hearted girl, and deservedly popular in the school.

When Harry went to bed that night he smelt the smoke of a candle, though he carried his own in his hand. Woodman was apparently fast asleep, but, on being questioned, he won Harry's heart by confessing without hesitation or excuse. He had *The Red Eric* and a candle-end under his pillow, and the wax was still soft when he gave them up. Harry sat on the side of his bed and duly lectured him on the disobedience and the danger of the detected crime, while the criminal lay with his great eyes wide open, and his hair almost as white as the pillow beneath it. When he had done the small boy said—

"If they had spoken to me like that, sir, last time, sir, I never should have done it again."

"You shouldn't have done it in any case," said Harry. "You've got to promise me that it's the last time."

"It's so hard to go asleep the first night of the term, sir," sighed Woodman. "You keep thinking of this time yesterday and this time last week, sir."

Harry's eye was on the little irons lying on top of the little heap of clothes, but he put on the firmest face he could.

"That's the same for all," he said. "How do you know I don't feel like that myself? Now, you've got to give me your word that you won't ever do this again!"

"But suppose they say what they said before, sir?"

"Give me your word," said Harry.

"Very well, sir, I never will."

"Then I give you mine, Woodman, to say nothing about this; but mind—I expect you to keep yours."

The great eyes grew greater, and then very bright. "I'll promise not to open another book this term, sir—if you like, sir," the little boy cried. But Harry told him that was nonsense and to go to sleep, and turned in himself glowing with new ideas. If he could but influence these small boys as Innes had influenced him! The thought kept him awake far into his first night at Teddington. His life there had begun more happily than he could have dared to hope.

Morning brought the day-boys and work which was indeed within even Harry's capacity. It consisted principally in "hearing" lessons set by Mrs. Bickersteth; and it revealed the educational system in vogue in that lady's school. It was the system of question and answer, the question read from a book by the teacher, the answer repeated by rote by the boy, and on no condition to be explained or enlarged upon by extemporary word of mouth. Harry fell into this error, but was promptly and publicly checked by the headmistress, with whom some of the elder boys were studying English history (from the point of view of Mrs. Markham and her domestic circle) at the other end of the baize-covered dining-table.

"It is quite unnecessary for you to enter into explanations, Mr. Ringrose," said Mrs. Bickersteth down the length of the table. "I have used *Little Steps* for very many years, and I am sure that it explains itself, in a way that little people can understand, better than you can explain it. Where it does not go into particulars, *Little Arthur* does; so no impromptu explanations, I beg."

Whereafter Harry received the answers to the questions in *Little Steps to Great Events* without comment, and was equally careful to take no explanatory liberties with *Mangnall's Questions* or with the *Child's Guide to Knowledge* when these works came under his nose in due course.

Saturday was, of course, a half-holiday; nor could the term yet be said to have begun in earnest. It appeared there were some weekly boarders who would only return on the Monday, while Mr. Scrafton also was not due until that day. Meanwhile an event occurred on the Saturday afternoon which quite took the new master's mind off the boys who were beginning to fill it so pleasantly: an event which perplexed and distracted him on the very threshold of this new life, and yet one with a deeper and more sinister significance than even Harry Ringrose supposed.

CHAPTER XVII.

AT FAULT.

Harry had been requested to put on his boots in order to take the elder boys for a walk. He was to keep them out for about an hour and a half, but nothing had been said as to the direction he should take, and he was indiscreet enough to start without seeking definite instruction on the point.

"Do you always walk two-and-two?" he asked the boys, as they made for the High Street in this doleful order.

"Yes, sir," said two or three.

"But we needn't if you give us leave not to," added the younger Wren, with a small boy's quickness to take advantage.

"No, you must do as you always do, at any rate until we get out of the village," said Harry as they came to the street. "Now which way do you generally go?"

The boys saw their chance of the irregular, and were not slow to air their views. Bushey Park appeared to be the customary resort, and the proverbial mischief of familiarity was discernible in the glowing description which one boy gave of Kingston Market on a Saturday afternoon and in the enthusiasm with which another spoke for Kneller Hall. Richmond Park, said a third, would be better than Bushey Park, only it was rather a long walk.

To Harry, however, who had come round by Wimbledon the day before, it was news, and rather thrilling news, that Richmond Park was within a walk at all. The boys told him it would be near enough when they made a bridge at Teddington.

"There's the ferry," said one; and when Harry said, "Oh, there is a ferry, then?" a little absently, his bias was apparent to the boys.

"The ferry, the ferry," they wheedled, jumping at the idea of such an adventure.

"It's splendid over Ham Common, sir."

"The ferry, sir, the ferry!"

Of course it was very weak in Harry, but the notion of giving the boys a little extra pleasure had its own attraction for him, and his only scruple was the personal extravagance involved. However, he had some silver in his pocket, and the ferryman's toll only came to pennies that Harry could not grudge when he saw the delight of the boys as they tumbled aboard. One of them, indeed, nearly fell into the river—which caused the greatest boy of them all his first misgivings. But across Ham fields they hung upon his arms in the friendliest and pleasantest fashion, begging and coaxing him to tell them things about Africa; and he was actually in the midst of the yarn that had failed on paper, when there occurred on the Common that which was to puzzle him in the future even more than it startled him at the moment. A lady and gentleman strolled into his ken from the opposite direction, and that instant the story ceased.

"Go on, sir, go on! What happened then?"

"I'll tell you presently; here are some friends of mine, and you fellows must wait a moment."

He shook them off and stepped across the road to where his friends were passing without seeing him. Thus his back was turned to the boys, who fortunately could not see how he blushed as he raised his hat.

"It's Mr. Ringrose!" cried Fanny Lowndes.

"The deuce it is!" her father exclaimed. "Why, Ringrose, what the blazes are you doing down here, and who are your young friends?"

"I'm awfully sorry I didn't let you know," said Harry, "but the whole thing was so sudden. As I told you when you came to see us, Miss Lowndes, I have been trying for a mastership for some time; and just as I had given it up——"

"You have got one!"

"Yes, quite unexpectedly, at the beginning of this week."

The girl looked both glad and sorry, but her father's nose was twitching with amusement and his eyes twinkling in their gold frames.

"You did well to take what you could get," said he, lowering his voice so that nothing could be heard across the road. "Writing for your living means writing for your life, and that's no catch; but by Jove, Ringrose, you ought to get off some good things with such a capital safety-valve as boys always on hand! When you can't think of a rhyme, run round and box their ears till one comes. When you get a rejected manuscript, try hammering their knuckles with the ruler! Where's the school, Ringrose, and who keeps it?"

Harry hung his head.

"I am almost ashamed to tell you. It's a dame's school—at Teddington."

"A dame's school at Teddington! Not Mrs. Bickersteth's?"

"Yes—do you know it?"

Harry had looked up in time to catch the other's expression, and it was a very singular one. The lad had never seen such a look on any other face, but on this face he had seen it once before. He had seen it in the train, during the journey back to London, on the day that he could never forget. It was the look that had afterwards struck him as a guilty look, though, to be sure, he had never thought about it from the moment when he took up his father's letter, and saw at a glance that it was genuine, until this one.

"Do I know it?" echoed Lowndes, recovering himself. "Only by repute—only by repute. So you have gone there!" he added below his breath, strangely off his guard again in a moment.

"Come," said Harry, "do you know something against the school, or what?"

"Oh, dear, no; nothing against it, and very little about it," replied Lowndes. "Only the school is known in these parts—people in Richmond send their boys there—that is all. I have heard very good accounts of it. Are you the only master?"

"No, there's a daily pedagogue, named Scrafton, who seems to be something of a character, but I haven't seen him yet. Do you know anything about him?"

The question was innocently asked, for Harry's curiosity had been aroused by the repeated necessity of preventing the boys from opening their hearts to him about Mr. Scrafton. If he had stopped to think, he would have seen that he had the answer already—and Lowndes would not have lost his temper.

"How should I know anything about him?" he cried. "Haven't I just asked you if you were the only master? Either your wits are deserting you, Ringrose, or you wish to insult me, my good fellow. In any case we must be pushing on, and so, I have no doubt, must you."

Harry could not understand this ebullition, which was uttered with every sign of personal offence, from the ridiculously stiff tones to the remarkably red face. He simply replied that he had spoken without thinking and had evidently been misunderstood, and he turned without more ado to shake hands with Miss Lowndes. The father's goodwill had long ceased to be a matter of vital importance to him; but it went to his heart to see how pale Miss Fanny had turned during this exchange of words, and to feel the trembling pressure of that true friend's hand. It was as though she were asking him to forgive her father, at whose side she walked so dejectedly away that it was not pure selfishness which made Harry Ringrose long just then to change places with Gordon Lowndes.

The whole colloquy had not lasted more than two or three minutes; yet it had ended in the most distinct rupture that had occurred, so far, between

Harry and his parents' friend; and that about the most minute and seemingly insignificant point which had ever been at issue between them.

The boys found their new master poor company after this. He finished his story in perfunctory fashion, nor would he tell another. He not only became absent-minded and unsociable, but displayed an unsuspected capacity for strictness which was really irritability. More than one young wiseacre whispered a romantic explanation, but the majority remembered that it was to the gentleman old Ring-o'-ring-o'-roses had chiefly addressed himself; and the general and correct impression was that the former had been "waxy" with old Ring-in-the-nose. Harry's nickname was not yet fixed.

Those, however, with whom he had been "waxy" in his turn had a satisfaction in store for them at the school, where Mrs. Bickersteth awaited them, watch in hand, and with an angry spot on each fresh-coloured cheek. She ordered the boys downstairs to take their boots off, and in the same breath requested Mr. Ringrose to speak to her in the study, in a tone whose significance the boys knew better than Harry.

"I was under the impression, Mr. Ringrose, that I said an hour and a half?" began the lady, with much bitter-sweetness of voice and manner.

Harry pulled out his own watch, and began apologising freely; he was some twenty minutes late.

"When I say an hour and a half," continued the schoolmistress, "I do not mean two hours. I beg you will remember that in future. May I ask where you have been?"

Harry said they had been to Richmond Park. The lady's eyes literally blazed.

"You have walked my boys to Richmond Park and back? Really, Mr. Ringrose, I should have thought you would know better. The distance is much too great. I am excessively angry to hear they have been so far."

"I beg your pardon," said Harry, with humility, "but I don't think the distance was quite so great as you imagine. Though we have walked back through Kingston, we made a short cut in going, for I took the liberty of taking the boys across the river in the ferry-boat."

This was the last straw, and for some moments Mrs. Bickersteth was practically speechless with indignation. Then with a portentous inclination of her yellow head, "It *was* a liberty," said she; "a very great liberty indeed, I call it! I requested you to take them for a walk. I never dreamt of your risking their lives on the river. Have the goodness to understand in future, Mr. Ringrose, that I strongly disapprove of the boys going near the river. It is a most undesirable place for them—most unsootable in every way. Excessively angry I am!"

This speech might have been heard over half the house, and by the end Harry was fairly angry himself. But for his mother, and for a resolution he had made not to take Mrs. Bickersteth seriously, but to put up with all he possibly could, it is highly probable that the Hollies, Teddington, would have known Harry Ringrose for twenty-four hours only. As it was he maintained a sarcastic silence, and, when the wrathful lady had quite finished, left her with a bow and the assurance that what had happened should not occur again; he merely permitted himself to put some slight irony into his tone.

And, indeed, the insulting character of a reprimand which was not, however, altogether unmerited, worried him far less in early retrospect than the inexplicable manner of Gordon Lowndes on Ham Common. What did he know about the school? What could have brought that odd look back to his face? And why in the world should the master of an excellent temper have lost it on provocation so ludicrously slight? These were the questions that kept Harry Ringrose awake and restless in the still small hours of the Sabbath morning.

CHAPTER XVIII.

MR. SCRAFTON.

In the basement was a good-sized but ill-lighted room where three long tables, resting on trestles, were sufficiently crowded on the four days of the week when the day-boys stayed to dinner. On the two half-holidays only one table was in use, and the boarders scarcely filled it, with Miss Maudsley and Mr. Ringrose in state at either end. But on Sundays all meals were in the big schoolroom, and were graced by the presence of Mrs. Bickersteth's City sons, who brought with them a refreshing whiff of the outside world, besides contributing to Harry's enjoyment in other ways. He never forgot those Sunday meals. He was fond of describing them to his friends in after years.

At breakfast on his first Sunday he was quite sure that Mrs. Bickersteth had heard of the death of a near relative. Her face and voice were those of a chief mourner, and she appeared to be shedding tears as she heard the boys their Collect at the breakfast table, rewarding those who knew it with half a cold sausage apiece. The boys were by no means badly fed, but that half-sausage was their one weekly variant from porridge and bread-and-butter for breakfast, and they used to make pathetically small bites of it. Mrs. Bickersteth, however, scarcely broke her fast, but would suffer all day, and every Sabbath, from what Harry came to consider some acute though intermittent form of religious melancholia. Towards the end of breakfast the sons would come down in wool-work slippers, a little heavy after "sleeping in," and it was not at this meal that they were most entertaining.

The next hour was one of the few which Harry had entirely to himself. Most days he was on duty from eight in the morning to half-past eight at night, but the hour between Sunday breakfast and morning service was the new master's very own, and he spent it in a way which surely would have made Mrs. Bickersteth's remarkable hair stand straight on end. Even Sunday letter-writing was forbidden in her Sabbatarian household, and yet Harry had the temerity to spend this hour in composing vulgar verses for the *Tiddler*. He had discovered that contributions for the Saturday's issue must reach the office on the Monday, and it is to be feared that the consequent urgency of the enterprise led him into still more reprehensible excesses. What he could not finish in his bedroom he would mentally continue in church, whither it was his duty to take the majority of the boys, while the rest accompanied the Bickersteths to chapel.

The dinner that followed was what Harry enjoyed. It was an excellent dinner, and all but Mrs. Bickersteth were invariably in the best of spirits. This lady used to stand at the head of her table and carve the hissing round of secular beef with an air of Christian martyrdom quite painful to watch. Not that it affected her play with the carving-knife, which was so skilful that Harry Ringrose used to wonder why the schoolmistress must needs lap a serviette round either forearm, and a third about her ample waist, for the better protection of her Sunday silk. This, however, was a trick of the whole family, who might have formed the nucleus of a Society for the Preservation of Sunday Clothes. Thus Reggie, the younger and more dapper son, used to appear on these occasions in a brown velvet coat and waistcoat, with his monogram on every button, but would mar the effect by tucking his table-napkin well in at the neck and spreading it out so as to cover as much as possible of his person. Lennie, the elder and more sedate, though he had no such grandeur to protect, nevertheless took similar precautions; while the good-natured Baby used to pull off a pair of immensely long cuffs, the height of a recent fashion, and solemnly place them on the table beside her tumbler, before running any risks.

Water was the beverage of one and all, yet the spirits of the majority would rise with the progress of the meal. Reggie, who was a very facetious person, would begin to say things nicely calculated to make the boys titter; the elder brother would air a grumpy wit of his own; and Mrs. Bickersteth would shake the cap awry on her yellow head and beg them both to desist. The good-hearted Baby would add her word in vindication of the harmless character of her brothers' jokes, and at the foot of the table the governess would trim her sails with great dexterity, looking duly depressed when she caught Mrs. Bickersteth's eye and coyly tickled on encountering those of the gentlemen. Harry sat between Leonard Bickersteth and a line of little boys, and facing the flaxen-haired Baby, who gave him several kindly, reassuring smiles for which he liked her. The young men also treated him in a friendly fashion; but he was quite as careful as his fair colleague not to commit himself to too open an appreciation of their sallies.

The boys were in Harry's charge for the afternoon, but it seemed that on Sundays they never went for a walk for walking's sake. Occasionally, as it turned out, he would be requested to take them to some children's service; but on that first Sunday, and as a rule, they spent the afternoon in the smaller school-room upstairs, where some strictly Sabbatarian periodicals were given out for the day's use, and only such books as *Sunday Echoes in Week-day Hours*, and the stories of Miss Hesba Stretton, permitted to be read. Harry used to feel sorry for little Woodman on these occasions. He would catch the small boy's great eyes wandering wistfully to the shelf in which his *Mangnall's Questions* and *The Red Eric* showed side by side; or the eyes would stare into vacancy by the hour together, seeing doubtless his Devonshire home, and all that his "very superior people" would be doing there at the moment. Harry liked Woodman the best of the boys, partly because he had a variety of complaints but never uttered one. The new master was much too human, and perhaps as much too unsuited by temperament for his work, not to have favourites from the first, and Woodman and Gifford were their names.

After tea they all went off to evening service, and after that came a peaceful half-hour in the pretty drawing-room, where the boys sang hymns till bedtime. There was something sympathetic in this proceeding, the conduct of which was in Baby Bickersteth's kindly hands. The young lady presided at the piano, which she played admirably, and the boys stood round her in a semicircle, and each boy chose his favourite hymn. Lennie and Reggie joined in from their chairs, and Mrs. Bickersteth's lips would move as she followed the words in a hymn-book. When the last hymn had been sung, the schoolmistress read prayers; and when the boys said good-night she kissed each of them in a way that quite touched Harry on the Sunday evening after his arrival. He saw the boys to bed in a less captious frame of mind than had been his all day, and when he turned in himself he was rather ashamed of some of his previous sentiments towards the schoolmistress. He had seen the pathos of her pious depression, and he was beginning to divine the hourly irritants of keeping school at Mrs. Bickersteth's time of life. Instead of his cynical resolve not to take her seriously, he lay down chivalrously vowing to resent nothing from a woman who was also old. He seemed to have seen a new side of the schoolmistress, and henceforth she had his sympathy.

Indeed there was a something human in all these people; they had kind hearts, when all was said; and Harry Ringrose began to feel that for a time at any rate, he need not be unhappy in their midst. He had still to encounter the master spirit of the place.

When all the boys were standing round the long dining-table next morning, having taken turns in reading a Chapter aloud, Mrs. Bickersteth made an announcement as she closed her Testament.

"This term," said she, "Mr. Scrafton is coming at half-past ten instead of at eleven, and those boys who are to go to him will be in their places in the upper schoolroom at twenty-five minutes past ten each morning."

A list followed of the boys who were promoted to go to Mr. Scrafton that term; it ended with the name of little Woodman. Harry happened to be engaged in the background in the intellectual task of teaching a tiny child his alphabet. He could not help seeing some ruddy cheeks turn pale as the list was read; but Woodman, with a fine regardlessness, was reading a letter from Devonshire behind another boy's back.

Punctually at ten-thirty a thunderous knock resounded from the front door, and Harry was sorry that he had not been looking out of the window. He saw Mrs. Bickersteth jump up and bustle from the room with a most solicitous expression, and he heard a loud voice greeting her heartily in the hall. Heavy feet ran creaking up the stairs a few minutes later, and Mrs. Bickersteth returned to her task of hearing tables and setting sums.

Meanwhile Harry was devoting himself to the very smallest boys in the school, mites of five and six, whose nurses brought them in the morning and came back for them at one o'clock. About eleven, however, Mrs. Bickersteth suggested that these little men would be the better for a breath of air, and would Mr. Ringrose kindly take them into the back-garden for ten minutes, and see that they did not run on the grass? Now, Harry's pocket was still loaded with a missive addressed to the editor of *Tommy Tiddler*, which obviously must be posted by his own hand, and might even now be too late. He therefore asked permission to go as far as the pillar-box at the corner, in order to post a letter; and Mrs. Bickersteth, who was luckily in the best of tempers, not only nodded blandly, but added that she would be excessively obliged if Mr. Ringrose would also post some letters of hers which he would find upon the hall-table. So Harry sallied forth, with an infant in sailor-clothes holding each of his hands, and whom should he find loitering at the corner but Gordon Lowndes?

"Why, Ringrose," cried he, "this is well met indeed! I was just on my way to have a word with you. I was looking for the house."

The hearty manner and the genial tone would have been enough for Harry at an earlier stage of his acquaintance with this man; but now instinctively he knew them for a cloak, and he would not relinquish the small boys' hands for the one which he felt was awaiting his, though his eyes had never fallen from Lowndes's spectacles.

"I am not sure that you would have been able to see me," was his reply. "I am on duty even now. What was the point?"

"Is it impossible for me to have a word with you alone?"

Harry told the little boys to walk on slowly to the pillar. "It will literally have to be a word," he added pointedly. Yet his curiosity was whetted. What could the man want with him here and now?

"Very well—very well," said Lowndes briskly. "I merely desire to apologise for my—my hastiness when we met on Saturday. I fear—that is, my daughter tells me—but indeed I am conscious myself—that I quite misunderstood your meaning, Ringrose, on a point in itself too trifling to be worth naming. You may remember, however, that you asked me if I knew anything about a person of whose very existence I had just exposed my ignorance?"

"I remember," said Harry. "A mere slip of the tongue, due to my curiosity about the man."

"And is your curiosity satisfied?" inquired Lowndes, becoming suddenly preoccupied in wiping the dust from his eye-glasses.

"Well, I haven't seen him yet, though he is in the house."

"Ah!" said Lowndes, as though he had not listened. "Well, Ringrose, all I wanted was to tell you frankly that I didn't mean to be rude to you on Saturday afternoon; so I took the train on here before going to the City; and now I've just time to catch one back—so good-bye."

"It was hardly worth while taking so much trouble," said Harry dryly; for he knew there was some other meaning in the move, though as yet he could not divine what.

"Hardly worth while?" said Lowndes. "My dear boy, that's not very kind. I have always been fond of you, Ringrose, and for your own sake as well as on every other ground I should be exceedingly sorry to offend you. Things are looking up with the Company, you know, and I can't afford to quarrel with our future Secretary!"

And with that cunning unction he walked away laughing, but Harry knew there was no laughter in his heart, and that every word he had spoken was insincere. What then was the meaning? To keep friendly with him, doubtless; but why? And such were the possibilities of Gordon Lowndes, and such the imagination of Harry Ringrose, that the latter took his little boys back to the school with the very wildest and most far-fetched explanations surging through his brain.

In the hall he heard a strident voice raging in the schoolroom overhead. He could not help going a little way upstairs to discover whether anything serious was the matter. And outside the schoolroom door stood one of the biggest boys, crying bitterly, with his collar torn from its stud, and one ear and one cheek as crimson as though that side of his face had been roasted before a fire.

At one o'clock the whole school went for a walk before dinner, and it was then that Harry at last set eyes on the formidable Scrafton, as he came downstairs in his creaking shoes, with his snuff-box open in his hand, and his extraordinary head thrown back to take a pinch. There are some faces which one has to see many times before one knows them, as it were, by heart; there are others which one passes in the street with a shudder, and can never afterwards forget; and here was a face that would have haunted Harry Ringrose even though he had never seen it but this once.

A magnificent forehead was its one fine feature; the light blue eyes beneath were spoilt by their fiery rims, and yet they gleamed with a fierce humour and a keen intelligence which lent them distinction of a kind. These were the sole redeeming points. The rest was either cruel or unclean or both. The creature's skin was very smooth and yellow, and it shone with an unwholesome gloss. Abundant hair, of a dirty iron-grey, was combed back from the forehead without a parting, and gathered in unspeakable curls on the nape of a happily invisible neck. A long, lean nose, like a vulture's beak, overhung a grey moustache with a snuffy zone in the centre, and lost pinches of snuff lingered in a flowing beard of great length. The man wore a suit of pristine black, now brown with age and snuff, and Harry noticed a sallow gleam between his shoes and his trousers as he came creaking down the stairs. In warm weather he wore no socks.

"This is the new master of whom I spoke to you," said Mrs. Bickersteth, who was waiting in the hall to introduce Harry to Mr. Scrafton.

"That a master?" bellowed Scrafton. "Why, I thought it was a new boy!" And he let out a roar of laughter that left his blue eyes full of water; then he strode across the hall with a horrible hand out-stretched; the long nails had jagged, black rims, and in another moment Harry was shuddering from a clasp that was at once clammy and strong.

"What's your name?" asked Mr. Scrafton, grinning like a demon in Harry's face.

"Mr. Ringrose," said Mrs. Bickersteth.

"What name?" roared Scrafton. He had turned from Harry to the schoolmistress. Harry saw her quail, and he took the liberty of repeating his surname in a very distinct voice.

"Where do you come from?" demanded Scrafton, turning back to Harry, or rather upon him, with his red-rimmed eyes glaring out of an absolutely bloodless face.

Harry answered the question with his head held high.

"Son of Henry Ringrose, the ironmaster?"

"I am."

"I thought so! A word with you, ma'am," cried Scrafton—and himself led the way into Mrs. Bickersteth's study.

CHAPTER XIX.

ASSAULT AND BATTERY.

Harry was left alone in the hall. The boys were in the basement, putting on their boots. There were high words in the study, and yet Scrafton seemed to be speaking much below his normal pitch. Harry sauntered into the deserted schoolroom to avoid eavesdropping. And as if in spite of him, the voices rose, and this much reached his ears:

"I tell you it will ruin the school!"

"Then let me tell you, Mr. Scrafton, that the school is mine, and I have done it with my eyes open."

"The son of a common swindler! I know it to my cost———"

To his cost! How could he know it to his cost, this suburban schoolmaster? Harry had shut the door; he stood against it in a torment of rage and shame, his fingers on the handle, only listening, only waiting, for that other door to open. So in the end the two doors opened as one, and the two masters met in the hall and glared in each other's faces without a word.

"Mr. Ringrose!" cried Mrs. Bickersteth hastily.

Harry turned from the baleful yellow face in a paroxysm of contempt and loathing, and was next moment closeted with a trembling old woman whose pitiable agitation was another tribute to the terrible Scrafton.

Mrs. Bickersteth's observations were both brief and broken. She had just heard from Mr. Scrafton what indeed was not exactly new to her. The name was uncommon. Her sons had recalled the case on the arrival of Harry's application for the junior mastership. They had not painted the case quite so black as Mr. Scrafton had done, and they had all agreed that the—the sin of the father—should not disqualify the son. She had not meant to let Mr. Ringrose know that she knew (Harry thanked her in a heartfelt voice), but she had hoped that nobody else would know: and Mr. Scrafton knew for one.

"Do you want to get rid of me?" asked Harry bluntly.

The lady winced.

"Not unless you want to go. No—no—I have neither the inclination nor the right to take such a course. But if, after this, you would rather not stay, I—I would not stand in your way, Mr. Ringrose."

Harry saw how it was with Mrs. Bickersteth. She did not want to be unjust, she did not want to give in to Scrafton, but oh! if Mr. Ringrose would save the situation by going of his own accord!

"Will you give me the afternoon to think it over?" said he.

"Certainly," said Mrs. Bickersteth. "I wish you to consult your own feelings only. I wish to be just, Mr. Ringrose, and—and to meet your ideas. If you are going to town, any time before ten o'clock will be time enough for your return."

Harry expressed his gratitude, and said that in that case it would be unnecessary for him to absent himself before the close of afternoon school; nor did he do so; for he was not going to town at all.

He was going straight to Richmond Hill, to put the whole matter before Gordon Lowndes, and to beg the explanation he felt certain the other could give. Why should Scrafton have lost his colour and his temper at the bare mention of the name of Ringrose? Was it true that he knew that name already "to his cost"? Then how did he know it to his cost, and since when, and what was the subtle connection between Mr. Ringrose and this same Scrafton? Was Lowndes aware of any?

Yes, there was something that Lowndes knew, something that he had known on the Saturday afternoon, something to account for his surprise on learning to what school Harry had gone as master. He had indignantly denied all knowledge of Scrafton, but Harry could no longer accept that gratuitous and inexplicable repudiation. It was the very fact that he did know something about Scrafton, something which he wished to keep to himself, that had made him angrily disclaim such knowledge.

Harry was coming back to his old idea that Lowndes had been more deeply implicated in his father's flight than anybody supposed. He no longer suspected foul play—that was impossible in the face of the letter from Dieppe—but he did suspect complicity on the part of Lowndes. What if Lowndes had swindled wholesale in the ironmaster's name, and what if Scrafton were one of his victims?

What if Lowndes could tell him where his father lay in hiding abroad!

The thought brought a happy moment and an hour of bitterness; no, it were better they should never know; better still if he were dead. And the bitter hour that followed was the last and the loveliest of a warm September day; and Harry Ringrose spent it in walking across Ham Common and through Richmond Park, in the mellow sunset, on his way to Richmond Hill.

When he got there it was dusk, and two men were pacing up and down the little garden in front of Lowndes's house. Harry paused at the gate. The men had their heads close together, and were conversing so earnestly that they never saw him. They were Lowndes and Scrafton.

Harry stepped back without a sound. All his suppositions had been built upon the hypothesis that these two were enemies; it had never entered his head that they might be friends. To find them together was the last thing he had expected, and the discovery chilled him in a way for which he could not instantly account. He knew there was good reason for it, but in his first discomfiture he could not find the reason.

He stole back along the road, a shower of new suspicions sticking like arrows in his soul. The very vagueness of his sensations added to their sickening effect. His brain heaved as though with wine, and when he clapped a hand to his head it came back dripping. He was at the corner of the road before he knew what he was going to do, and there he spent minutes hesitating and considering. Unable to make up his mind, he crossed over and returned to reconnoitre from the other side. To and fro walked Lowndes and Scrafton, on the gravel path in front of the lighted window opposite; and faster than their feet, but lower than their footfalls, went their tongues.

Harry had not heard a word before. At this distance it was impossible for him to catch a syllable, and he was glad of it. He would watch his men and bide his time. It might be his best policy to do nothing, to say nothing, for the present; but he would keep an eye on the house while he thought it over.

The difficulty was for the observer himself to escape observation. The road was so quiet that if he strolled up and down, those other saunterers in the garden could not fail to have their attention attracted to him sooner or later. It was so narrow that they had only to look up in order to see him leaning against the paling of the opposite house. This house, however, was unoccupied, and behind the paling, in the segment of a circle formed by the shortest of suburban carriage drives, grew a clump of laurels which tempted Harry to do a very foolish thing. He crept into the garden of the unoccupied house, and from a point of vantage among the laurels he watched the two men in the garden over the way.

Up and down they walked, backward and forward, and their low voices never ceased; backward and forward, up and down; and now the light of a lamp made oval flames of Lowndes's glasses, now the taller Scrafton's cormorant profile was stamped for an instant on the lighted blinds, while the loathsome sound of his snuff-taking came again and again across the quiet road.

So these men were friends: and Lowndes had carefully implied that they were not even acquainted. Why should he have gone out of his way to do that? He had flown into a temper when that careful implication was inadvertently ignored; and had afterwards so feared the tell-tale effect of this unguarded outbreak that he had gone all the way to Teddington with elaborate apologies and ingenious explanations.

Stay: no: he had gone to Teddington with an ulterior motive, which only this instant dawned upon Harry Ringrose. Now he thought of it, there had been an obvious absence of premeditation about both the apology and the explanation; in fact, he had never before heard the fluent Lowndes hesitate so often for a word. Why? Because he had gone to Teddington that morning with quite another object, and at last Harry saw what it was.

He remembered Mrs. Bickersteth's announcement that this term Mr. Scrafton was coming half-an-hour earlier than formerly. He remembered how cleverly Lowndes had contrived to discover that Scrafton was already in the house. He had never forgotten Scrafton's face on hearing the new master's name. The thing was plain as daylight, and Harry only wondered how and why he had not seen it at once. Gordon Lowndes had gone to Teddington simply and solely to intercept his friend Scrafton, and to warn him that he was about to meet a son of the missing Henry Ringrose.

But why warn him? What had Harry's father been to Scrafton, or Scrafton to Harry's father? The lad's blood ran hot with suspicion, ran cold with surmise: there were the two men who could tell him the truth, there within twenty yards of him: he heard their every footfall in the gravel, heard one taking snuff, and the other talking, talking, talking in an endless whisper. Yet he could not walk boldly across the road and challenge them to tell him the truth! He was not sure that it would be a wise thing to do, but it galled him to feel that he could not do it. Lowndes loved a scene as much as he hated one, but Harry felt he could have stood up to Lowndes alone. Scrafton was a loathly being, but he would not have daunted Harry by himself. It was the two together, the coarse bully and the keen-witted man of the world, strong men both, whom the lad could not bring himself to challenge in cold blood. He had, indeed, too much sense; but, in an agony of self-upbraiding consciousness, he kept blaming and hating himself for having too little pluck. He thought of the motto on his bedroom wall at home. He would have it down; it was not for him. It was only for those who had some pluck to lose.

And as he cowered in the garden of the empty house, a white face among the leaves, impotent, bewildered, self-tormenting, the front door opened across the road, and a supple, strong figure stood so straight in the mouth of the lighted passage, a silhouette crowned with gold by the lamp within. For an instant Harry's heart seemed to stop, and the next instant to rush from his keeping to that lighted door. He had forgotten the existence of Fanny Lowndes.

"Dinner is ready," she said. Harry heard the words distinctly: there was no reason to lower that honest voice. But he thought that he detected an unwonted note of fear—one of disgust he could swear to—and instantly his mind was going over every conversation he had ever had with the girl, hunting for that unwonted note which was yet not entirely unfamiliar. He felt certain that he had heard it before.

"One moment," replied Lowndes; and his voice sank once more, and so continued volubly for some minutes: then the pair went in.

But Harry lingered among his laurels, strongly impelled to go incontinently with his questions and his suspicions to the one friend of whose sympathy he felt sure, of whose truth and honour there was no question. Yet to that one friend he could never go, for was she not also the only child of Gordon Lowndes?

And what then was his wisest course? Should he do nothing, for the present, but return to Teddington, continue in the school, and watch this Scrafton from day to day? Or should he wait until Scrafton was gone, and then confront Lowndes with an uncompromising demand for explanations? Prudence advised one course, gallantry another; but the question was to receive a sufficiently sensational solution. It so happened that the burglary season had set in early that autumn in the Thames valley, and the Richmond police in particular were already greatly on their mettle. A certain young constable, at once desirous of his stripes and yet not a little alarmed by his own enterprise, had obtained leave to go on his beat in noiseless boots, and he came into Greville Road about the time that Lowndes and Scrafton went indoors. Not a sound came from his muffled feet, but that only seemed to make his heart beat the louder; for it was a very human young constable, and the majority of the recent burglaries had taken place at this very hour, while the families were at dinner.

Suddenly the young policeman stood still and all but shaking in his soundless boots: for a few feet from his nose, where he least expected it, in the garden of an empty house, was a pale face among the laurels, with dark eyes upon the house across the road. A palpable burglar choosing his window. A desperate fellow, judging by his face, and yet one to be taken single-handed if he were alone.

Harry did not hear the hand feeling for the truncheon, nor yet the leather tongue leaping from the brass button; but he smelt the dark lantern burning about a second before the light was flashed in his face.

"Wad-you-doing-there?"

The low voice was drunken in its excitement.

Harry recoiled among the laurels, guiltily enough, for he was horribly startled.

"Come-out-o'-that!" growled the young constable through his teeth to prevent their chattering, and with his words still running together. "Come-out-o'-that; you've-got-to-come-along-with-me!"

"Why?" cried Harry, frightened into self-possession on the spot.

"You know why! Think I didn't see you watching that house? Out you come!"

The constable also was becoming master of his nerves. Harry, indeed, neither looked nor spoke like a very desperate person.

"Look here, officer," said he, "you're making a mistake. Do I look a burglar?"

"Come out and I'll tell you."

"Well, but look here: you're not going to run me in if I do?"

"I'm not so sure about that."

"You can't!" cried Harry, losing his temper. "What charge have you to bring against me?"

"Trespassing with intent! You may satisfy the sergeant, and if you do he won't detain you. But I've got to do my dooty, and if you won't come out I'll make you, but if you take my advice you'll come quietly."

"Oh, I'll come quietly," said Harry, "if I've got to come."

His tone was one of unaffected resignation. To be haled before the police was a new and most grotesque experience, at which he could have laughed outright but for the dread lest his superior officers might prove as crass as this callow constable. That he would have to go, however, appeared inevitable; and though the thought of calling Lowndes to vouch for his respectability did occur to him, it was instantly dismissed, and that of resistance never occurred to him at all. Harry was a very peaceable person, but he was also very excitable and impulsive, and what he now did was done without a moment's thought. He had opened the gate, which was wide and heavy, with the kind of latch which allows a gate to swing past the post on either side, and on the pavement stood a young police man with his lantern and something glittering in its light. It was a pair of handcuffs, and the sight of them was responsible for what followed. Instead of passing through the gate, as he seemed in the act of doing, Harry clapped both hands to the bar and rushed at the policeman with the gate in front of him. Every bar struck a different section of the man's body: his lantern fell with a clatter, his handcuffs with a tinkle, and he himself was hurled heavily into the road, along which Harry was scampering like a wild thing. At the corner he stopped to look back, because no footsteps were following and no whistle had been blown. The lantern had not gone out, for a jet of light spouted from the pavement half-way across the road, where it ran into a dark-blue heap. Otherwise the little road was quite deserted.

Some minutes later, when the whistles began to blow, the man they blew for just heard them from the heights of the hill; but he had had the presence of mind to walk up to the park gates, and through them at a pace almost leisurely; and long before ten o'clock he was sitting over little Woodman's fire in his room at the Hollies, Teddington, and wondering whether it was he or another who had been through the adventures of the evening.

He had decided to remain at the school, and Mrs. Bickersteth had accepted his decision without comment. The schoolmistress little dreamt to whom a paragraph referred which caught her eye in the next issue of the *Surrey Comet*:—

RICHMOND BURGLARS.
ASSAULT ON THE POLICE.

As Constable John Tinsley, Richmond division, Metropolitan Police, was on his rounds on Monday evening last, he noticed a man lurking in the garden of an empty house on the hill, and, on demanding an explanation, was savagely assaulted and left senseless in the road. There can be little doubt, from the bruises on Tinsley's body, that the ruffian felled him with some blunt instrument, and afterwards kicked him as he lay insensible. Tinsley is now on duty again, but considers he has had a lucky escape. He describes his assailant as a thick-set and powerful young fellow of the working class, and has little doubt that he was one of the brutal and impudent thieves who are at present a pest of the neighbourhood.

Harry Ringrose would not have recognised himself had he not been on the look-out for some such item: when he did, he breathed more freely, though not freely enough to show himself unnecessarily on Richmond Hill. The paragraph he cut out and treasured for many years.

CHAPTER XX.

BIDING HIS TIME.

When Scrafton's knock thundered through the house on the morning after Harry's adventure, Mrs. Bickersteth again rose hastily and bustled from the schoolroom; and for the next five minutes the ears of the junior master had some cause to tingle. When the schoolmistress returned she would not look at Harry, who was well aware that she had secretly wished him to resign, and that conscience alone forbade her to send him away in obedience to Scrafton's demands. That such demands had been made the day before, and reiterated this morning, Harry was as certain as though he had heard them; but the certainty only cemented his resolve to stay where he was, to give not the smallest pretext for his dismissal, and to watch Scrafton, patiently, steadily, day after day, for some explanation of his animus against himself and of his mysterious relations with Gordon Lowndes.

It chanced that the middle of that September was as warm as midsummer, and on the first Wednesday of the term a whisper of cricket went round the school. It appeared that on Wednesday and Friday afternoons, throughout the summer, the boys played cricket in Bushey Park, and as it was still summer weather they were to do so this afternoon.

"Are you going to take us, sir?" asked Gifford, as they were changing into flannels, under Harry's supervision, in their dormitory, after dinner.

"Not that I know of," said Harry. "Who generally does?"

"Mr. Scrafton, and he doesn't know the rules———"

"Read 'em through once, years ago———"

"And thinks he understands the game———"

"And scores and umpires———"

"And gives two men out at once!"

Here, duty compelled Harry to administer a general snub; but he determined to go to Bushey Park and see the cricket for himself; and when the day-boys had assembled in flannels also, and Mr. Scrafton, flourishing a long blackthorn, had marched them all off in double file, the junior master had his chance. Little Woodman was left behind. He was not allowed to play cricket. Harry was requested to take him for a walk instead; and, on inquiring whether there would be any objection to their going to Bushey Park to watch the game, received permission to do so on the understanding that Woodman was not to sit on the grass or to stand about too long.

The wickets had just been pitched when they arrived, and Scrafton and the biggest boy, kneeling behind either middle stump, were taking sights for a common block-hole which Scrafton proceeded to dig at great depth at either end. When the game began no player was allowed to take an independent guard; but meanwhile Scrafton had caught sight of Harry and his charge, and had borne down upon them with his blue eyes flashing suspicion and animosity.

"What have you come for?" he thundered in Harry's face.

"To—watch you," replied Harry, watching him very calmly as he spoke.

"Who gave you leave?"

"Mrs. Bickersteth. Do you dislike being watched?"

So mild was the look, so bland the tone, that it was impossible to tell whether the ambiguity was intentional or accidental. Scrafton glared at Harry for one eloquent moment; then his blue eyes fell and fastened furiously upon the little fellow at Harry's side.

"And you," he roared, flourishing his blackthorn over the small boy's head, "what right have you here? A blockhead who can't say his first declension has no right idling out o' doors. Take care, Master Woodman—take very great care to-morrow!"

And with the grin of an ogre behind the lifted blackthorn, Mr. Scrafton turned on the heels of the shoes he wore next his skin, and rushed back to the pitch.

"I expect Mr. Scrafton's bark is worse than his bite," Harry could not help saying to the trembling child at his side. "The brute!" he cried in the same breath. He could not help that either. The blackthorn had fallen heavily across the shoulders of a boy who had been throwing catches without leave. Little Woodman never said a word.

After this Harry could not trust himself to remain without interfering, and he knew only too well what the result of such interference would be. So Woodman and he walked to the far side of the ground, and only watched the game for a few minutes, from a safe distance; yet it left as vivid an impression in Harry's mind as the finest cricket he had ever seen at Lord's. There stood Scrafton in his rusty suit, the murderous blackthorn tucked under an arm, his pocket-book and snuff-box in one hand, the pencil with which he scored in the other. Never was game played in more sombre earnest, for neither side had the temerity to applaud, and the umpire and scorer was also judge and flagellator of the fielders, who pursued the ball slowly at the risk of being themselves pursued with the blackthorn. Just before Harry went he saw his friend Gifford given out because the ball had rolled against the stumps without removing the bails. The boy had been making runs, and he seemed dissatisfied. Scrafton took a pinch of snuff, put his pencil in his pocket, and advanced flourishing his blackthorn in a manner that made Harry turn his back on the game for good. But that night, when the boarders undressed, there was a long, lean bruise across Gifford's shoulders.

The blackthorn remained in the umbrella-stand while Scrafton roared and blustered in the upper schoolroom. But when it was he who took the boys for their walk, the blackthorn went too—and was busy. And on the chimney-piece upstairs there used to lie a long black ruler which was said to hurt even more, which Harry yearned to pitch into the middle of the Thames.

During the first half of the term he never saw the inside of that room under Scrafton's terrific rule; but his roaring voice could be heard all over the house; and now and then, when Harry had occasion to pass the door, he would pause to listen to the words.

"Look at the sweat on my hand," was what he once heard. "Look at the sweat on my hand! It's sweating to give Master Murray what he deserves!"

With that Scrafton could be heard taking a tremendous pinch of snuff; but Harry was still on the stairs when a couple of resounding smacks, followed by a storm of sobs, announced that Master Murray (aetat. 11) had received his alleged deserts. The boy's ears were red and swollen for the rest of that day.

At first Harry could not understand how a religious woman like Mrs. Bickersteth could countenance and keep such a flagrant bully, since what he heard at odd times must be heard morning after morning by some member of the household. The explanation dawned upon him by degrees. Scrafton had been there so many years that he had gained an almost complete ascendency over every adult in the establishment. The one instance in which Harry knew Mrs. Bickersteth to stand firm was that of his own continuance in the school. The one member of the Bickersteth family whom he ever heard breathe a syllable against Scrafton was the good-hearted, golden-haired Baby. Harry once met her face to face on the stairs when a roaring and a thumping and a sobbing were going on behind that terrible closed door. Harry looked at her grimly. Miss Bickersteth reddened to the roots of her yellow hair.

"It does sound dreadful," she admitted. "But—but Mr. Scrafton's kinder than you think; he sounds worse than he is. And he teaches them so well; and—and he has been here so many years!"

Harry thought there was a catch in her voice as she brushed past him; for one thump had sounded louder than the rest; and first a slate had fallen, and then a boy. Indeed it was a common thing to hear the boys whispering that so-and-so had been knocked down that day. But the fiend was clever enough to keep his fist for their bodies, his flat hand for their faces; the wretched little victims were never actually disfigured.

That he was a clever teacher Harry did not doubt. With quick receptive material he was probably something more, and there were one or two boys whom that baleful face, that ready hand, and that roaring voice did not instantly daze and stupefy, and who were consequently getting on remarkably well under Mr. Scrafton. With his repulsive personality, and his more repulsive practices, the man had yet a touch of genius. He wrote the boys' names in their Latin Grammars in the most perfect and beautiful copperplate hand that Harry had ever seen. And those quicker boys would show him sums worked out by no recognised rule, but with half the figures expended in the "key": for Scrafton had a shorter and better rule of his own for every rule in arithmetic.

Weeks went by before Harry and this man exchanged another word; but daily they met and looked each other in the face, and daily the younger man became surer and surer that the look those blue eyes shot at him was instinct with a special venom, a peculiar malice, only to be explained by the unravelment of that mystery which he was as far as ever from unravelling. And every night of all these weeks he lay awake wondering, wondering; yet every day the daily duties claimed and absorbed his whole attention; and he took no step because he had found no clue, and was still determined to find one; also because there were certain cogent reasons for his keeping this mastership, for its own sake, for one term at least. Mrs. Ringrose was still at the seaside with the Walthews. She wrote to tell Harry how kind they were to her; when they returned she was to remain with them until he rejoined her. Meanwhile the flat was costing nothing but its rent, and Harry was not only earning his board, lodgings, and ten pounds for the term, but from ten to fifteen shillings a week from the excellent and munificent *Tiddler*. If he chose to throw up the mastership at Christmas, they would be able to start the New Year on a much sounder financial basis than would have been possible had he never obtained it.

So October wore into November, and the autumn tints became warmer and richer in Bushey Park, and Harry grew fond of his walks with the boys, and very fond of the boys themselves. Somehow his discovery on Richmond Hill came to seem less significant than it had appeared at the time. The idea grew upon Harry Ringrose (who was fully alive to the defects of his own imaginative quality) that very likely there was a much simpler explanation of Lowndes's lie than he had suspected at the time: and though he loathed Scrafton for his brutality to the boys, and never failed to meet that baleful eye as though he saw through its bloodshot blue into the brain beyond, the look became a mechanical part of his day's routine, and it was only in the long nights that the old suspicions haunted him. So it was when the clash came between Harry Ringrose and "I, Jeremiah Scrafton" (as the harpy loved to call himself to the boys); and with the clash, not suspicion any more, but the dire conviction of some rank and nameless, yet undiscovered, villainy.

CHAPTER XXI.

HAND TO HAND.

It all came of the junior master's clandestine connection with the *Tiddler*.

Harry Ringrose used many precautions in the matter of his little journalistic skeleton. He imagined it safe enough in the locked drawer in which he treasured such copies of the lively periodical as contained his stealthy contributions. But, just as the most cautious criminal is often guilty of the greatest carelessness, so Harry committed one gross blunder every week; and, again like so many malefactors, his own vanity was the cause of his undoing. He must see himself in print each week at the earliest possible opportunity.

The boys began by wondering why they always passed Teddington Station on the Saturday walk, and why they were invariably left outside for at least a minute. Then they wondered what paper it was the master bought. He never let them see it. Yet he habitually took a good look at it before rejoining them, which he nearly always did in the best of tempers, though once or twice it was just the opposite. At last one sophisticated boy bet another that it was a sporting paper, and the other boy stole into the station at Harry's heels and with great gallantry discovered what it was. The same Saturday Harry was observed scribbling things (probably puns) on his shirt cuff, and referring to these that evening when he said he had to write a letter, and writing the letter in irregular short lines. It is to be feared that a few of the boys then turned unscrupulous detectives, and the discovery of an envelope addressed to the editor of *Tommy Tiddler* proved a mere question of time.

The next thing was to find out what he wrote, and about this time Harry had a shock. A day-boy was convicted of bringing a *Tiddler* to lessons at the instigation of a boarder, and the whole school heard of it after Bible-reading, when the incriminating pennyworth was taken between the tongs and publicly cremated for a "low, pernicious, disreputable paper, which I hope never to see in my school again." Harry was not present at the time, but these were Mrs. Bickersteth's words when she told him what she had done, and begged him to be good enough to keep a sharp look-out for future numbers of the "degrading thing." He had the new one in his pocket as he bowed.

About this time young Woodman was laid up in the bedroom at the top of the house, and Harry had to keep the fire in and the kettle steaming all night. The little fellow had grown upon him more and more, and yet for a child he was extraordinarily reserved. Harry could never tell whether Scrafton knocked him about or not; and once when Woodman attributed a set of bruised knuckles to his having struck another boy (a thing he was never known to do), Harry could have laughed at the pious lie if he had not been too angry at the thought of anybody ill-treating such a shadow of a boy. Yet nobody was especially good to little Woodman: for Baby Bickersteth was good to all.

Once or twice the boy's parents came to see him, young, wealthy people, against whom Harry formed a possibly unwarrantable prejudice; and on these occasions, before being sent downstairs to see them, the child was first taken upstairs and his light hair made lank and rank with pomatum, and his pale face burnished with much soap. While he was ill, however, the Woodmans ran down from their hotel in town one Sunday morning and spent an hour in the sick-room before hurrying back. Harry was present when Mrs. Bickersteth came in from chapel and heard of it. He followed the irate lady upstairs (to put away his Sunday hat), and he heard her tell the invalid what she thought of his father for coming up into her bedrooms in her absence. Gentlemen in her bedrooms she did not allow; it was a most ungentlemanly liberty to take; and so on and so on, until Harry saw such tears in the boy's eyes as Scrafton himself could not have wrung. A new book was lying on the bed when Harry quitted this painful scene. He saw it next under Mrs. Bickersteth's arm; and he had to go upstairs again to say a word to the boy, though it should cost him his beggarly place fifty times over.

"I don't mind what they say to me," whimpered Woodman. "I only mind what they say about my people."

Harry found it possible to take the other side without unkindness. Mrs. Bickersteth had said more than she meant. Most people did when they were angry. Ladies were always sensitive about untidiness, and, of course, the room was untidy. She had not meant to hurt Woodman's feelings.

"But my mater brought me a new Ballantyne, sir," said the boy. "It was the one that's just come out, and Bick—Mrs. Bickersteth—has taken it away from me."

His tears ran again.

"Well, I'll lend you something instead," said Harry.

"Thanks awfully, sir."

"I'll lend you anything you like!" quoth Harry recklessly.

He was thinking of some novels in the locked drawer.

"Honest Injun, sir?"

Harry laughed. The boy had a quaint way with him that never went too far, he was the one fellow with whom it was quite safe to joke, and it was delightful to see his dark eyes drying beneath the bright look that only left them when Woodman was really miserable.

"Honest Injun, Woodman."

"Then lend me a *Tiddler*."

"A what?"

"A *Tommy Tiddler*, sir," said Woodman demurely.

"How on earth do you know I have one?" cried Harry aghast.

"Everybody knows you get it every Saturday from the station, sir."

"But how?"

"Oh, I don't know," said Woodman. "But—but I do wish you'd show me what you write in it, sir. I swear I won't tell the other fellows!"

Harry was temporarily dumb. Then he burst out in an excited whisper: how in the wide world did they know he wrote for the thing? Woodman would not say. A lot of them did know it, but they had agreed not to sneak—for which observation he apologised in the same breath. Woodman whispered too; never were two such conspirators.

And the immediate result was altogether inevitable. Harry loved a word of praise from anybody, like many a better man, and Woodman was as much above the average boy in sense of humour as he was below him in the ordinary endowments. That Sunday, before he went to sleep, he had read every false rhyme and every unblushing inversion of Harry's which had yet found their way into print. It may have been very demoralising—it has never been held that Harry had even the makings of an ideal pedagogue—but the small boy actually went to sleep with a *T.T.* under his pillow. And next day when he was permitted abroad in his room, and, after the doctor's visit, to go down to Mr. Scrafton for an hour, it was with *T.T.* stowed hastily in his jacket pocket that Woodman made his reappearance in the upper schoolroom.

Unaware that he had been allowed to leave his bed, Harry contrived to run upstairs during the morning with a boy's magazine which one of the other boarders had received from home that morning. Finding the room empty, Harry only hoped his convalescent was breaking the journey from bed to Scrafton in some more temperate zone, but on his way downstairs he could not help pausing at that sinister shut door, and this was what he heard.

"Where did you get it?" No answer—thud. "Where—did—you—get it?" No answer—thud—and so on some four or five times, with a dull thud after each fruitless reiteration.

Cold breath seemed to gather on Harry's forehead as on glass; an instinct told him what was happening.

"I am going on, you know," continued Scrafton, dropping his normal bluster for a snarl of subtler malice, "until—you—tell—me—where—you—got——"

A blow was falling between each word, and what Harry saw as he entered was Scrafton leaning across a corner of the table, with his ogre's face glaring into little Woodman's, and the unlucky *Tiddler* grasped in his left hand, while with his right fist he kept punching, punching, punching, with unvarying aim and precision, between the shoulder and the chest of the child. No single blow would have drawn a tear, nor might the series have left a mark, but the little white face was positively deathly with the cumulative pain, and, though his lips might have been sewn together, a tear dropped on Woodman's slate as Harry entered softly. Next instant Scrafton was seated on the floor, and Harry Ringrose standing over him, brandishing the chair that he had tugged from under the bully's body.

"You infernal villain!" cried the younger man. "I've a good mind to brain you where you sit!"

It was more easily said than done. Scrafton seized a leg of the chair in either hand, and, leaping up, began jabbing Harry with the back, while his yellow face worked hideously, and his blue eyes flamed with blood. Not a word was said as the two men stood swaying with the chair between them; and Mrs. Bickersteth, who had heard the fall and Harry's voice, was in time for this tableau, with its ring of small scared faces raised in horror.

"Mr. Scrafton!" she cried. "Mr. Ringrose! pray what are *you* doing here?"

"What am I doing?" shouted Harry. "Teaching this brute you keep to torture these children—teaching him what I ought to have taught him weeks ago. Oh, I had some idea of what went on, but none that it was so bad! I have seen these boys' bruises caused by this bully. I ought to have told you long ago. I tell you now, and I dare you to keep him in your school. If you do I call in the police!"

Poor Harry was quite beside himself. He had lost his head and his temper too completely to do justice to his case. His chest was heaving, his face flaming, and even now he looked at Scrafton as though about to tear that foul beard out by the roots. Scrafton grinned like a fiend, and took three tremendous pinches of snuff.

"Mr. Scrafton has been with me twenty-two years," said Mrs. Bickersteth. "I shall hear him first. Then I will deal with you once and for all. Meanwhile I shall be excessively obliged if you will retire to your room."

"I shall do nothing of the kind," retorted Harry Ringrose.

"Then you are no longer a master in my school."

"Thank God for that!"

Mrs. Bickersteth turned her back upon him, and through all his righteous heat the youth felt suddenly ashamed. In an instant he was cool.

Scrafton was telling his story. Mrs. Bickersteth had forbidden the low paper, *Tommy Tiddler*, to be brought into the school, and Master Woodman not only had a copy in his pocket, but stubbornly refused to say how he had come by it. A little persuasion was being used, when Mr. Ringrose rushed in, said Scrafton, and committed a murderous assault upon him with that chair.

"A little persuasion!" jeered Harry, breaking out again. "A little torture, you brute! Now I will tell you where he came by that paper. I lent it him."

"You—a paid master in my school—lend one of my boys that vulgar, vicious, abominable paper, after I have forbidden it in the school?"

"Yes—I did wrong. I beg your pardon, Mrs. Bickersteth, for that and for the way I spoke just now—to you—not to him," Harry took care to add, with a contemptuous jerk of the head towards Scrafton. "As for this unlucky rag," picking it up, "it may or may not be vulgar, but I deny that it is either vicious or abominable. I shouldn't write for it if it were."

"You *write* for it?"

"Have done ever since I was here."

"Then," cried Mrs. Bickersteth, "even if you had not behaved as you have behaved this morning—even if you had not spoken as you have spoken—in my presence—in the presence of the boys—you should leave my school this day. You are not fit for your position."

"And never was," roared Scrafton, taking another huge pinch and snapping the snuff from his fingers; "and perhaps, ma'am, you'll listen to Jeremiah Scrafton another time. What did I tell you the first time I saw him. A common swindler's whelp—like father, like son."

So Scrafton took his chance, but now it was Harry's. He walked up to the other and stared him steadily in the face. It was the look Harry had given him five days out of the seven for many a week, but never had it been quite so steady or so cool.

"I won't strike you, Scrafton," said he; "no, thank you! But we're not done with each other yet. You've not heard the last of me—or of my father."

"There's plenty wish they hadn't heard the last of him," rejoined Scrafton brutally.

"Well, you haven't, any way; and when you hear of him again, you ruffian," continued Harry, under his breath, "it will be to some purpose. I know something—I mean to know all. And it surprises you! What do you suppose I stayed here for except to watch you? And I'll have you watched still, Scrafton. Trust me not to lose sight of you till I am at the bottom of your villainy."

Not a word of this was heard by Mrs. Bickersteth or by the boys; they merely saw Scrafton's face set in a grin that had suddenly become ghastly, and the snuff spilling from the box between his blue-nailed fingers, as Harry Ringrose turned upon his heel and strode from the room.

He took the stairs three at a time, in his eagerness to throw his things into his portmanteau and to go straight from the guilty man downstairs to the guilty man in Leadenhall Street or on Richmond Hill; he would find him wherever he was; he would tear the truth from that false friend's tongue. And this new and consuming excitement so lifted him outside of his present surroundings, that it was as though the school was not, as though the last two months had not been; and it was only when he rose perspiring from his strapped portmanteau that the glint of medicine bottles caught his eye, bringing the still lingering odours of the sick-room back to his nostrils, and to his heart a tumult of forgotten considerations.

Instead of hurrying downstairs he strode up and down his room until a note was brought to him from Mrs. Bickersteth. It begged him as a gentleman to go quietly and at once, and it enclosed a cheque for ten pounds, or his full salary for the unfinished term. Harry felt touched and troubled. The lady wrote a good bold hand, but her cheque was so tremulously signed that he wondered whether they would cash it at the bank. He had qualms, too, about accepting the full amount; but the thought of his mother overcame them, and that of the boys fortified him to send down a stamped receipt with a line in which he declined to go before Mrs. Bickersteth's sons returned from the City.

He remained upstairs all day, however, in order to cause no additional embarrassment before the boys, and, when his ears told him that afternoon school had begun, he was still further touched at the arrival of his dinner on a tray. On the strength of this he begged for an interview with Mrs. Bickersteth, and, when Baby Bickersteth came up to say her mother was quite unequal to seeing him, Harry apologised freely and from his heart for the violence to which he had given way in his indignation. But he said that he must see her brothers before he went, as nothing could alter his opinion of the ferocious Scrafton, or of the monstrosity of retaining such a man in such a position.

"And you," he cried, looking boldly into the doll-like eyes, "you agree with me! Then back me up this evening, and you will never, never, never regret it!"

The girl coloured as she left him without a word; but he thought the blue eyes were going to fill, and he hoped for the best in the evening. Alas! he was leaning on reeds, and putting his faith in a couple of sober, unimaginative citizens, who, seeing Harry excited, deducted some seventy per cent. from his indictment, and met his every charge with the same stolid answer.

"We were under him ourselves," they said, "and you see, we are none the worse."

"But you were Mrs. Bickersteth's sons. And I don't say these boys will be any the worse when they grow up. I only say it is a crime to let such little chaps be so foully used."

"You have said quite enough," replied Leonard, gruffly. "It's not the slightest use your saying any more."

"So I see!" cried Harry bitterly.

"You've upset my mother," put in Reggie, "but you don't bully us."

"No!" exclaimed Harry. "I'll leave that to Scrafton—since even the men of the house daren't stand up to him!"

This brought them to their feet.

"Will you have the goodness to go?" thundered Lennie.

"Or have we to make you?" drawled Reginald.

"You may try," said Harry, truculently. "I'm on to have it out with anybody, though I'd rather it were a brute like Scrafton than otherwise good fellows who refuse to see what a brute he is. But you will have to see. You haven't heard the last of this; you'll be sorry you didn't hear the last of it from me."

"You threaten us?" cried Lennie Bickersteth, throwing the drawing-room door open in a way that was in itself a threat. Harry stalked through with an eye that dared them to use their hands. He put on his hat and overcoat, flung open the front door, picked up his portmanteau and his hat-box, and so wheeled round on the threshold.

"I mean," he said, "to communicate with the parents of every boy who has been under Scrafton this term. They shall question the boys themselves."

He turned again, and went slowly down the steps; before he was at the bottom the big door had slammed behind him for ever. And yet again did he turn at the wooden gate between the stucco pillars. There was his window, the end window of the top row, the window with the warm red light behind the blind. Even as he watched, the blind was pulled back, and a little lean figure in white stood between it and the glass.

It was a moonlight night, made lighter yet by a fall of snow that afternoon, and Harry saw the little fellow so distinctly for the last time! He was alternately waving a handkerchief with all his might and digging at his eyes with it as though he meant to blacken them. It was Harry's first sight of Woodman since the scene in the schoolroom, and it was destined to be his last in life.

CHAPTER XXII.

MAN TO MAN.

The flat was in utter darkness when Harry arrived between nine and ten. He was disappointed, and yet not surprised. He knew that his mother was to have returned from the sea by this time, but that was all he did know. He found the porter, and asked him how he was redirecting the letters.

The man gave Mr. Walthew's address. Harry groaned.

"Mrs. Ringrose has never been back since she first went away?"

"No, sir."

"You have the key of the flat?"

"Yes, sir; my wife goes up there every day."

"Then get her to go up now and light the gas stove and lay the table. I'll bring in the provisions if she'll do that and make my bed for me. Tell her I know it's late, but——"

"That's all right, sir," interrupted the porter, a familiar but obliging soul; and when Harry returned in ten minutes, with his slices of pressed beef and his French rolls and butter, from the delightful shop round a couple of corners, the flat was lighted like a public-house, and you lost sight of your breath in the minute dining-room where the asbestos was reddening in the grate.

Yet it was a sorry home-coming, that put Harry painfully in mind of his last, and he felt very wistful and lonely when he had finished his supper and written a few lines to his mother. He came in from posting them with an ounce of birdseye, and dragged an easy chair from under its dust-sheet in the other room, and so arranged himself comfortably enough in front of the gas stove. But his first pipe for several weeks did no more for him than Weber's Last Waltz, which duly welcomed him through the ceiling. He was unused to solitude, and the morrow's interview with Lowndes sat heavily on his nerves. His one consolation was that it would take place before his mother's return. She must know nothing until he knew all. And he had begged her not to hurry back on his account.

In the sideboard that was so many sizes too large for the room—the schoolroom sideboard of the old home—he at last laid hands upon some whisky, and in his loneliness and suppressed excitement he certainly drank more than was good for him before going to bed. Immense and immediate confidence accrued, only to evaporate before it was wanted; and morning found him nervous, depressed, and dearly wishing that he had gone hot from

Scrafton to Lowndes the day before. But the bravest man is he who goes trembling and yet smiling into action, and, after all, it was a sufficiently determined face that Harry Ringrose carried through the sloppy City streets that foggy forenoon.

In the outer office the same small clerk was perched on the same tall stool: but Bacchus sat solitary, in his top-coat and with a redder nose than ever, at the desk in the inner office, the door of which was standing open.

"Good-morning, Mr. Backhouse," said Harry entering. "Mr. Lowndes is out?"

"Very much out."

"Doesn't he come here now?"

"No."

"I'm sorry to trouble you, Mr. Backhouse, but can you tell me where I can find him?"

"Offices of the Crofter Fisheries."

"Where are they?"

"Hartington House, Cornhill."

So brusque was his manner, so different from Harry's recollection of the red-nosed man, that the young fellow thanked him for his information with marked stiffness, whereupon the other sprang up and clapped on his hat.

"I don't mean to be rude to you, Mr. Ringrose, but I'm sick of that man's name," cried he: "it gives me a thirst every time I hear it. Didn't you know about the Company? It comes out next week—they're going to have a solid page in every morning paper on Monday—capital one million, and everything but Royalty on the board! Lowndes has made himself General Manager with God knows how many thousand a year, and I was to be Secretary with five hundred. He promised it to me again and again—he had the use of these offices rent free for months—and used to borrow from the housekeeper when I had nothing—and now he gives it over my head to one of his aristocratic pals. I tell you, Mr. Ringrose, it makes me dry to think of it! Come and let me buy you a drink."

Harry thanked him but declined, and, on the way downstairs, asked whether Lowndes still lived at Richmond.

"He may be there still," said Bacchus, "but I hear he's going to move into an abbey or castle—I forget which—as soon as the Company comes out. He's renting it furnished from one of these belted blokes he's got in with. So you won't have the least little split? Well, good-bye then, Mr. Ringrose, and may Gordon Lowndes prove a better friend to you than he has to me!"

Harry could not help smiling grimly as he headed for Cornhill. The grievance of Bacchus was as much his own. Most heartily he wished he had no worse.

Hartington House proved to be a modern pile with a lift worked by a smart boy in buttons; and the offices of the Crofter Fisheries, Limited, occupied the whole of one floor. If Harry had felt nervous when climbing the familiar stairs in Leadenhall Street, he might well have been overpowered by the palatial character of the new premises. A commissionaire with as many medals as a Field-Marshal handed his card to one gentleman, who passed it on to another gentleman, who carried it through a ground-glass door. Harry was then conducted into a luxurious waiting-room in which two or three busy-looking men were glancing alternately at their watches and at the illustrated papers which strewed the table. A single gigantic salmon occupied a glass case running the length of the mantelpiece, while several new oil paintings hung upon the walls. Harry noticed that the subjects were exclusively Scottish, and that one at least was by a distinguished Academician, of whose name the most was made in black letters on a gilt tablet.

In such surroundings the visitor found it a little difficult to rehearse what he had determined to say to Lowndes, and it was no misfortune that kept him waiting the better part of an hour. The delay gave him time to gather his wits and to recollect his points. It prepared him for a new Gordon Lowndes. It steadied his feet when they sank into the rich carpet of a still more sumptuous apartment, in the middle of which stood the most magnificent desk he had ever seen; it kept his eye from being distracted from the resplendent gentleman who sat at the desk, the gentleman with the orchid in the silken lapel of his frock-coat, and with everything new upon him but the gold eye-glasses that bridged the twitching nose.

Before his mouth opened beneath his waxed moustache, Harry felt convinced that Lowndes had seen Scrafton, and was fully prepared for this visit.

"Well, Ringrose, what can I do for you?" he cried, as Harry advanced, and his tone was both cold and sharp.

"Ask your typist to step into another room," replied Harry, glancing towards the young girl at the clicking Remington.

Lowndes opened his eyes. Indeed, Harry had begun better than he himself expected, and his confidence increased as the other turned to his typist.

"Be good enough to leave us for a minute, Miss Neilson; we shan't be longer," said Lowndes pointedly. "Now," he added, "kindly take a seat, Ringrose."

But Harry came and stood at the other side of the magnificent desk.

"I want to ask you two or three questions, Mr. Lowndes," said he quietly.

"About the Company, eh?"

"No, not about the Company, Mr. Lowndes."

"Then this is neither the time nor place, and it will have to be a very short minute. But blaze away."

"What is there between you and that man Scrafton?" asked Harry, and for the life of him he could steady his voice no longer. His very lip was trembling now.

"Which man Scrafton?" asked Lowndes, beginning to smile.

"You know as well as I do!" Harry almost shouted. "The other master in the school at Teddington—the man whose existence you pretended not to know of when I met you that afternoon on Ham Common. I ask you what there is between you. I ask you why you pretended there was nothing that Saturday afternoon—that Monday morning when you came to intercept him and pretended you had come to see me. I ask you what there was between that ruffian and—my father!"

His voice was almost breaking in his passion and his agony, but he was no longer nervous and self-conscious. That agony of doubt and of suspicion—that passionate determination to know the truth—had already floated him beyond the shoals of self. Lowndes waved a soothing hand, and his tone altered instantly. It was as though he realised that he was dealing with a dangerous fellow.

"Steady, Ringrose, steady!" said he. "You must answer me one question if you want answers to all those."

And there was a touch of the old kindness in his tone, a strange and disconcerting touch, for it sounded genuine.

"As many as you like—*I have nothing to hide*," cried Harry. And he had the satisfaction of making Lowndes wince.

"What makes you think I am acquainted with the man you mention?"

"What makes me think it?" echoed Harry, with a hard laugh. "Why, I've seen you together!"

"When?" cried Lowndes.

"The very day I saw you last. I came over to tell you something I'd heard the fellow say. I wanted to consult you of all men! And there were the two of you walking up and down your garden path."

"Was it the evening?"

"Yes, it was, and you walked up and down by the hour—like conspirators—like confederates!"

Lowndes had started up and was leaning across his desk. His hands gripped the edge of it. His face was ghastly.

"Spy!" he hissed. "You listened to what we were saying."

"I didn't," retorted Harry. "You knew one gentleman even then."

There were several sorts of folly in this speech: no sooner was it uttered than Harry saw one. Had he been less ready to deny the eavesdropping he might have learnt something now. By pretending to know much he might have learnt all. He had lost a chance.

And Gordon Lowndes—that arch-exponent of the game of bluff—was quick as lightning to appreciate his good fortune. The blood rushed back to his face, his hands came away from the mahogany (two little tell-tale dabs they left behind them), and he sank back into his luxurious chair—with a droop of the eyelids and ever so slight a shake of the head—an artist deploring the inartistic for art's sake while he welcomed it for his own.

Harry was furious at his false move, and at this frank though tacit recognition of the lost advantage.

"I wish I had listened!" he cried. "God knows what I should have heard, but something you dare not tell me, that I can see. There! I have been fool enough to answer your questions; now it's your turn to answer mine, and to tell me what there is between you and Scrafton."

"Well, he's a man I've had a slight acquaintance with for a year or two. He lodges—or he did lodge—in Richmond. I scraped acquaintance with him because his face interested me. But it isn't more interesting than the man himself, who is the one genius I know—the one walking anachronism——"

"I know all about that," interrupted Harry. "Why did you pretend you knew nothing about him? That's what I want to get at. You don't deny you led me to think you had never heard of him?"

"No—I did my best to do so."

"You admit it now! And why did you do your best? What was the meaning of it? What had you to gain?"

"Nothing."

"Then why did you do it?"

"My good fellow, that's my business."

"Mine too," said Harry thickly. "This man knows something of my father; you know something of this man; and first you pretend you don't—and then you try to prepare him for meeting me. I suppose you admit it was Scrafton you came to see that morning?"

"Well, I confess I wanted to put salt on the fellow; and, as he'd left Richmond, that was my only way."

"Exactly!" cried Harry. "You wanted to put salt on him because there was some mystery between the two of you and my father, and you were frightened he'd let something out. By God, Lowndes, there's some treachery too, if there isn't crime! Sit still. I'm not going to stop. Ring your bell if you like, and I'll tell every man in the office—I'll tell every big-wig on the board. There's treachery somewhere—there may be crime—and I've suspected it from the beginning. Yes, I suspected you the first time I set eyes upon you. I suspected you when we talked about my poor father in his own room and in the train. You looked a guilty man then—you look a guilty man now. Confess your guilt, or, by the living Lord, I'll tell every director of this Company! Ah, you may laugh—that's your dodge when you're in a corner—you've told me so often enough—but you were white a minute ago!"

The laugh had stopped and the whiteness returned as Lowndes sprang up and walked quickly round the desk to where Harry stood. He laid a hand on Harry's arm. The boy shook it off. And yet there was a kindness behind the other's glasses—the old kindness that had disconcerted Harry once already.

"Consider what you are saying, Ringrose," said Lowndes quietly. "You're going on like a young madman. Pull yourself together and just consider. You talk of telling tales in a way that is neither nice nor wise. What do you know to tell?"

This simple question was like ice on the hot young head.

"Enough, at any rate," he stammered presently, "to put me on the track of more."

"Then I advise you to find out the more before you make use of threats."

"I intend to do so. I'll be at the bottom of your villainy yet!"

Lowndes darkened.

"Do you want to force me to have you turned out?" he asked fiercely. "Upon my word, Ringrose, you try the patience of the best friend you ever had.

Didn't I stand by you when you landed? Didn't I do the best I could for you when I was on the rocks myself? Now I'm afloat again I want to stand by you still, but you make it devilish difficult. I honestly meant to make you Secretary of this Company, but when the chap who helped me to pull it through asked for the billet, what could I do? Here's an envelope that will show you I haven't forgotten you; take it, Ringrose, and look at it at your convenience, and try to think more charitably of an old friend. Recollect that I was your father's friend first."

"So you say," said Harry, taking the long thick envelope and looking straight through the gold-rimmed glasses. "I will believe you when you tell me where he is."

"I know no more than the man in the moon."

"You were at the bottom of his disappearance!"

"I give you my word that I was not."

"You know whether he is dead or alive!"

"I do not, Ringrose."

"Then tell me where you saw him last!"

"You sicken me," cried Lowndes, losing his temper suddenly. "I told you the whole story six months ago, and now you want me to tell it you again so that you may challenge every point. I'll answer no more of your insolent questions, and I'll tell the commissionaire to mark you down and never to admit you again. You hold in your hand fifty shares in this Company. Next week they will be worth a hundred pounds—next month perhaps a thousand—next year very likely five. Take them for your mother's sake, if not for your own, and for God's sake let me never see your face again!"

"From the man who may be at the bottom of our disgrace? No, thank you—not until you tell me what you did with my father—you and Scrafton between you!"

"I have already answered you."

"Then so much for your fifty shares."

The long envelope spun into the fire. Lowndes darted to his desk, caught the electric bell that dangled over it, and pressed the button. Harry stalked to the door, turned round, and faced him for the last time.

"You will not tell me the truth; very well, I will find it out. I will find it out," cried Harry Ringrose in a breaking voice, "if I have to spend my whole life in doing so. And if you have wronged my father I will have no mercy on you; and if you have not—all I ask is—that you—have no mercy on me!"

CHAPTER XXIII.

THE END OF THE BEGINNING.

Harry drifted through the fog, the sport of misery and rage. He was a beaten man, and slow as another to own it to himself. Now he swore that he and he alone would unravel the mystery of his father's fate; now the sense of his own impotence appalled him; but at last the bitter fact of his defeat came home to him in all its nakedness.

Yes, he had been beaten by a readier and a keener wit, and the most plausible tongue a villain ever wagged. He had been at the mercy of that specious charlatan, that unscrupulous blackleg, that scoundrel self-confessed. He knew it now. Lowndes had put him in the wrong. He was no match for a man like that. Nevertheless, he was in the right, and one day it would be proved—and one day Lowndes would get his deserts.

And yet—and yet—there were words and looks and tones that had sounded genuine enough. The man was not wholly false or bad. His good side, his staunch side, had shown itself again and again, in good and staunch actions performed without ostentation, and in motive transparently pure. That side existed in him still, and Harry felt that he had spoken as though it did not. He was sorry for many things he had said. He wished he had said other things instead or as well. He wished he had not flung those shares into the fire, though they proved that Lowndes had expected him, and they must have been intended for a sop. Still he was sorry he had thrown them on the fire; and he wished he could unsay that boast about his being a gentleman because he had not listened; other considerations apart, it struck him now almost as a contradiction in terms.

So to existing tortures he must needs add that of savage self-criticism. It was the morbid wont of Harry Ringrose, the penalty of a temperament. In a little, however, sheer perplexity gripped his mind again, and wrenched it from himself. The old unanswered questions were upon him once more.

What had there been between Lowndes and Scrafton and his own poor father? Were these men in league with the fugitive? Had they planned the wrong which had ruined and disgraced his family? Lowndes had long ago confessed that the raising of the £20,000 was his idea, that the actual acquisition of the £10,000 was his deed. The chances were that his scheme had gone further and cut deeper, and that at least a part of the plunder was for himself. Then what had he done with his share—and what had Scrafton done with his?

How else could Scrafton come in?

Harry thought of that ghoulish face, of those cruel hands, and the blood ran cold in every vessel. If ever he had seen a man capable of any crime, a man without bowels, as Lowndes was without principle, that man was Jeremiah Scrafton. What if between them they had murdered the ironmaster for those ten thousand pounds? What if they had driven him out of his mind and clapped him into an asylum, or into some vile den of Scrafton's? Ever quicker to imagine than to reason, the young fellow tasted all the horror of his theories before he realised their absurdity: where, again, were the proceeds of the crime? Lowndes was only now emerging from the very depths of poverty, while as for Scrafton, he was either an extremely poor man, or a stage miser come to life. Besides, there was the letter from Dieppe.

So he went from one blind alley of the brain to another; and of all the faces that passed him in the fog, there was none he knew—he had no friend to turn to in his sore dilemma. And he was trudging westward, going back to face his mother and to live with her in the little flat, with this miserable mystery unsolved, with these haunting suspicions unconfirmed, and therefore to be locked indefinitely in his own bosom. Vultures for his vitals, and yet he must face them, and alone.

No one to tell—no friend to consult. The words were a dirge in his heart. Suddenly they changed their tune and became a question. He stopped dead in the street. It was the Strand. He had just passed the gulf of fog which hid Waterloo Bridge.

He stood some minutes, ostensibly studying the engravings in the shop at the Adam Street corner, and looking again and again at his watch as though anxious to know the time, but too absent to bear it in mind. It was five minutes to one when he looked first; by five minutes past that shop-window and the Strand itself knew Harry Ringrose no more. He was deep in the yellow gulf, which was dimly bridged by the lights of the bridge.

The train took an hour to feel its way to Richmond: it was worse than the hour spent in the waiting-room of the Crofter Fisheries, Limited.

At Richmond the fog was white. To make an end of it, Harry took a cab, and kept the man waiting while he asked if Miss Lowndes was in. A smart parlour-maid told him that she was; otherwise there was no change.

Fanny rose hastily from a low chair in front of a blazing fire; her face was flushed but smiling, and she held up a paper in one hand while she gave Harry the other.

He took it mechanically. He had not meant to take it at all. It was the wretched *Tiddler*, of all papers, which disarmed him.

"I was just thinking about you," said his friend. "I was trying to find out which is yours this week."

"Yes?"

There was no life in his voice. His heart had leapt with pleasure, only to begin aching in a new place.

"We take it in every week on your account," said Fanny Lowndes.

"You mean that you do," said Harry, pointedly.

She coloured afresh.

"No; it is my father who brings it home from the City."

"Then he never will again!"

For some seconds their eyes were locked.

"Mr. Ringrose, what do you mean? Your tone is so strange. Has anything happened?"

"Not to your father. He and I have quarrelled—that's all."

"When?"

"This morning."

"And you have come to tell me about that!"

"I didn't mean to do so. I came to speak to one of the only two friends I have in the world besides my mother. I came to speak to you while—while you would speak to me. And now I've gone and spoilt it all!"

"Of course you haven't," said the girl, with her kind smile. "Sit down and tell me all about it. I think all the more of you for saying the worst thing first." Yet she looked alarmed, and her tone was only less agitated than his.

"It is not the worst," groaned Harry Ringrose, "and I can't sit down to say the sort of thing I've come to say. Oh, but I was a coward to come to you at all! It was because I had no one else to turn to; and you have always been my friend; but it was a cowardly thing to do! I will go away again without saying a word."

She had sunk down upon her low chair, and was leaning forward so that he could not see her face, but only the red gold of her hair in the ruddy firelight.

"No; now you must go on," she said, without raising her face.

"It is about your father—and mine."

"I expected that."

"I asked him some plain questions which he could not—or would not—answer. In desperation—in distraction—I have come to put those questions to you!"

"It is useless," was the low reply. "I cannot answer them—either."

"Wait until you hear what they are. They are very simple. What was there between Scrafton and your father and mine? What had your father and Scrafton to do with my father's flight? That's all I ask—that's all I want to know."

"I cannot tell you what you want to know."

"Cannot," he said gently, "or dare not?"

"Cannot!" she cried, and was on her feet with the word, her burning face flung back and her grey eyes flashing indignation.

Harry bowed.

"That is enough for me," he said, "and I apologise for those last words—but you would understand them if you had heard all that passed this morning."

"I do not want to know what passed. My father's affairs are not necessarily mine. I cannot tell you what you want to know because—I do not know myself."

"You have made that clear to me," said Harry, staring out of the window and through the fog. He could see the gate with the ridiculous name still painted upon it. It stood wide open as he had left it in his haste. He thought of the first time he had seen it and entered by it; he thought of the second time, which had also been the last; and all at once he thought of a question asked upon the other side of the gate, and never answered, nor repeated, nor yet remembered, from that day to this.

He turned to his companion.

"You once told me that you knew my father?"

"Yes, I knew him."

"You have seen him here in this house?"

"Yes."

"I am going to ask you what I asked you once before. You did not answer then. I entreat you to do so now. When was the last time you saw my father in this house?"

The girl drew back in dismay; not a syllable came from her parted lips.

"Was it since I asked you the question last?" cried Harry, his imagination at its wildest work in a moment.

"No."

"Was it after he was supposed to have disappeared?"

"No."

"Was it after he left my mother up north?"

Miss Lowndes turned away, but there was a mirror over the mantelpiece, and in it he could see her scarlet anguish. Harry set his teeth. He must know the truth—the truth came first.

"So he was here on his way through town. I understood it was my mother who saw him last. I have to thank you—I do so from my heart—for setting me so far upon the right track. Oh, I know what it must be to you to have such things forced from you! I hate to press you like this. No, Miss Lowndes, duty or no duty, you have only to say the word, and I will leave you alone." He could not bear the sight of her quivering shoulders, of the pretty pink ear that was all her hands now let him see of her face. Unconsciously, however, he had made his strongest appeal in his latest words; his magnanimity fired that of the girl, his consideration touched her to the quick, and she turned to him with noble impulse in her frank, wet eyes.

"I will tell you of the last time I saw your father," she cried, "on one condition. You are to question me no more when I have finished."

Harry took her hand.

"I promise," he said, and released it instantly. It was no time to think of her. He must think only of his purpose—his duty—his sacred obligation as a son.

"It was on Easter Eve," said his friend steadily. "I was up in my room—it was just dinner-time—and I saw him come in at the gate." She could not conceal a shudder. "He looked terrible—terrible—so sad and so old! My father must have seen him too. I heard their voices, but I did not hear what they said; my father lowered his voice, and I thought I heard him telling Mr. Ringrose to do the same. It was all I did hear. My father came upstairs and said a business friend had come unexpectedly, and would I mind not coming down? So my dinner was sent up to me, and afterwards in the dark I saw them go together to the gate; and at the very gate they met that dreadful man—that man whose face alone is enough to haunt one. Oh, you know him better than any of us! You are a master in the same school."

"Not now," said Harry. "I left yesterday on that man's account. Didn't he come here yesterday to tell your father?"

"Not here. He may have been to the new offices. I saw last night there had been some unpleasantness. Unpleasantness! If you knew what we have suffered from that monster! One reason why we got in such difficulties was because he was always coming——" She checked herself suddenly, with a gesture of disgust and of some underlying emotion.

"And is that all?" asked Harry gently. "Am I to know nothing beyond that meeting at the gate?"

"No, I will tell you the very last I saw of your father—and I will tell you what I think. The very last I saw of him was when they all three went out together after talking for a few minutes in the dining-room below mine. I did not hear a word. What I think is—may God forgive me, whether I am right or wrong—that the flight was arranged in those few minutes."

"You think your father knew all about it?"

"I cannot help thinking that."

"When did he come back?"

The girl turned white.

"Your promise!" she gasped. "You promised to ask no more questions!"

"I see," said Harry, grimly. "Your father crossed the Channel with mine. This is news indeed!"

"It is not!" cried Miss Lowndes. "I don't admit it. I don't know it. I don't believe it. He told me he had been up in Scotland; he was always going up to Scotland then. Oh, why do you try to wring more from me than I know? I have told you all I know for a fact. Why do you break your promise?"

"I didn't mean to," he answered brokenly. "And yet—it was my duty—to my poor father."

"Your father is gone," she cried. "Spare mine—and me."

"Do you mean that he is—dead?"

She looked at him an instant with startled eyes, as though his had read the secret suspicion of her heart; then with a wild sob, "I do not know, I do not know," she cried piteously. With that she burst into tears. He tried to soothe her. "Leave me—leave me," was all her answer, and in his helplessness he turned to do so—to leave her bowed down and weeping passionately—weeping as he had never seen woman weep before—in the chair from which she had risen to welcome him—with that foolish paper still lying crumpled at her feet.

It was so he saw her when he turned again at the door, for a last look at his friend. The white fog pressed against the panes; a little mist there was in the room, but the fire burnt very brightly, and against the glow were those small ears pink with shame, those strong hands racked with anguish, that fine head bowed low, that lissom figure bent double in the beautiful abandon of a woman's grief. Young blood took fire. He forgot everything but her. He could not and he would not leave her so; in an instant his arms were about her, he was kissing her hair.

"I love you—I love you—I love you!" he whispered. "Let us think of nothing else. If we are never to see each other again, thank God I have told you that!"

She pushed him back in horror.

"But it is dreadful, if it is true," she said; and yet she held her breath until he vowed it was.

"I have loved you for months," he said, "though I didn't know it at first. I never meant to love you. I couldn't help myself—it makes me love you all the more." And his arms were round her once more, in the first earnest passion of his life, in the first sweet flood of that passion.

"If you love me," she whispered, "will you ask no more questions of me—or of anybody? They will not bring your father back. They may only implicate—my ather—just as he is coming through his hard, hard struggles. Can you not leave it in the hands of Providence—for my sake? It is all I ask; and I think—if you do—it may all come right—some day."

"With you?" he cried. "With you and me?"

"Who knows?" she answered. "You may not care for me so long; but when there are no more mysteries—well, yes—perhaps."

"Shall I ever see you meanwhile?"

"Not until there are no more mysteries—or quarrels."

"Yet you will not let me try to clear them up."

"I want you to leave them in the hands of Providence—for my sake."

"It is hard!"

"But if you love me you will promise."

The cab was still waiting in the mist. Harry sprang into it, wild with unhidden grief, as one fresh from a death-bed. His perplexity was returning—his conscience was beginning to gnaw—yet one difficulty was solved.

He had promised.

A hansom stood at the curb below the flats; the porter was taking down the luggage; a lady and a gentleman were on the stairs.

"I hope, for every reason, that we shall find him in," the gentleman was saying. "If not I must wait a little, for I feel that a few words from me may be of value to him at this juncture, quite apart from the little proposal I have to make."

"I would not count on his accepting it," the lady ventured to observe.

"My dear Mary———"

Uncle Spencer got no further. Harry's arms were round his mother's neck. And in a few moments they were all three in the flat, where the porter's wife had the fires lighted and everything comfortable in response to a telegram from Mrs. Ringrose.

"But we must have the gas lit," cried the lady. "I want to look at you, my dear, and I cannot in this fog."

"It'll keep, mother, it'll keep," said Harry, who had his own reasons for not courting a close inspection.

"I quite agree with Henry," said Mr. Walthew. "To light the gas before it is actually dark is an extravagance which *I* cannot afford. I do not permit it in my house, Mary." Harry promptly struck a match.

"Come, my boy, and let me have a look at you," said Mrs. Ringrose when the blinds were drawn. She drew his face close to hers. "Let him say what he likes," she whispered: "I have been with them all this time. Never mind, my darling," she cried aloud; "it must have been a horrid place, and I am thankful to have you back."

Mr. Walthew prepared to say what he liked, his pulpit the hearthrug, and his theme the fiasco of the day before.

"I must say, Mary, that your sentiments are astounding. Naturally he looks troubled. He has lost the post it took him four months to secure. I confess, Henry, that I, for my part, was less surprised this morning than when I heard you had obtained your late situation. With the very serious limitations which I learnt from your own lips, however, you could scarcely hope to hold your own in a scholastic avocation. I told you so, in effect, at the time, if you remember. Was it the Greek or the mathematics that caused your downfall?"

Harry had not said what it was in his letter. He now explained, with a grim smile as he thought of *Mangnall's Questions* and *Little Steps to Great Events*. He described Scrafton's brutality in a few words, and in fewer still the scene of the day before. His mother's indignation was even louder than her applause. Uncle Spencer looked horrified at them both.

"So it was insubordination!" cried he. "You took the side of the boys against their master and your elder! Really, Henry, there is no more to be said. Your mother's sympathy I consider most misplaced. I tell you frankly that you need expect none from me."

"Did I say I expected any, Uncle Spencer?"

"That," said Mr. Walthew, "is a remark worthy of your friend Mr. Lowndes, the most impudent fellow I ever met in my life."

"He is no longer a friend of mine," said Harry Ringrose.

"I am glad to hear it, Henry."

"Do you mean that you have quarrelled?" cried Mrs. Ringrose.

"For good, mother; you shall hear about it afterwards. I can't forgive a liar, and no more must you. I have bowled Lowndes out in a thundering lie—and told him what I thought of him—that's all."

Mrs. Ringrose looked troubled, but inquisitive for particulars. Her brother did not smile, but for an instant his expression ceased to be that of a professional mute.

"'Liar' and 'lie,'" said he, "are stronger language than I approve of, Henry; but if anybody deserves such epithets I feel sure it is Mr. Gordon Lowndes. The man impressed me as a falsehood-teller when he came to my house, and I feel sure that the prospectus of this new Crofter Company, which reached me this morning, is nothing but a tissue of untruths from beginning to end. A thoroughly bad man, Henry, a lost and irredeemable sinner, who might have dragged you with him to fire eternal!"

"I did not find him thoroughly bad, Uncle Spencer," said his nephew civilly. "On the contrary, I believe there is more good in him than in most of us; but—you can't depend upon him, and there you are."

"Yet you would defend him!" exclaimed Mr. Walthew, with a sneer. "Well, well, I have no time to argue with you, Henry; *my* time is precious, so may I ask how you propose to fill yours now? You have tried and failed for the City; you have tried and failed for the Law; and now you have tried schoolmastering, and failed still more conspicuously. What do you think of trying next?"

"Something that I have been trying for some time without failing so badly as at the other things."

"Literature!" cried Mrs. Ringrose.

"Literature, forsooth!" echoed the clergyman, before Harry had time to repudiate the word. "I suppose, Mary, that you are alluding to the productions you have shown me in the paper with the unspeakable name? Well, Henry, if that's your literature, let's say no more about it; only I am almost sorry you did not fail there, too. You cannot, however, devote all or even much of your time to such buffoonery, and it was to speak to you about some permanent occupation that I accompanied your mother this afternoon. What should you say to the Civil Service?"

"I couldn't possibly get into it, uncle."

"Into the higher branches you certainly could not, Henry. But a second-class clerkship in one of the lower branches I think you might obtain, with ordinary application and perseverance. I am only sorry it did not occur to me before."

"What are the lower branches?" asked Harry, doubtfully.

"The Excise and the Customs are two."

"And the salary?"

"From eighty-five to two hundred pounds in the Excise, which is the service I recommend. I have been making inquiries about it this morning. A parishioner of mine is sending his son in for it. The lad is to attend classes at Exeter Hall, under the auspices of the Young Men's Christian Association, and I understand that mensuration is the only really difficult subject. What I propose to do, Henry, is to present you to-morrow with a ticket for the course of these classes which commences next week."

"You are very kind, Uncle Spencer——"

Mr. Walthew waved his hand as though not totally unaware of it.

"But——"

"But what?" cried Uncle Spencer.

"I believe before very, very long I should make as much money with my pen."

"You decline my offer?"

"I am exceedingly grateful for it."

"Yet you elect to go on writing rubbish for an extremely vulgar paper for the rest of your days."

"Not for the rest of my days, I hope, Uncle Spencer. I mean it to be a stepping-stone to better things."

"So you think you can earn eighty-five pounds a year by your pen!" sneered the clergyman, buttoning up his overcoat.

"I mean to try," said Harry, provoked into a firmer tone.

"Is this your deliberate decision?"

"It is."

"Then I am sorry I wasted my time by coming so far to hold out a helping hand to you. It is the last time, Henry. You may go your own way after this. Only, when your pen brings you to the poorhouse, don't come to me—that's all!"

Harry contrived to keep his temper without effort. Pinpricks do not hurt a man with a mortal wound. As for Mrs. Ringrose, she had fled before the proposal which she knew was coming, and of the result of which she felt equally sure. But she came to her door to bid the offended clergyman good-bye, and at last her boy and she were alone. He flung his arms round her neck.

"I am never going to leave you again!" he cried passionately. "I am not going to look for any more work. I am going to stop at home and write for *T.T.* until I can teach myself to write something better. I am going to work for you and for us both. I am going to do my work beside you, and you're going to help me. We ought never to have separated. Nothing shall ever separate us again!"

"Until you marry," murmured Mrs. Ringrose.

"I will never marry!" cried her boy.

CHAPTER XXIV.

YOUNG INK.

So it was that Harry Ringrose took finally to his pen towards the close of the most momentous year of his existence; for four years from that date there was but one sort of dramatic interest in his life. There was the dramatic interest of the electric bell; and that was all.

In the early days, when the roll of the little steel drum broke a silence or cut short a speech, the eyes of mother and son would meet involuntarily with the same look. Her needles would cease clicking. His pen would spring from the unfinished word. Each had the other's thought, and neither uttered it. Many a man had fled the country in his panic, to pluck up courage and return in his cooler senses. Many a man effaced himself for a time, but few for ever. The ironmaster's last letter confessed flight and promised self-effacement. He might have thought better of it—that might be he at the bell. One of the two within got over this feeling in time; the other never did.

The dogged plodder at the desk endured other heartburnings of which the little steel drum beat the signal. Knockers these flats had not, and the postman usually rang a second before he thrust the letter through the door. It was a breathless second for Harry Ringrose. He developed an incredibly fine ear for what came through. He was never deceived in the thud of a rejected manuscript. He used to vow that a proof fell with peculiar softness, and, later, that a press-cutting was unmistakable because you could not hear it fall. He had an essay on the subject in his second book, published when he was twenty-five.

His first book had been one of the minor successes of its season. It had made a small, a very small, name for Harry, but had developed his character more than his fame. It is an ominous coincidence, however, that in conception his first book was as barefaced and as cold-blooded as his first verses in *Uncle Tom's Magazine.*

For nearly three years he had been writing up, for as many guineas as possible, those African anecdotes which he had brought home with him for conversational purposes. In this way he had wasted much excellent material, to which, however, he was not too proud to return when he knew better. Heaven knows how many times he used the lion in the moonlight and his friend the Portuguese murderer of Zambesi blacks. One would have thought—he thought himself—that he had squeezed the last drop from his African orange, when one fine day he saw the way to make the pulp pay better than the juice. It was not his own way. It was the way of the greatest humorist then living. Harry took the whole of his two years abroad, and eyed them afresh from that humorist's point of view, as he apprehended it. He saw the things the great man would have seized upon, and the way it seemed to Harry he would have treated them. The result was a comic lion in the moonlight, and a more or less amusing murderer. He had treated these things tragically hitherto.

The book purported to be fact, and was certainly not fiction, for which, indeed, our young author had no definite aptitude. It earned him an ambiguous compliment from various reviewers who insisted on dubbing him the English So-and-so; but it was lucky for Harry that the new humour was then an unmade phrase. His humour was not new, but that would not have saved it from the category. It was keen enough, however, in its way, and not too desperately subtle for the man on the knifeboard. Yet Harry's first book, after "going" for a few weeks, showed a want of staying power, and was but a very moderate success after all. A few papers hailed Mr. Ringrose as the humorist for whom England had been sighing since the death of Charles Dickens, and predicted that his book would be the book of the season and of many seasons to come. Such enthusiasm was inevitable from organs which let loose at least one genius a week; but Harry did not realise the inevitability all at once. For a week or two he could not give his name in a shop without a wholly unnecessary blush; while he took his mother to look at empty houses in West End squares, thanks to indiscriminate praise from irresponsible quarters. On the whole, however, Harry had no reason to complain of the treatment accorded to his first-born; and, to descend to lower details, he sold the copyright for a small sum, which was, nevertheless, quite as much as the publishers could possibly have made out of it.

But it was in indirect ways that this book did most for Harry Ringrose. It made new friends for him at a time when his acquaintance was badly in need of some fresh blood. Years of immersion in solitary work must narrow and may warp a man; and the almost exclusive companionship of his dear mother, whose only interest he was in the present, and who vastly overrated his merits, was a joy too great not to be purchased at a price. It kept the lad's heart tender and his life of fair report, but it tended to monopolise his sympathies, and it did not increase his knowledge of the outside world. In the world of letters he had made but one friend in those first three years. This was a youth of Harry's own age, who, with a board-school education, was on the staff of an evening paper, in a position which the public-school boy was certainly not competent to fill. Harry stormed this fortress with a little article on "Portuguese Africa"—which the Editor would label "By an Afrikander"—and the acquaintance was struck up outside that gentleman's door. It ripened in a bar to which the young fellows used to repair whenever Harry was in the Strand. There, over a glass of bitter—or two—or three— he used to hear at first hand of the great novelists whom he longed to meet, but with whom his friend the journalist seemed on enviable terms. It was merely that the latter was in the heart of the big game, whereas Harry was playing a very little game of his own, in an exceedingly remote corner of the field.

His book was not a huge success, but it succeeded well enough to take him out of his corner. His friend the journalist (who managed to review the thing himself in his paper) wrote to tell Harry of a distinguished lady who was so enchanted with it that she begged him to take the author to see her. Harry had no means of knowing that the lady's enchantment was as chronic as the enthusiasm of the paper which had hailed him as a genius, and that the demand was not for himself, but for the latest name. He was still a very simple-minded person, and he waited on this lady with all alacrity, and under her wing made his bow in the sort of society of which he had heard with envy in the Gaiety bar. It cannot be said, however, that he did anybody much credit; he had been too long in his corner, and had an awkward manner when not perfectly at home. Yet a number of other ladies asked him to go and see them, and one invited him to dinner at her smart house—where the wretched Harry distinguished himself by freezing into a solid block of self-consciousness and hardly opening his mouth.

But it was all very valuable experience, and, instead of two or three, he knew a good many people by the end of that winter. He became a member of a club, and got on intimate terms with men whose names and work had become familiar to him in these years. They enlarged his sympathies—they extended his boundaries on every side. And they made him know himself as he had not known himself before. All at once he realised that he had fewer interests than other men, that his nose had been too close to his own grindstone, that the mind he had been slaving to develop had grown narrow in the process. It was a rather bitter discovery, until one day it struck him there was another side to narrowness, and he sat down and began his "Plea for Narrow Minds" on the spot. This article secured a better place in the periodicals than anything Harry Ringrose had then written. It attracted some attention during the month of its appearance, and even on republication in his second book. But it was generally considered a frivolous adventure in mere paradox (on a par with a companion paper "On Enjoying Bad Health"), whereas it was really a reaction against the writer's own self-criticism.

"Cant is not necessarily humbug," declared our scribe, "and there is probably less hypocrisy in the cant of breadth than in any other kind of cant. It may spring from a laudable ambition to be on the side of the good angels in all things. But it is apt to crystallise in a pose. For my part, when I meet a typically broad-minded man, who sees good in everybody and merit in everything, either I suspect his sincerity or I doubt his depth. I want to know if he is saying (*a*) what he thinks, or (*b*) what he thinks he ought to think.

Either he is insincere and a prig, or he means what he says and is shallow. Those wonderfully wide sympathies are too often sympathy spread thin. The odds are against your being very deep as well as very broad."

There were those critics who remarked that the sapient essayist came under both his own categories, whereupon Harry lay awake all night wondering whether he did. And it was "A Plea for Narrow Minds" that drew from Miss Lowndes the letter which she never posted, but which came into Harry's hands long afterwards. She agreed with him in part, but by no means on the whole; in fact, her letter was a remonstrance, written impulsively in a dainty boudoir of Berkeley Square, and found long afterwards in an escritoire. Harry often wondered whether the woman he loved ever read what he wrote. She read everything he signed, and would never have dropped *Tommy Tiddler* had she dreamt he was still a comic singer in its columns. But Harry saw nothing and heard but little of his quondam friends. He knew they lived in Berkeley Square—he knew they were very rich. He had heard of the dividend the Crofter Fisheries were paying, and what he would have to give now for the shares which he had committed to the flames. He had also read *Truth's* opinion of the concern, and wondered why the action for so obvious a libel hung fire. He sometimes wondered, too, how it was that he never met either the father or the daughter from whom he had severed with such different emotions on the same thick November day. He did not know that the daughter once fled from a party on hearing he was expected—and was sorry afterwards.

Curiously enough, the very article which failed to gain the good opinion he coveted most, was so fortunate as to secure that of Harry's most severe and least respected critic. The Reverend Spencer Walthew read religion between the lines, and, having written to thank his nephew for his spirited though veiled attack on the Broad Church party, concluded by begging him to have a go at the Ritualists.

"I have seldom had a more unexpected pleasure," wrote the Evangelical divine, "than you have given me by this shrewd blow against the vice of tolerance and the ultra-charitable spirit which I regard as one of the great dangers of the age. We want no charity for the heretic and the ritualist—with whom I trust you will deal unmercifully without delay. I cannot conclude, Henry, without telling you what a relief it is to me to see you at last turning your attention to serious subjects. I feel sure that they are the only ones worthy of a Christian's pen. I have never concealed from you my pain and disgust at the levity of almost all your writings hitherto, although I have tried to do justice to the literary quality, which, on the whole, has been distinctly better than might have been expected. It is the greater pleasure to me, therefore, to recognise the serious purpose and the lofty aim of your latest essay. May you never again descend to 'humorous' accounts of your 'adventures,' or to inferior versifying for papers which are not to be seen in respectable houses!"

Harry, however, had never ceased his connection with the *Tiddler*, although it was not one of the things he mentioned to the notorious interviewer who came to patronise him in those days, and to whom he caught his mother showing the parody on Gray's Elegy. *T.T.* had been a good friend to Harry at the foot of the hill, and he was not going to desert just yet, even if he could have afforded to do so. Of the £51 10s. 9d. which he managed to make in the first year, £34 4s. was from the *Tiddler's* coffers; of the third year's £223 14s. 6d. (a mighty leap from the intermediate year), £55 12s. was from the same genial source. And so we find him towards the end of the fourth year—not quite such a good one as the last—fighting hard to touch the second hundred for the second time, and writing verses in his pyjamas at midnight at the close of a long day's work on an ungrateful book.

The flat is no longer that in which Harry Ringrose found his mother; it is a slightly larger one in the same mansions on a higher floor; and instead of Weber's Last Waltz, a lusty youth, who arrived there on the same night as Harry, supplies the unsolicited accompaniment inseparable from life in a flat.

Only one room has been gained by the change; but in it sleeps a servant, an old retainer of the family; and the sitting-room is larger, so that there is ample room in it for the rather luxurious desk which Harry has bought himself, and at which we find him seated, his back to the books and his nose in his rhyming dictionary, taking his most trivial task seriously, as was ever his wont, on a warm night in the middle of September.

He is a little altered—not much. He is thicker set; the legs in the pyjamas are less lean. His face is older, but still extremely young. He has tried to grow a moustache, but failed, and given it up; and the two blots of whisker show that he has no candid girl friend now; and the blue stubble on his chin means that his mother is away. His black hair inclines to length, not altogether because he thinks it looks interesting, but chiefly because he has been too busy to get it cut. He has not yet affected the *pince-nez* or the spectacles of the average literary man. But he is smoking at his desk; he will be smoking presently in his bed; and on a small table stand a bottle of whisky and a syphon.

Suddenly a ring at the bell.

At half-past twelve at night a prolonged tattoo on the little steel drum!

Harry was greatly startled, as a man may easily be who is working at night after working all day. Yet he would have been much more startled the September before.

Since then his books had come out, and he had made a number of friends. Only the night before a play-actor had looked in after his "show," and they had sat up reading Keats against Shelley, and capping Swinburne with Rossetti, until the whisky was finished and daylight shamed them in their cups. Harry thoroughly enjoyed a Bohemian life in his mother's absence, though indeed she let him do exactly as he liked when she was there. Was it the actor again, or was it....

Not for months had the old fancy seized him with the ringing of the bell. It was only the lateness of the hour which brought it back to-night. Yet the look with which the young fellow rose was one that he wore often enough when there were none to see. It was a look of utter misery barbed with shame unspeakable and undying. Sometimes the mother had seen it—and taken the shame and the misery for his share of their common hidden grief. She little knew!

The gas was burning in the passage, but lowered on the common landing outside. Harry could see nothing through the ground glass which formed the upper portion of the door. He flung it open. A tall man was standing on the mat.

"Good evening, Mr. Ringrose," said he, and took a tremendous pinch of snuff as Harry drew back in dismay.

It was Jeremiah Scrafton.

CHAPTER XXV.

SCRAFTON'S STORY.

Harry had not heard of him for nearly four years, had not set eyes on him since their scuffle at the school. But only a few days later Leonard Bickersteth had called at the flat with strange news of Scrafton. He had never returned to the Hollies; he had disappeared from his lodgings; it was impossible to trace his whereabouts. The motive of his flight, on the other hand, seemed pretty clear. Mrs. Bickersteth had been questioning the boys, with the result that Harry's charges were sufficiently proved, as Scrafton must have known they would be, and hence his sudden desertion. Leonard Bickersteth had proceeded, on his mother's behalf, to make Harry an apology and an offer which did that lady equal credit. But the younger man was too perturbed either to accept the one or to decline the other as cordially or as civilly as he desired. He had his own explanation of Scrafton's flight. It had been a nightmare to him ever since. And here was the central figure of that nightmare standing before him in the flesh, with his snuff-box in his hand, and the old ferocious grin upon his pallid glistening face.

"Surprised to see me, are you?" cried Scrafton, taking another pinch.

"I am," said Harry, looking the other in the face, and yet reflecting its pallor.

"You'll be still more surprised when you hear what I've come to tell you. Ain't you going to ask me in?"

"Come in by all means, if you wish," said Harry, coldly.

"I do wish," was the answer. "Are you alone?"

"Absolutely," said Harry, as he closed the door and led the way into the sitting-room.

"I thought you lived with your mother?"

"She is away."

"Do you keep a servant?"

"Yes."

"Not next door, I hope?" said Scrafton, tapping the wall to gauge its thickness.

"No, at the other end of the flat; and she's used to late comers."

Scrafton glanced at Harry obliquely out of his light-blue eyes. Then they fell on the whisky bottle, and he favoured Harry with a different look.

"Help yourself."

Scrafton did so with his left hand so clasped about the glass that it was impossible to see how much he took. His hand seemed bonier than formerly, but it was no less grimy, and the fingernails were still rimmed with black. He was dressed as of old, only better. It was a moderately new frock-coat, and as he sat down with his glass Harry saw that he did wear socks. His beard and moustache were whiter; they showed the snuff-stains all the more.

It was the rocking-chair this man was desecrating with his pestilent person; while Harry, having shut the door, had reseated himself at his desk, but turned his chair so that he sat facing Scrafton, with an elbow on his blotting-pad.

"I have come," said the visitor, putting his glass down empty, "to tell you the truth about your father."

"I thought as much."

"The truth, the whole truth, and nothing but the truth," continued Scrafton, eying the bottle wistfully. "Do you suppose now that he is living or dead?"

"I have no idea."

"He is dead."

Harry did not open his mouth. He could not appreciate the news of his father's death, but then he would have been equally slow to realise that he was alive. So completely had the missing ironmaster passed out of the world of ascertainable fact and of positive statement; so dead was he already to his son.

"When did he die?" asked the latter presently; and his voice was unmoved.

"On the night between Good Friday and Easter Day."

"This year?"

"No; over four years ago."

Harry leapt to his feet.

"Where was it he died?"

"At sea——"

"At sea!"

"Between Newhaven and Dieppe."

"But how—how?"

"He was murdered."

Harry seemed to have known it all along. He could not utter another syllable. But his wild eyes and his outstretched hands asked their question plainly.

"By your friend Gordon Lowndes," said Scrafton coolly.

Harry came down heavily in his chair, and his hands lay on the desk, and his face lay in his hands; but he was acutely conscious, and he heard the furtive trickle as Scrafton seized the opportunity of replenishing his glass. The man drank. To anybody but an innocent it might have been obvious four years ago. He was one of those whom drink made pallid and ferocious; to get more from him while still sober, Harry started up as suddenly as he had subsided, causing the other to spill some liquor in his beard.

"Take all you want," cried Harry, "only tell me everything first. I must know everything now. I have suspected it so long."

He leant forward to listen, this time with an elbow on each knee, but with his face again buried in his hands. Scrafton kept a gleaming eye upon him, as he dried his beard with his coat-sleeve, and supplemented the spirit with a couple of his most sickening inhalations.

"I will begin at the beginning," said he; "but you needn't have any fears about my not reaching the end, for I've never had less than a bottle a night when I could get it, and the man doesn't breathe who ever saw Jeremiah Scrafton the worse. What you have here is only enough to make me thirsty, and I may want another bottle broached before I'm done. Meanwhile, to begin at the beginning, you must know that it is some years now since I made our friend's acquaintance at Richmond. We spotted each other one night by the river, and though he was old enough to be your father, and I was old enough to be his, I'm hanged if it wasn't like a man and a woman! He took to me, and I took to him. We were both clever men, and we were both poor men. His head was full of ways of making his pile, and my head was full of one way worth all his put together. You're a dunce at mathematics, Master Ringrose. Have you ever played roulette?"

"Never."

"Then you wouldn't understand my system, even if I was to tell it you, and I wouldn't do that for a thousand pounds. Lowndes has offered me more than that for it—wanted to form a syndicate to work it—offered me half profits; but not for Jeremiah! I'll double the capital that's put in, and I'll pay it back with cent. per cent. interest, but I'll rot before I do more. I told him so years ago, and I've never budged. I never told him or anybody else my system, and I never will. I may not live to work it now. I may never get another chance of the capital. But if I don't benefit from it, nobody else ever shall; it's my secret, and it'll go with me to the worm. One comfort is that nobody else is likely to hit upon it—no other living mathematician has the brain!"

Harry could not help looking up; and there sat Scrafton in his mother's chair, his head thrown sublimely back, a grin of exultation amid the rank hair upon his face, and the light of drunken genius in his fiery blue eyes. There was something arrestive about the man; a certain vile distinction; a certain demoniac fascination, which diverted Harry's attention in spite of himself. It was with an effort that he shook the creature from his brain, and asked how all this affected his poor father's fate.

"There is a weak point common to every system," replied Scrafton, "and want of money was the one weak point of mine. Without capital it was no use."

"Well?"

"With a thousand I'd have backed myself to bring it off; with five it was a moral certainty; with ten a dead certainty. Now do you see where your father came in?"

"It was ten thousand pounds Lowndes got him!"

"And twenty I'd have handed him, cent. per cent., on what he put in."

"Go on," said Harry, hoarsely.

Scrafton grinned until his yellow fangs gleamed through their snuffy screen; he took another pinch before complying. "It's waste of breath," said he, "for you must see for yourself what happened next. Lowndes knows I've been waiting all my life for a man with ten thousand pounds and the nerve to trust me, but he comes to make sure of me before going down to your father with the ten thousand and the dodge of making it twenty. I'm his man, of course; but your father won't listen to it; as good as shows our friend the door, but keeps the money, and says he'll pay it back himself, and then fail like an honest man. Back comes old Lowndes to Richmond, with his tail between his legs, on the Thursday night. Next day's Good Friday, and your father spends it at home—thinking about it—thinking about it—saying good-bye to everything—making up his mind to fail next day. All right, I'll stop if you like; he couldn't do it, that's all; and on the Saturday evening, just as I was going to ask Lowndes if the crash had come, and if we couldn't run down together and try again before it did, who should I meet coming out of the gate but Lowndes and the man himself! He'd caved in of his own accord. I was the very man they wanted, and in five minutes we were all three on our way to the station. It was then after eight, I recollect, but we just caught a fast train to Waterloo, and from there we galloped to London Bridge, and jumped into the boat-train as she was moving out of the station at nine sharp."

"Which boat-train?" asked Harry suspiciously. It was his first chance of cross-examination. Up to this point every statement tallied with the statements of Fanny Lowndes, made now nearly four years ago, but unforgettable in the smallest detail. And for an instant he was back in the little room at Richmond, the bright fire within, the white fog without, and the face of his beloved red with shame and wet with agony. Good God, what a barrier it had been! Her father the murderer of his! He remembered that the thought had occurred to him, but only in his wild moments, never seriously. And she must have suspected—might even have known it—at the time!

"What did you say?" said Harry, for, in the sudden tumult of his thoughts, Scrafton's answer had been lost upon him.

"It was the train for Newhaven, that runs in connection with the boat to Dieppe."

"What was your destination?" asked Harry, alert and suspicious once more.

"Monte Carlo."

"That was no way to go."

"It was an unusual way; your father insisted upon it on that account; he was the less likely to be seen and recognised."

Harry started up, mixed some whisky and soda water for himself, and tossed it off at a gulp.

"Now," he said, "tell me the worst—tell me the end—and you shall finish the bottle."

"As you like," said the other. "It isn't the most hospitable way of treating a man; but as you like—especially as there's very little to tell. I'll tell you exactly what I saw and discovered; neither more nor less; for, first of all, you must understand that we were all three to travel separately. I went third in the train and second on the boat, but they took first-class tickets right through. They were not to look at me, nor I at them. At Newhaven I saw them, but turned my back. They were both very quiet, and I foresaw no trouble. Of foul play I never dreamt until Lowndes stole into the second saloon and touched me on the shoulder. Nobody saw him, for it was a nasty night, and all but me were sick and prostrate. But I was practising my little combination with a pencil and a bit of paper, and I tell you his face gave me a turn. He said it was sea-sickness; but I knew better even then.

"I was to go aft and see Ringrose that minute. What was the matter? He was trying to back out—swearing he'd return by the next boat and face his creditors like a man. Would I go and reassure him of the absolute certainty of doubling his ten thousand? So I got up, and Lowndes led the way to the private cabin your father had taken for the night.

"And a wicked night it was! I recollect holding on for dear life as we made our way aft along the gallery where the private berths were. On one side the rail hung over the sea, on the other a line of doors and portholes hung over us, and underneath you had a wet deck at an angle that felt like forty-five. It was very dark, just light enough to see that we had the lee-side down there to ourselves. And when Lowndes opened one of the doors and climbed into one of the cabins he nearly fell out again on top of me. Or so he pretended. The cabin was empty. I pushed him in and shut the door, and stood with my back to it. Your father had vanished; yet there were his ulster and his travelling cap on the settee; and Lowndes's teeth were chattering in his head.

"'He's jumped overboard!' says he.

"'You pushed him over,' says I. 'You may as well make a clean breast of it, for I see it in your face.'

"In another minute he had confessed the whole thing. Your father had been leaning over that rail, feeling fit to die, and swearing he was going back by the next boat. In a fit of passion Lowndes had tipped him over the side, and in the black darkness, and the noise of the wind and the engines, he had gone down without a cry. That was the end of Henry Ringrose. He was drowned in the Channel in the small hours of Easter Day, four years and a half ago. Instead of a runaway swindler he was a murdered man—and now you know who murdered him!"

Harry never spoke. His face was still in his hands.

Scrafton opened his snuff-box and took an impatient pinch.

"I tell you that your father is a murdered man," he cried, "and Gordon Lowndes is his murderer!"

Harry looked up with a curious smile.

"It's a lie," said he. "He wrote to my mother from Dieppe."

"Show me the letter."

"I can't; and wouldn't if I could."

"It was a forgery."

"But I have seen it."

"I can't help that."

"I thought it might be a forgery until I came to examine it," admitted Harry.

"It was one. You can only have examined the first page."

"What do you mean?"

"It was genuine; the next was not. The letter was written on both sides of half a sheet, and the other half torn off. If you could get hold of it I would show you in a minute."

"You shall show me!" cried Harry Ringrose. "If you prove what you say——"

He checked himself with a gesture of misery and bewilderment. What was he to do if the man proved what he said? What would it be his duty to do?

He knew where his mother kept the letters she most prized, the ones that he had himself written her from Africa, and this last letter from her husband. He went into her room and broke open her desk without compunction. It was no time for nice scruples on so vital a point. And yet when he returned to the other room, and found Scrafton smacking his lips over the tumbler that he had filled and almost drained in those few moments, it seemed a sacrilege to let such eyes see such a letter. Instinctively he drew back from those outstretched unclean talons; but Scrafton only burst into hoarse laughter.

"Don't I tell you it's more than half a forgery?" cried he. "Oh, keep it yourself, by all manner of means. I've seen it before, thank you. But it's waste of time looking at the front page; that's genuine, I tell you; turn over and try the other."

"I believe that's genuine too."

"Then you'd believe anything. Why, it's written in different ink, to begin with. Hold it to the light and you'll see."

Harry did so; and the ink on both sides looked black at first sight; but closer inspection revealed a subtle difference.

"It was begun in blue-black ink," gasped Harry, "and finished in some other kind."

"Exactly."

"But the pen seems to have been the same."

"It was the gold pen your father used to carry about with him in his waistcoat pocket. But it seems he felt hot when he returned to the berth, after writing this letter in the saloon, for I found his waistcoat hanging on one of the hooks, and the pen was in the pocket."

"You say 'after writing this letter.'"

"I meant the first page of it. The second is a forgery. Look again at both, and you will see that whereas there is a kind of regular irregularity about the first page, due to the motion of the boat, the irregularity of the second is a sham. It was the most difficult part to imitate."

Harry could see that it was so; but at these last words he looked up suddenly from the letter.

"You speak as though you had committed the forgery yourself," said he.

"I did," was the calm reply. "Lowndes couldn't have used his pen like that to save his life. Don't excite yourself, young fellow. I make no secret that I was his accessory after the fact. I am going to confess that in open court, and I don't much care what they do with me—so long as they hang the dog who refused to give me a sixpence this evening."

He glared horribly out of his now bloodshot eyes, and took snuff with a truculent snap of his filthy fingers.

"So that's what brings you to me?" said Harry Ringrose. "You would have done better to take your confession straight to the police; but since you are here you had better go on if you want to convince me. You say my father went overboard in mid-Channel. How was it he was afterwards seen in Dieppe?"

Scrafton leant forward with his demon's grin.

"He wasn't," said he. "*I* was seen in his ulster, with his comforter round my beard, and his travelling cap over my eyes. It was I who walked into thin air, as the papers said, from the *café* in Dieppe. And it was in the *café* the second page of the letter was written, as you see it now. As your father wrote it, the letter finished on the fourth page, the two in between being left blank. I finished it on the second page, and then tore off the fourth. I have it here."

And he produced the greasy pocket-book which he had used as a score-book in Bushey Park.

"Let me see it," whispered Harry.

"Will you give me your word to return it instantly?"

"My word of honour."

The page of writing that was now put into Harry's trembling hands is printed underneath the genuine beginning of his father's letter, and above the forgery.

"S.S. *Seine*,
"Easter Morning,
"188—

"My dearest Wife,

"Half frantic with remorse, degradation, sorrow, and shame, I sit down to write you the last letter you may ever receive from your unhappy husband.

"When I said good-bye to you this morning I could not tell you that it might be good-bye for ever. I told you I was going up to town on business. How could I tell you that the business was to take my passage for the Continent? Yet it was nothing else, and I write this midway between Newhaven and Dieppe, where I shall post it.

"My wife, I could not bear to give back the ten thousand pounds that was only half enough to save us. I am going where I hope to

(genuine)

double it in a night. A man is going with me who has an infallible system; also another man who swears by the first man, and whom I myself can trust. I know that it is a mad as well as a wicked thing to do. I am going to gamble with other men's money—to play for my home and for my life. Yes; if I lose, my end will be the end of many another dishonest fool at Monte Carlo. You will never see me again.

"I am altogether beside myself. I am not mad, but I am near to madness. I do not think I should have done such a wild thing in my sane senses—and yet these men are so sure! Forgive me whether I win or lose, whether I live or die, and let our boy profit by my example and my end. I can say no more. My brain is on fire. I may or may not post this. But I was obliged to tell you. God bless you! God bless you!

"Your distracted husband."

(forgery)

"be forgotten altogether, going with other men's money! I know that it is a mad as well as a wicked thing to do. I do not think I should have done such a wild thing in my sane senses, but I am altogether beside myself. I am not mad, but I am near to madness.

"Good-bye for ever. You will never see me again. Forgive me whether I live or die; and let our boy profit by my example and my end. I can say no more. My brain is on fire. God bless you! God bless you!

"Your distracted husband."

The devilish ingenuity of the fraud was not lost upon the reader. Hardly a word, hardly a phrase was used in the forgery for which there was not a definite model in the original, and the imitation was no less miraculous as a whole than when taken word by word. The very incoherence of the letter was one of its most convincing features; the way in which it began by saying it might be "good-bye for ever," and ended by confessing that it was, was just the way a maddened man might choose for breaking the news of his terrible intention.

Judged impartially, side by side, the genuine page looked no more genuine than the other.

The clock struck two: the younger man raised his face from a long reverie, and there were the terrible eyes of Scrafton still upon him. He was equally at a loss what to think, what to believe, what to do; but all at once his eyes fell upon the "copy" on his desk; it must go by the three o'clock post, or it would be too late for the next issue.

Mechanically he began folding up his various contributions—punning paragraphs—four-line quips—a set of verses that he had completed. The other set, upon which he had been engaged on Scrafton's entry, he tossed aside, but all that was ready he put into a long envelope, which he addressed, weighed, and stamped as though nobody had been there. Scrafton watched him with his grinning eyes, but leapt up and overtook Harry as he was leaving the room.

"You're not going out, are you?"

"Yes, to the post."

"What, like that?"

"Not a soul will be about, and there's a pillar just under the windows."

"What is it you want to post?"

"Nonsense for a comic paper."

Harry held up his envelope. The other read the address, and it quenched the suspicion in his fiery eyes, but opened them very wide.

"So you can think of your comic paper after this!"

"I must think of something, or I shall go mad."

"Well, where's another bottle of whisky before you go?"

Harry fetched one from the dining-room, and in another moment he was on the stairs, with an overcoat over his pyjamas, and the latch-key in his hand. His brain was in a whirl. He had no idea what to do when he returned, what steps to take, and no clear sight of his duty by his dead father. If he was dead, there was an end. But how could he believe the word of that ghoul upstairs? And yet, was there anything to be gained by his returning with the police? For the very idea had occurred to Harry, of which Scrafton had at first suspected and then acquitted him.

He could see his way no farther than the posting of his "copy"; that little commonplace necessity had come as a timely godsend to him; he only wished the pillar was a mile instead of a yard away.

As he emerged from the mansions a couple of men retired farther into the shadow of the opposite houses; as he turned from the pillar-box one of these men was crossing the road towards him, having recognised Harry; and it was the very man of whom he was thinking—of whom he was trying to think as his own father's murderer.

CHAPTER XXVI.

A MASTERSTROKE.

"Well, Ringrose!"

Gordon Lowndes did not look a day older since Harry had seen him last. He wore a light cape over his evening dress, a crush-hat on his head, and behind and below the same gold-rimmed glasses there twinkled and trembled the shrewd eyes and the singular sharp-pointed nose. The eyes were as full of friendship as in the earliest days of the intimacy that had come to a violent end nearly four years ago. And they had lost the old furtive look which had inspired vague suspicion from the first; nothing could have been franker or kindlier than their glance; but Harry recoiled with a ghastly face.

The story he had just heard was still ringing in his ears. It might not be true in every detail, but it was circumstantial, there was the proof of the letter, and much of the rest bore the stamp of truth. Certain it was that a foul crime had been committed, and that one of these two men had been the other's accomplice, if not in its commission then after the fact. And what was Lowndes doing here, and what was Scrafton doing upstairs, unless they were accomplices still?

A vague feeling that he had been tricked and trapped, to what end he could not conceive, made Harry put his back to the railings, clench his fists, and set his teeth; yet there was nothing in the other's look to support such a theory.

"Come, Ringrose," said he, "I think I know what's the matter! I know whom you've got upstairs. I can guess what he's been telling you."

"You can?"

"Certainly I can. In point of fact, it's not guesswork at all. He was good enough to warn me of his intention."

"Well?"

"He's been telling you that I did what he did himself."

"Which of you am I to believe?" cried Harry in a frenzy. "You are villains both! I believe you did it between you!"

"Steady, Ringrose, steady. I have given you provocation in the past, but I am not provoking you now. That your father's fate was different from what I led you to believe it would be idle to deny any longer, especially as I am here to clear up the mystery once and for all. Take me upstairs and you shall know the truth."

"What! Trust myself to the two of you?"

Lowndes pointed to the shadowy figure across the road.

"And to the man who is with me."

"Who is he?"

"The first detective in London," whispered Lowndes, in his pat, decisive way. "Now, will you take me up to bowl out Scrafton, or shall I call to him to come down, and make a scene here in the street? My dear Ringrose, I may have my faults, but do you seriously mean to take his word before mine?"

"Come up if you like," said Harry, shortly; and Lowndes turned to the man in the shadow.

"When I throw up a window," Harry heard him say, and he led the way upstairs, feeling once more as though he were walking into a trap with his eyes open.

"Leave the key in the door," whispered Lowndes again as they stood on the mat. "Then he will be able to come and help us if necessary."

There was something strangely trustworthy in his face and his voice; something new in Harry's knowledge of the man. He left the key in the door, and he felt next moment that he had done right. Scrafton had leapt to his feet with fear and ferocity in his face, and the empty spirit-bottle caught up in his hand.

"What do *you* want?" he roared. "What are *you* doing here? You fool, I've told him everything! Shut the door, you, young fellow; now he's come we won't let him slip."

Harry humoured him by shutting it. He had only to look on their two faces to see which was the villain now.

"I've told him!" repeated Scrafton, in a loud, jeering voice. "I told you I'd round on you if ever you went back on me, and I've been as good as my word. He knows now who persuaded his father to go abroad, and he knows why. He knows who went with him. He knows who pushed him overboard and took the money."

"It's pretty plain, isn't it?" said Lowndes to Harry. "Be prepared to close with him the moment he lifts that bottle higher than his shoulder, and I'll tell you honestly what I did do. It will save time, however, if you first tell me what this fellow says I did."

Harry did so in the fewest words, while they both stood watching Scrafton, grinning in their faces as he held the empty bottle in rest. His grin broadened as the tale proceeded. And so strange was the growing triumph in the fierce blue eyes, if it were all untrue, that at the end Harry turned to Lowndes and asked him point-blank whether there was any truth in it at all.

"Heaps," was the reply. "It's nothing but the truth up to a certain point. I am not here to exonerate myself from fault, Ringrose, and not even altogether from crime. It is perfectly true that it was at my instigation your father consented to go abroad and put his faith in this fellow's system. It was a wild scheme, if you like, but it was either that or certain ruin, and I'd have risked it myself without the slightest hesitation. I firmly believe, too, that it would have come off if we'd kept cool and played well together—for make no mistake about the mere ability of our friend with the bottle—but it never came to that. Your father weakened on it halfway across the Channel, and vowed he'd go back by the next boat and fail like a man. That's true enough, and it's also true that after reasoning with him in vain I went to send Scrafton to reassure him about the system; and here's where the lies begin. I didn't go back with him to the empty cabin. I followed him in a few minutes, and there he was alone, and there and then he started accusing me of what he'd obviously done himself."

"Obviously!" jeered Scrafton. "So obviously that he made no attempt to prove it at the time!"

"I stood no chance of doing so. It would have been oath against oath. And meanwhile, Ringrose, there were the two of us in a tight place together—and the French lights in sight! There was nothing for it but to pull together for the time being, and to avoid discovery of your father's disappearance at all costs. What was done couldn't be undone; and discovery would have meant destruction to us both, without anybody else being a bit the better. So Scrafton went ashore muffled up in your father's ulster, as he has told you himself; and, indeed, the rest of his story is—only too true."

"You consented to this?" cried Harry, recoiling from both men, as one stood shamefaced and the other took snuff with a triumphant flourish.

"Consented to it?" roared Scrafton. "He proposed it, bless you!"

"That's not true, Lowndes?"

"I'm ashamed to say it is, Ringrose. We were in a frightful hole. Something had to be done right there and then."

"So you went ashore together?"

"No; we arranged to meet."

"To concoct the forgery I've been shown to-night? You had a hand in that, had you?"

"I had a voice."

"Yet none of the guilt is yours!"

The tone cut like a knife. Lowndes had been hanging his head, but his spectacles flashed as he raised it now.

"I never said that!" cried he. "God knows I was guilty enough after the event; and God knows, also, that I did what I could to make it up to you and yours in every other way later on. You may smile in my face—I deserve it—but what would you have gained if I had blown the gaff? Nothing at all; whereas I should have been bowled out in getting your father abroad with the very money I'd raised to save the ship; and that alone would have been the very devil for me. No Crofter Fisheries! Very likely Wormwood Scrubs instead! I couldn't face it; so I held my tongue, and I've been paying for it to this ruffian ever since."

"Paying for it!" echoed Scrafton. "Paying *me* to hold *my* tongue; that's what he means!"

"It is true enough," said Lowndes quietly, in answer to a look from Harry.

"He admits it!" cried Scrafton, snuffing horribly in his exultation; "he might just as well admit the whole thing. Who but a guilty man pays another to hold his tongue?"

"I have confessed the full extent of my guilt," said Lowndes, in the same quiet voice.

"Then why were you such a blockhead as to put yourself at my mercy tonight?" roared the other, his bloodshot eyes breaking into a sudden blaze of fury.

Lowndes stood a little without replying; and Harry Ringrose, still wavering between the two men, and as yet distrusting and condemning them equally in his heart, saw all at once a twinkle in the spectacled eyes which weighed more with him than words. A twitch of the sharp nose completed a characteristic look which Harry could neither forget nor misunderstand; it was not that of the losing side; and now, for the first time, the lad could believe it was a real detective, and not a third accomplice, who was waiting in the street below.

"Do you think I am the man to put myself at your mercy?" asked Lowndes at length, and with increased serenity.

"You've done so, you blockhead! You've put the rope round your own neck!"

"On the contrary, my good Scrafton, I've simply waited until I was certain of slipping it round yours. You would see that for yourself if you hadn't drunk your brain to a pulp. You would have seen it by the way I sent you to the devil this evening. However, I think you're beginning to see it now!"

"I see nothing," snarled Scrafton; "and you can prove nothing! But if I can't hang you, I can tell enough to make you glad to go out and hang yourself. It doesn't much matter what happens to me. I'm old and poor, and about done for in any case, or I might think more of my own skin. But you're on the top of the wave—and I'll have you back in the trough! You're living on the fat of the land—you shall see how you like skilly! Never mind who did the trick; who took the money when it was done?"

Harry turned once more to Lowndes, and, despite his late convictions, the question was reflected in his face.

"The notes went overboard with your father," said Lowndes. "The gold we found in his bag in the cabin."

"And what did you do with the gold?"

Scrafton echoed the question with his jeering laugh.

"Ringrose," said Lowndes, "it didn't amount to very much; what I consented to take I used for your mother and you, so help me God!"

"Your mother and my eye!" cried Scrafton. "A likely yarn!"

"I believe it," said Harry, after a pause.

"You believe him?" screamed Scrafton.

"Certainly—before you."

"After all the lies he's owned up to?"

"After everything!"

Scrafton gnashed his teeth, and his bloodshot eyes blazed again.

"You had my version first, you blockhead!" he burst out. "You never would have had his otherwise. Can't you see he's only trying to turn the tables on me? I tell you he threw your father into the sea, so he turns round and says I did it! Let him prove a word of it. Do you hear, you lying devil? Prove it; prove it if you can!"

Lowndes stepped over to the window and threw up the centre sash very casually.

"It's a warm night for this sort of thing," he remarked. "Prove it, do you say? That's exactly what I'm going to do, if you'll give me time. Steady with that bottle, though—watch him, Ringrose—that's better! So you still insist on having a proof, eh? Do you think I'd have refused your demands this evening if I hadn't had one? My good fellow, there was a man in my house at the time who is in a position to convict you at last. He has been on your track for years—and here he is!"

As the door opened, Harry kept his eyes on Scrafton, and on the empty bottle he still gripped by the neck. Instead of being raised, it slipped through his slackened fingers and fell upon the hearthrug. A moment later Scrafton himself crashed in a heap where he stood.

Harry turned round; a bronzed gentleman with snow-white whiskers had entered the room and was holding out his arms to him, the tears standing thick in his eyes.

"My son—my son!"

The mist was clearing from Harry's eyes; a trembling hand held each of his; trembling lips had touched his forehead.

"Father—father—is it really you?"

"By God's mercy—only."

"They said you were drowned!"

"I was saved by a miracle."

"Yet you have kept away from us all these years!"

"It was the least I could do, Harry. The slur was on you and your mother. I had cast it on you; it was for me to remove it; or never to show my face again. God has been very good to me. I will tell you all. I am only sorry I consented to this scene."

Lowndes was kneeling over the prostrate Scrafton, loosening the snuffy raiment, feeling the feeble heart, pouring more whisky into the fallen mouth that reeked of it already.

"Is there nothing we can do?" said Mr. Ringrose.

"He will be all right in a minute or two."

"I am sorry I was a party to this business!"

"Not a bit of it, my dear sir! It was what he deserved. Sorry I told you your father was a detective, Ringrose. I wanted you to believe me for once before you saw him, that was all. You'll never believe me again—and that's what *I* deserve."

He had looked round for a moment from the senseless man; now he bent over him once more; and father and son stepped forward anxiously. The high forehead, the dirty, iron-grey hair, and the long lean nose, were all that they could see; the glistening skin was of a leaden pallor.

"Is it more than a faint?" asked Mr. Ringrose. "Ah! I am thankful."

The blue eyes had opened; the flowing beard was moving from side to side; a feeble hand feeling for a waistcoat pocket.

"My snuff-box," he whined. "I want my snuff-box."

Harry found it and gave it to him; and after the first pinch Scrafton was sitting upright; after the second he was struggling to his feet with their help, and scowling at them all in turn. He shook off their hands as soon as he felt his feet under him; and with a fine effort he tried to stalk, but could only totter, to the door. Harry was very loth to let him go, but it was his father who held the door open, while Lowndes nodded his approval of the course.

But in the doorway Scrafton turned and glared at the trio like a sick grey wolf, and shook an unclean fist in their faces before he went.

They heard him taking snuff upon the stairs.

CHAPTER XXVII.

RESTITUTION.

Shortly after Scrafton's departure, Gordon Lowndes also took his leave. It was not, however, until he had offered Harry his hand with much diffidence, and the younger man had grasped it without a moment's hesitation. At this the other coloured and dropped his eyes, but stood for some moments returning Harry's pressure twofold.

"Ringrose," he faltered, "I would give all I'm worth to-night to have told the truth in the beginning. But how could I? I might as well have blown my brains out. I—I tried to be your friend instead. I suppose you'll never let me be your friend any more?"

It is doubtful whether any man could have said these words to Harry Ringrose, in any conceivable circumstances, without receiving some such response as that which instantly burst from his lips. Want of generosity was not one of Harry's faults; yet he had no sooner forgiven Lowndes, once and for all, and with a whole heart, than an inner voice reminded him that he had but served self-interest in doing so; and the reason, coming home to him like a bullet, gave a strange turn to his emotions.

The father was sitting in a deep reverie in his wife's chair: his face was in his hands: he neither saw nor heard. Harry looked at him, hesitated, and in the end not only saw Lowndes to the door but accompanied him downstairs in the first leaden light of the September morning. He had something more to say.

He merely wanted to know whether Miss Lowndes was in town, and whether he might call. Yet he only got it out as they were shaking hands for the last time.

"You mean at Berkeley Square?" said Lowndes.

"Yes—if I may."

"You'll have to be quick about it, Ringrose. We leave there in a day or two. The men are already in the house. Still, I've no doubt she'll be glad to see you."

"Taking a country seat?" asked Harry, smiling.

"No, a suburban one: the sort of thing we had at Richmond, only rather better."

"You don't mean it!"

"A fact."

"But the Crofters are paying such a dividend?"

Gordon Lowndes shrugged his shoulders with a gesture that reminded Harry of former days.

"A paltry fourteen per cent.!" said he. "I'm sick of it. I thought we should all be millionaires by this time. I've sold out, and, of course, at a good enough figure; but we've been doing ourselves pretty well these last few years, and I haven't got much change out of the Crofters after all. In point of fact, it would take a few thousands to clear me; but, on the other hand, the credit's better than ever it was, and I'm simply chock-a-block with new plans. Loaded to the muzzle, Ringrose, and just spoiling for the fray! I know my nature better than ever I knew it before. I wasn't built for sitting in a chair and drawing my salary and receiving my dividends. I've found that out. It's worrying the thing through that I enjoy; there's some sport in that. However, I'm as lively as an old cheese with schemes and ideas; and one of them, at least, should appeal to you. It's a composite daily paper on absolutely new lines—that is, on all existing lines run parallel for a penny. My idea is to knock out the *Times* and the *Guardian* on one hand, and *Punch* and the *Pink 'Un* on the other. What should you say to coming in as comic editor at a four-figure screw?"

"Where's the capitalist?" was what Harry said.

"Where is he not?" cried Lowndes. "Every man Jack of them would jump at it! I made such a success of the Crofters that I could raise a million to-morrow for any crack-brained scheme I liked to put my name to. Yes, my boy, I'll have my pick of the capitalists this time; have them coming to me with their hats in one hand and their cheque-books in the other; but, between ourselves, I don't think we shall have far to seek for our man, Ringrose!"

"What do you mean?" cried Harry, his curiosity whetted by the other's tone.

"Ask your father," was the reply. "I may be mistaken, and he mayn't have made such a pile as I imagine; but he'll tell you as soon as he has you to himself; and meanwhile I'll warn Fanny that you're going to look her up."

A hansom tinkled and twinkled across the jaws of Earl's Court Road; and as the light-hearted rapscallion darted off in pursuit, few would have believed with what a deed he had been connected; fewer still with what emotion he had lamented his wickedness not five minutes ago.

The father had not stirred, but he looked up as Harry burst in, breathless and ashamed.

"What, have you been out?"

"Yes, father," with deep humility.

"And where is Lowndes?"

"I have been seeing him off."

"I never heard him go," said Mr. Ringrose, with a deep sigh. "The old things about me—they carried me back into the past. One question, Harry, and then you shall hear all you care to know. We found out from the commissionaire that your mother is at Eastbourne. What is she doing there?"

"I thought it would set her up for the winter."

"Is she not well?"

"Perfectly, father; but—she likes it, and—we were able to do it last year."

"She is in lodgings, then, and alone?"

"Yes."

"When does the next train leave?"

"Eight-ten," said Harry, a minute later.

Mr. Ringrose had shaded his eyes once more. They shone like a young man's as with a sudden gesture he whisked his hand away and snatched at his watch.

"Only five hours more! Thank God—thank God—that I can look her in the face to-day!"

"Do you remember how I taught you to swim when you were a tiny shrimp? It was my one accomplishment in my own boyhood, my one love among outdoor sports, and I sometimes think it must have been implanted in me for the express purpose of saving my life when the time came. Certainly nothing else could have saved it; and I cannot think that I was spared by mere chance, Harry, but intentionally, for better things. Mine had been an easy life up to that time; even in my difficulties it had been an easy life. Well, it has not been easy since!

"He stunned me first—that's how it happened. He struck me a murderous blow as I was leaving him to go in search of Lowndes. I knew no more until I was in the water. Then, before my head was clear, my limbs were doing their work. I was keeping myself afloat. I kept myself afloat until close upon daylight, when a French fisherman picked me up. He carried me to his cottage on the coast, and treated me from first to last with a kindness which I hope still to reward. At the time I bought his silence, with but little faith in his sticking to his bargain; now I know how loyally he must have done so. When I left him it was to find my way to Havre, and at Havre I took ship for Naples. I had still a little paper-money which had not come to me from Lowndes, and which I did not think likely to leave traces. With this money I transhipped at Naples, after reading of my own mysterious disappearance from Dieppe. Yes, that puzzled me; but I thought and thought, and hit at last upon something not altogether unlike the actual explanation. No, I never contemplated returning to unmask the villain who had attempted my murder. I was beginning to feel almost grateful to him. It was to him I owed such a fresh start as no ruined man ever had before.... Harry, Harry, don't look like that! My ruin was complete in any case. How could I come back and say I had been running away with the money, but had thought better of it? I could have come back in the beginning, and met my creditors without telling them what I had been tempted to do. This was impossible now. It was too late to undo the immediate effects of my disappearance; it was not too late to begin life afresh under another name and in another land. Rightly or wrongly, that is what I resolved to do—for my family's sake as much as for my own. They must forgive me, or my heart will break!"

It was to Durban that the fugitive had taken ship at Naples. He had landed on those shores within a month of the day on which his son had quitted them. And the first man he met there was one who recognised him on the spot. But good came of it; the man was an old friend, and proved a true one; he was down from Johannesburg on business, and when he returned Mr. Ringrose accompanied him. With this staunch friend the ironmaster's secret was safe; and partly through him, and partly with him—for within the year the pair were partners—the man who had lost a fortune bit by bit in the old country had made another by leaps and bounds in the new. Which was a sufficiently romantic story when Harry came to hear it in detail at a later date. At the time it was but the bare fact that the father cared to chronicle or the son to hear. It was the result on which Mr. Ringrose preferred to dwell. That very day he had returned with interest (before he knew that his wife had been paying it all these years) the money those four old friends had lent him through Gordon Lowndes. He had barely touched it, and would have returned it long ago, only he did not want his wife and son to know that he was alive until he could come back to them a rich enough man to atone in some degree for the wrong that he had done them—for the poverty and the shame they had endured for his sake.

Harry said that Lowndes had spoken as though his father was a millionaire. Mr. Ringrose smiled slightly as he shook his head.

"That's entirely his own idea," said he. "There might have been some truth in it in a few more years; but, as it is, it was no great pile I set myself to make, and I am more than content in having made it. In point of fact I am a poorer man than I was when you were born, but I am a free man for the first time for many years. This very day I have paid every penny that I owed here in town. A cheque is also on its way to the old firm, with which they can settle to-morrow any outstanding liabilities, and put the rest into the works in my name. And now I can face your mother. I could not do it until I could tell her this."

Yet he had not been a dozen hours in England; the cheques had been written on board, and posted the moment he landed. On reaching London he had gone straight to Gordon Lowndes, and it was only the almost simultaneous arrival of Scrafton which had kept him so long from seeking his own. Scrafton, who had latterly taken to pestering his victim almost daily, had ultimately left him (to the delight of Lowndes) with the avowed intention of carrying out his old threat and going straight to Harry Ringrose. In what followed Harry's father had once more yielded, against his better judgment, to Gordon Lowndes.

"It was his frankness that did it," said Mr. Ringrose; "he told me everything, before he need have told me anything at all, in his sheer joy at seeing me alive. He told me everything that he has since told you, and upon my word I am not sure that you or I would have acted very differently in his place. It was while we were talking that Scrafton called, and I learned for myself how Lowndes had suffered at his hands. I could not refuse to give him his revenge, though I should have vastly preferred to give it him there. Scrafton had gone, however, and Lowndes seemed almost equally anxious that you should judge between them, as it were, on their merits. So he had his way ... I am glad you have made it up with him, Harry. He is a strange mixture of good and bad, but which of us is not? And which of us does not need forgiveness from the other? I—most of all—need it from you!"

"And I from you," said Harry in a low voice.

"You? Why?"

"Four years ago I suspected foul play. I was sure of it. Some other time I will tell you why."

"I rather think Lowndes has told me already. Well?"

"I held my tongue! I found out most on the promise of not trying to find out any more. I shall never forgive myself for making that promise—and keeping it."

"Nay; thank God you did that!"

"You don't know what I mean."

"I think I do."

"Every day I have felt a traitor to you!"

"I think there has been a little morbid exaggeration," said Mr. Ringrose, with his worn smile. "What good could you have done? And to whom did you make this promise?"

Harry told him with a red face.

The night was at an end. Milk-carts clattered in the streets; milkmen clattered on the stairs. Harry put out the single light that had been burning all night in the sober front of the many-windowed mansions; and in the early morning he took his father over the flat. The rooms had never seemed so few—so tiny. Mr. Ringrose made no remark until he was back in the only good one that the flat contained.

"And your mother has made shift here all these years!" he exclaimed then, and the remorse in his voice had never sounded so acute.

"Oh, no; we have only been here a year."

"Where were you before?"

"In a smaller flat downstairs."

"A smaller one than this? God forgive me! I was not prepared for much; but from what I read I did expect more than this!"

"From what you read?" cried Harry. "Read where?"

A new light shone in the father's face. "In some paragraphs I once stumbled across in some paper—I have them in my pocket at this moment!" said he. "Did you suppose I never saw your name in the papers, Harry? It has been my one link with you both. I saw it first by accident, and ever since I have searched for it, and sent for everything I could hear of that had your name to it. So I have always had good news of you; and sometimes between the lines I have thought I read good news of your mother too. God bless you ... God bless you ... for working for her ... and taking my place."

The old servant wept over her old master as though her heart would break with gladness. Her breakfast was a sorry thing, but no sooner was it on the table than she was sent down for a hansom, and she was still whistling when the gentlemen rushed after her and flew to find one for themselves. It was ten minutes to eight, and their train left Victoria at ten minutes past.

Mrs. Ringrose was reading quietly in her room—reading some proof-sheets which Harry had posted to her the day before—when she heard the bell ring and her boy's own step upon the stairs. "You have news!" she cried as he entered; then at his face—"He has come back!"

"Mother, did you expect it?"

"I have expected it every morning of all these years. I have prayed for it every night."

"Your prayer is answered!"

"Where is he?"

"I left him in the cab——"

"But he could not wait!" cried a broken voice; and as Harry stood aside to let his father pass, he could see nothing through his own tears, but he never forgot the next words he heard.

"I have paid them all—all—all!" his father cried. "I can look the world in the face once more!"

"I care nothing about that," his mother answered. "You have come back to me. Oh! you have come back!"

CHAPTER XXVIII.

A TALE APART.

Harry Ringrose used sometimes to complain of his life from a literary point of view. This piece of ingratitude he was wont to couch in the technical terminology with which his conversation was rather freely garnished. He acknowledged that his "African horse had good legs," as Gordon Lowndes would remind him; it was the later years that set him grumbling. In Harry's opinion they were full of "good stuff," which he longed to "handle"; but the facts were so badly "constructed" (as facts will be) that all the king's horses and all the king's men could not pull them to pieces and put them together again without spoiling them. Then there were the "unities": our author was not quite clear as to their meaning, but he had an uncomfortable presentiment that they would prove another difficulty. And the "dramatic interest" lacked continuity. It was also of too many different kinds. The play began in one theatre, went on in another, and finished across the river. Worst of all was the "love story:" it disappeared for years, and then came altogether in a lump.

This was true. It did. And if Harry Ringrose had essayed the task to which his innate subjectivity and the want of better ideas often drew him, there is no saying how much he would have made of scenes which the impersonal historian is content simply to mention. Of such was the meeting which took place within a few hours of that other meeting in the Eastbourne lodgings. Yet this proved to be the beginning of a new story rather than the end of an old one, which poor Harry meant it to be, as he returned alone to town the same afternoon, and drove straight to Berkeley Square.

His excitement is not to be described. It seemed but a day since the leave-taking in the little shabby drawing-room on Richmond Hill. He remembered his own words so clearly. He remembered her replies. There were no more mysteries now; there were no more quarrels; and he cared still, as he had always done, Heaven knew! If only she still cared for him—if only there was nobody else—what was there to hinder it for another minute?

Nothing, one would have thought: yet it was dusk when Harry rang the bell in a shivering glow of hope and fear, and nearly midnight when he came away downcast and disheartened: and during all those hours but one he had been pressing an unsuccessful suit: though he had her word for it that there was nobody else.

What was there, then?

Those six years which had once given Harry Ringrose a misleading sense of safety.

And literally nothing else!

He called again next day. He hindered the removal on the plea of making himself useful. And in season and out of season he tried his luck in vain.

In the broad light of day he was met by a new and awful argument: his beloved showed him what she declared to be a genuine and flagrant crow's-foot; and he only a boy of twenty-five!

The removal was soon over, and for Harry the town emptied itself just as it was filling for everybody else; so then he took to writing tremendous letters; and an answer was never wanting in the course of a day or so; only it was never the answer he besought.

Her fondness for him was obvious and not denied; only she had got it into her head that those six years between them were an insuperable bar, that a boy like Harry could not possibly know his own mind, and, therefore, that it would be manifestly unfair to take him at his word.

So the thing resolved itself into a question of time; and, in the midst of other changes in his life, Harry did his best to bury himself in his work; but his comic verses were as much as he could manage, and for several weeks in succession these were the feeblest feature in *Tommy Tiddler*.

Then he went to her in despair.

"I can't stand it any longer!"

"Then give it up."

"I've waited five months!"

"I said six."

"Surely five is enough to show whether a fellow knows his own mind?"

"Some of it may be mere obstinacy."

"Well, then, it's playing the very mischief with my work."

"Then what *will* it be when we are married?"

"I beg your pardon?"

"I mean to say if we ever are."

"Fanny, you said *when*!"

"I meant *if*."

"But you *said* WHEN!!"

It was the thin edge of the wedge.

This protracted siege had other sides. It was not a joke to either party. Yet each tried to treat it as one. The man tried to conceal his disappointment, his inevitable chagrin; the woman, her deep and selfless anxiety as to whether, in all the years before them, he would be happy always—truly happy—happy as a man could be. She looked so far ahead, and he such a little way. Sometimes they told each other their thoughts; sometimes they were less happy than lovers ought to be; but all these months their inner lives were very full. They did not stagnate in each other's love. They lived intensely and they felt acutely. And that is why, if Harry Ringrose were to tell his own love story, and tell it honestly, it would be a tale apart.

When the time came there was some little heart-burning as to who should perform the ceremony. Harry had set his heart on being married by his dear Mr. Innes. This man still filled a unique place in his life. Indeed the many friendships that he had struck up in the last year or two only emphasised the value of that friend of friends: there was no one like Mr. Innes. They had not seen a great deal of each other during these last years; but they had never quite lost touch; and of the many influences to which the younger man's nature responded only too readily, as strings to every wind, there was none so constant or so helpful as that of the old master to whom he was now content to be as a boy all his days. It was not that he had paid very many visits to the school at Guildford: it was that each had left its own indelible impress on his mind, its own high resolves and noble yearnings in his heart. So it was natural enough that Harry Ringrose should want that man to marry him to whom he vowed that he owed such shreds of virtue as he possessed. And Fanny wished it too, for she had been with Harry to Guildford, and caught his enthusiasm, and knelt by his side one summer evening in the chapel where he had knelt as a boy. But it was not to be; there was a clergyman in the family; it would be impossible to pass him over.

Harry thought it would be not only possible but highly desirable, since his Uncle Spencer disapproved so cordially of Gordon Lowndes; but Mrs. Ringrose (with whom her son had warm words on the subject) very justly observed that such disapproval had not once been expressed since the engagement was announced; nor had her brother uttered one syllable to mar her own great happiness in her husband's return, but had shown a more tender sympathy in her joy than in her trouble; after which he must marry them, or they could be married without their mother. The matter was settled by a private appeal to Innes himself, who sided against Harry, and by a note from Mr. Walthew, in which that gentleman accepted the responsibility with fewer reservations than Harry had ever known him make before.

"To tell you the truth," wrote Uncle Spencer, "it is against all my principles to make engagements so many weeks ahead; but every rule has its exception, and I shall be very happy to officiate on December 1st, if I am spared, and if it has not seemed good to you meanwhile to postpone the event. I must say that in my poor judgment a longer engagement would have shown greater wisdom: your Aunt and I waited some five years and a quarter! As you say that you are determined to depend (almost entirely) on your own efforts, it would have been well, in our opinion, to follow our example, and to wait until your literary position is more established than your warmest admirer can consider it to be at present. At the same time, my dear Henry, if marriage leads you into a less frivolous vein of writing (such as I once hoped you were about to adopt), I for one shall be thankful—if only you are also able to make both ends meet."

Gordon Lowndes read this letter with such uproarious delight that Harry was sorry he had shown it to him.

"There's that brother of mine," said he; "the chap we wired to for the tenner; *he* would want a finger in the pie if he knew. But he's forgotten our existence since we left Berkeley Square, and I'm hanged if I remember his again. Besides, he's as High as your uncle's Low, and they might set on each other in the church. On the whole I'm sorry it isn't to be your schoolmaster friend. I want to meet that man, Ringrose. I want to turn that school of his into a Limited Liability Company."

It took place very quietly on a bright keen winter's day. Harry's parents were there, and Gordon Lowndes, and another. Mr. Walthew performed the ceremony in a slow and sober fashion which added something to its solemnity; the church was very still and empty; and in one awful pause the bridegroom's voice deserted him, in the mere fulness of his boyish heart. But the hand that he was holding pressed his with the familiar, firm, kind pressure, and it was from his heart of hearts that the lagging words burst:

"I will!"

THE END.